DUNHUANG
DREAM

DUNHUANG DREAM

A Novel

XU XIAOBIN

TRANSLATED BY JOHN BALCOM

ATRIA INTERNATIONAL

New York   London   Toronto   Sydney

ATRIA INTERNATIONAL

A Division of Simon & Schuster, Inc.
1230 Avenue of the Americas
New York, NY 10020

Originally published in China in 1994 by Henan Arts & Literature Publishing House.

First Atria International edition May 2011

ATRIA INTERNATIONAL and colophon are trademarks of Simon & Schuster, Inc.

For information about special discounts for bulk purchases, please contact Simon & Schuster Special Sales at 1-866-506-1949 or business@simonandschuster.com.

The Simon & Schuster Speakers Bureau can bring authors to your live event. For more information or to book an event contact the Simon & Schuster Speakers Bureau at 1-866-248-3049 or visit our website at www.simonspeakers.com.

Manufactured in the United States of America

10 9 8 7 6 5 4 3 2 1

Library of Congress Cataloging-in-Publication Data
   Xu, Xiaobin.
      Dunhuang dream : a novel / Xu Xiaobin ; translated by John Balcom.
         p. cm
   1. Xu, Xiaobin.—Translations into English. I. Balcom, John. II. Title
   PL2862.U15627D8613 2011
   895.1'352—dc22
                                                    2011001282

ISBN 978-1-4165-8390-5

Dunhuang Dream, Xu Xiaobin's novel of romance, intrigue, and crime, is set in the exotic locale of the Mogao Caves in the far west of China. Buddhism, especially in its iconographic aspects and its esoteric Tantric form, pervade the novel and add to the mystery. Given the rich cultural dimensions of the novel, perhaps a very brief introduction is in order.

The main characters of the novel find themselves in the Mogao Caves, popularly known as the Dunhuang Caves, a UN World Heritage Site, which are located in the Hexi Corridor of Gansu Province, China, along what was once part of the fabled Silk Road. Zhang Shu is running away from a bad marriage and decides to travel to Dunhuang, a place he failed to reach as a student during the "Great Link-up," when revolutionary students traveled around China linking up with their counterparts all over the country during the Cultural Revolution (1966–1976). Xiao Xingxing, a noted artist, is also fleeing from the boredom of a stifling marriage and seeking inspiration from the art treasures contained in the Dunhuang Caves. Xiang Wuye, a young student of traditional Chinese medicine, is there out of curiosity. A number of secondary characters who live at Dunhuang, such as a collector of folktales, a fortune-teller, a local Tantric master, and corrupt officials, among others, contribute to the depth and richness of the novel.

The Mogao Caves are located southeast of the city of Dunhuang. They were an important religious site for centuries. The first cave was dug out in 366; eventually more than one thousand were dug over the years. From the fourth to the fourteenth centuries, as the caves were excavated, they were also painted; it is estimated that the paintings cover miles of wall. The caves became an important religious site, containing not only the impressive frescoes for which the site is known today, but also a huge repository containing important religious and philosophical manuscripts dating from 406 to 1002 AD. It is estimated that there were approximately fifty thousand manuscripts stored there. The caves were eventually abandoned and only rediscovered in the early 1900s. Today they are an important tourist destination.

Not surprisingly given the backdrop of the story, Buddhism pervades the novel. In fact, the reader will notice that the five chapters are titled with Buddhist terms and concepts: Tathagata, or "thus come one," a name for the Buddha; Lakshmi, the Hindu goddess of wealth who was absorbed into the Buddhist pantheon; Ganapati, another Hindu god that became a part of the Buddhist pantheon; Guanyin, the Buddhist goddess of mercy; the transformation of the Western Paradise, the Buddhist paradise; and "My mind is Buddha," an expression stating a fundamental truth of Buddhism that we all possess the Buddha nature.

This structural device is an essential element of the novel. The reader should in no way be intimidated by the detailed descriptions of Buddhist iconography—in point of fact, few Chinese readers of the novel know much about these things. What is important to remember is that the author is juxtaposing an ideal world of religious and philosophical aspirations, which, through its iconic representation, seems to take on a sense of permanence, with the transient, ever-changing world of human affairs and emotions. The lengthy and detailed descriptions of Buddhist deities create verbal frescoes incorporating the historical evolution of the imagery and the symbolic qualities that have accrued over time, creating a sense of timelessness. Thus, against the pervasive, transcendent backdrop of Buddhism, the actions of the characters begin to appear as insignificant and transient as they really are.

Tantric Buddhism is another feature that comes into play in the novel for a number of characters. Tantric Buddhism is also known as Esoteric Buddhism, Vajra Buddhism, and the Secret Sect. While there is a textual tradition to the school, it also places great stress upon ritual, including different forms of yoga. In terms of the artistic representation of such practices, most Western readers will think of Tibetan statues or paintings depicting couples in sexual embrace, one form of yoga practice. The transmission of certain of these teachings is secret and only occurs directly from teacher to student. Supposedly, if the teachings are not practiced properly, they can be quite dangerous or harmful. As pointed out, Tantric Buddhism made its way to China along the Silk Road. In fact, Dunhuang was a repository of Tantric texts, 350 of which are catalogued in the British Library; and, of course, there are a great many tantric paintings to be seen at the Mogao Caves, dating from the Tang dynasty (618–907) to the Yuan dynasty (1279–1367).

By the end of the novel, it becomes evident that perhaps there is a Buddhist moral to the tale. As the *Diamond Sutra* says: "Everything is like a dream, an illusion, bubbles, shadows, like drops of dew, and a flash of lightning: contemplate them thus."

J.B.
Monterey
June 2010

DUNHUANG
DREAM

I.

The Tathagata

1

Tathagata, it is said, refers to the absolute truth as spoken by the Buddha. Candrakirti, a transmitter of Tibetan Tantric Buddhism, said, "The Tathagata is a five-colored light."

Tson-kha-pa took it a step further and said, "The absolute truth is the mysterious appreciation of that light."

For a long time, I mistakenly believed that Tathagata was another name for Shakyamuni.[1] When I was young, I would point at an image of Shakyamuni and say, "That's the Tathagata Buddha."

It's not altogether untrue. In Mahayana Buddhism, Shakyamuni is the transformation body of the absolute truth.

Only in Buddhism are two opposing truths enshrined: the basic tenets of Buddhism advocate the practice of discipline, meditation, and wisdom and the avoidance of the three poisons of desire, anger, and ignorance. But Tibetan Tantric Buddhism holds that only when man and woman cultivate the esoteric together—which is to say in a union of the Buddha and the two sexual forces—can a particular state be achieved.

The light of the Tathagata is divided into five colors, most likely in order to suit people's differing conceptions.

2

Zhang Shu's wife died. She died in an auto accident.

I heard she was with her lover at the time.

Naturally this put Zhang Shu in an awkward position. But I must say

---

1. A spiritual teacher who founded Buddhism.

that he didn't look terribly heartbroken; rather, his expression was more one of resignation. He has aged a lot in the last two years and looks older than most men in their forties. Actually the onset of aging coincides with putting on weight, which is the result of the wasting power of an empty routine and the mediocre. This process is as implacable as the net of Heaven from which no one escapes; it tightens slowly and facilely around a fresh, vibrant life until it expires, ossified amid excessive warmth and comfort.

The ashen pallor preceding ossification had already appeared on Zhang Shu's face.

"She's dead and gone. You needn't take it so hard. You still have the child." I repeated this obligatory cliché.

He smiled coldly and with his coarse hand stroked his son's faded hair. "It occurred to me over the last couple of days," he said, unhappily, "that people don't have enough ways to express their grief. What is there other than the usual sobbing or tears?"

His words gave one the chills.

"You might have been better off if it had ended three years ago," I said.

"Who knows? I believe everything is predetermined, 'Poverty and power have been fixed since the beginning of time; meeting and parting are fated.'" His eyes drifted. "I never left her and the child. On this point I have no regrets."

Three years before, Zhang Shu had departed on a mysterious journey to the Hexi Corridor in Gansu Province. No one thought he would return, or at least not return to his wife.

But he did come back, as suddenly as he had left.

His wife, Wang Xiyi, was the daughter of the party secretary to one of the provincial committees. She was as lovely as her name and was known far and wide as a talented young woman. They had a cute and well-behaved son by the name of Zhang Gu. He's twelve years old now.

No one really understood the reason for the loneliness in Zhang Shu's eyes.

Not counting myself, of course. This is not to say that I have the ability to decipher the secret signs of the soul. It's quite simple—Zhang Shu told me everything. To be more precise, he chose me. We're not exactly close friends, and I'm usually too busy to sit down and have a chat, but that's probably why he chose me.

"How is Xiao Xingxing? Are you in touch with her?" Seeing his hairline, which had receded even more, a small path flashed before my eyes.

He shook his head. The small path was suddenly blocked.

"Perhaps she was right when she said a good man and a good woman will never be together, never. So stop daydreaming," he said.

3

Zhang Shu met Xiao Xingxing at the guesthouse on Sanwei Mountain at Dunhuang in Gansu.

It was on the third day after he arrived at Dunhuang on a damp, fresh morning, something rare in the Northwest. And it was the first time he had heard a pure Beijing accent since his arrival. Years later, he would remember that pleasing voice, which had allowed him to relax, feeling as if he had returned to familiar territory.

That clear ringing voice was talking about national ration coupons with the old manager.

"Do you need some coupons? I have some." He hastened over. He had never been so forward in his life, and those who knew him would have been surprised.

Standing, profile toward him, the young woman turned. The first thing he saw, of course, was her eyes, those eyes of hers—big, bright, and black as lacquer. Many years later he realized where he had gone wrong: he shouldn't have looked at her eyes first! That's because her other features were so ordinary. If at the time he had first looked at her nose or her forehead, he, in all likelihood, would not have been so absurdly infatuated.

The young woman seemed as fresh as the morning. She looked sharp and lively in her short, casually brushed hair. She fixed her large, bright eyes on him. The tip of her nose was slightly upturned (it was the sort of cute, small, upturned nose rarely seen among Chinese women!). Her full lips resembled a deep red rosebud. Her tanned face was lightly freckled, but from her neck down to her exposed collarbone, her skin was a brilliant white. She was dressed simply in a loose white cotton T-shirt and a pair of denim shorts. She was not tall, but full figured and light on her feet. As the morning breeze lifted her hair, she seemed bathed in the splendor of youth.

She was different and, from beginning to end, mysterious. She spoke to him in her gentle way, "Oh, you have ration coupons? That's so good of you!" He felt her manner of speech did not fit her appearance; she should have been more lively, more straightforward, more blunt and to the point. But her tone of voice never varied. Yes, from beginning to end, she maintained a distance between them, never once affording him the opportunity to get close.

Perhaps it was this distance that made her mysterious and beautiful, and why he never felt disappointed in her. Maybe it was cunning on her part.

"When did you arrive?" He took the ration coupons from his stiff, worn wallet and handed them to her as if he were moving a chess piece.

"Last night." She smiled as she accepted them. "I never expected to run into someone from home here. That's wonderful."

"What do you need the ration coupons for? The dining hall in the guesthouse doesn't require them."

"I don't feel like eating in the dining hall. I can get rice with the coupons and cook for myself."

Zhang Shu smiled. "What do you do?"

"I paint. Did you see the *Halfway Exhibition*? Do you recall that half of a bull's head? Xiao Xingxing." As she smiled, her eyes narrowed to slits.

"Ah, the painter," he said, hesitatingly. He had seen the *Halfway Exhibition* and remembered the name Xiao Xingxing. However, he seemed to recall that Xiao Xingxing the painter was about thirty years old and found it impossible to match her with the vibrant young woman before him.

"And what do you do?" Xiao Xingxing's eyes twinkled.

Zhang Shu laughed. "Nothing. I don't even have a job. I came here to see the Mogao Caves."

"You quit your job?"

"Yeah."

"That takes guts. I wish I could do the same; I've thought about it for years but could never bring myself to do it." As she spoke, she fanned herself with her hat. At first he thought it was because of the heat, but later he realized it was just a habit of hers.

"You don't strike me as someone lacking in nerve."

"Really? That's just the problem, I suppose. I look brave, but I'm not. Well, it's been nice meeting you. I've got to go buy some rice now."

"I have a couple of packages of instant noodles."

"That's okay. I really don't care for them." She had already moved away some distance. He found it strange that she could walk so fast. She was full figured, but stepped lightly as if her feet had wings. Her voice had a rhythm all its own; he was sure she could sing.

4

At that time, Zhang Shu was close to forty. His background was typical of his generation. He lived seriously in his youth. In that fanatical time, he was present seven of the eight times Chairman Mao received the Red Guards, but he always regretted missing that one time. It was traveling around the country during the "Great Link-up," as it was called in those days, that changed him. With thirty yuan in his book bag, he traveled to the far reaches of the country. Running wild and unrestrained, he learned the meaning of poverty and foolishness. He stood like a blockhead for long hours in foul-smelling, crowded trains. After returning to Beijing he would have nothing more to do with revolution. He just kept his mouth shut. In silence, calm and unhurried, he went to a police substation to cancel his Beijing residence registration and then left for a poverty-stricken village in the mountains of northern Shanxi province, where he would spend eight whole years. In order to make it back to Beijing in time to take advantage of the reforms in the high school exam system to compensate for their interrupted educations during the Cultural Revolution, many of the older intellectuals vied with one another to get on the last train, but not him. Watching the overloaded train depart before his very eyes, he handled it as he had handled so many things over the years—he took a long-term wait-and-see attitude.

He wasn't without accomplishments, though. Many of his friends said that he was lucky in love and that his wife had willingly walked into his trap. She was not only pretty and competent, but more important, she was the daughter of a provincial party secretary. This in itself was sufficient to increase respect for him. No one could figure out or explain how a quiet guy like him had managed to snare a woman like her. He was, needless to say, quite handsome—tall, thick hair, swarthy, with eminently proper looks. His unshakably cool and stern temperament, that "strong, silent type" that has been preferred by women the last few years. But the daughter of the provincial party secretary soon learned that "reserved" didn't necessarily translate into food on the table. She had married an incompetent husband, entirely out of step with the times. The worst was that they soon had a child and then it was too late for regrets. Wang Xiyi began to show her displeasure through her expressions, by breaking things, and by verbally abusing her husband. She went out to have fun and later to work, leaving the child at home with him. He silently assumed responsibility for raising the child. Days turned into years, and he fulfilled his duty as the "mother" of the house. Even in the days after he had an accident and scalded his feet, everyone saw him hobbling with the aid of two canes, struggling against a freezing wind, to pick up the child at the kindergarten. But gradually, the daughter of the provincial party secretary was moved, or perhaps, for some other reason, she suddenly decided to come home. The moment she decided he deserved better, she immediately decided to quit the job she had obtained through her father and join her husband in the northwest with which he was so familiar.

It was the second time he had traveled the Hexi Corridor[2] in Gansu Province. Unlike his first visit during the Cultural Revolution, this time it was different in that he rode a creaking bicycle on the Silk Road. For some inexplicable reason he had a special feeling for the area. When the scorching wind of the Gobi desert lifted his hair and burned his skin, he would delight at the sight of the crystalline peaks of the Qilian Mountains and the usual mirages that appeared and disappeared. For him it was an extreme pleasure, an unworldly enjoyment. Often he would forget himself and shout several times to hear the distant echo. He even dreamed of encountering a sandstorm that would swallow him and then spit him out far away. He lost his way in the sea of sand and wandered aimlessly. Surviving, he would think of this and a smile would appear on his cracked lips. To him it all seemed an impossible, extravagant dream.

It was the first time he had been to Dunhuang, though. During the Cultural Revolution, he had stopped at Yanguan Pass in Gansu. Bending over, the Red Guards had all started rummaging through the antiques at a stand looking for valuables. Their military pants had been washed white till they looked like patches of white mushrooms. One girl found a nice piece of Han dynasty tile, and showed it all around as if it were a great treasure, and then had slipped it quietly to Zhang Shu. Maybe I really am lucky in love? He smiled bitterly thinking about the women he had met in his life. But like smoke or mist, they were all vague and unclear.

5

Zhang Shu had not expected his soul to be so stirred by the bewitching experience of the Mogao Caves. He suddenly felt that what he had been dreaming about for years had arrived at that moment. He could not put his feelings into words at the time. It struck him that the only thing comparable was the first time he saw the ocean. He had been so excited

---

2. Refers to the historical route in Gansu province of China. As part of the Northern Silk Road running northwest from the bank of the Yellow River, it used to be the most important passage from North China to Xinjiang and Central Asia for traders and the military.

that the first thing he felt like doing was to strip off his clothes and cast himself into the water and become a bubble on the vast and boundless sea.

Those beautifully molded lotus and canopy ceilings; those inverted wheel-shaped lotuses in the blue sky; those dancing clouds and spirals of scattered flowers; those floating scarves, gorgeous decorative designs like grapes, curling tendrils and patterns linked the walls; the beautiful heavenly musicians with their floating sleeves in rolling clouds formed interlocking patterns on the walls, that beautiful paradise of roiling cloud mist and dancing garments was filled with a foreignness, displaying a decorative taste both elegant and pure.

There were countless Jataka tales[3] and stories from Buddhist legends and the sutras; there was a statue of the Maitreya Buddha[4] thirty-three meters high; there was a huge fresco forty square meters in size depicting the magic competition of Raudraksha; there was a statue of a reclining Buddha entering nirvana measuring ten meters in length; and the countless flying apsaras[5], yakshas, rain gods, heavenly musicians, plumed races, devas, Indra, Brahma, bodhisattvas, and others of the eight classes . . . like a waterfall in a deep and secluded valley surging with magnificent history, beautiful myths and wonderful legends, and majestic works of art.

Lashed by so much brilliant beauty, he felt dizzy.

Later, upon discovering that empty space in Cave 73, he was startled and found it unbearable, especially when he discovered from the necklace of jade and pearls that remained that it was once an exquisite fresco. When the old manager told him that it was a famous painting by the Tang dynasty monk, Yu-Chi Yiseng, titled *Lakshmi Bathing,* an unbearable curiosity, unlike anything he had experienced before,

---

3. Refers to a voluminous body of folklore-like literature native to India concerning the previous births (jāti) of the Buddha.

4. According to scriptures, Maitreya will be a successor of the historic Shakyamuni Buddha, the founder of Buddhism.

5. Female spirit of the clouds and waters in Hindu and Buddhist mythology.

burgeoned in his heart. That night, he, who normally didn't dream, had a dream. It was a misty mirage. The sea was in the foreground and out of the sea grew a lotus, rising from the heart of which was a crowned and naked auspicious goddess, reminiscent of *The Birth of Venus*. But the body of Venus was enveloped in a pure and holy light, and her beauty was of the sort that eliminated all feelings of lust; but Lakshmi, on the other hand, was like a living girl whose beauty inflamed the passions. What was even more startling to him was her big Flaubertian eyes, a frightened perplexity with a hint of malice. Who had endowed her with such eyes? That pair of eyes grew in size and finally swallowed him.

And the monk Yu-Chi Yiseng lived nine centuries before Botticelli![6]

"Isn't the Eastern Buddha greater than the Western God," he muttered as he dreamed.

6

It was out of loneliness that he approached the crude, old door in the dim light at dusk. He knocked on the door; she opened it and invited him in. Under the lamp, her just-washed face took on a transparent quality. She was happy as ever. When she spoke, she liked to grab her cap or some other object and fan herself, ever faster as she grew more excited.

"Some Jataka tales, those stories of the Buddha's earlier incarnations, are just horrible!" She spoke excitedly about her first day at Dunhuang. "In order to save a mother tiger and her cubs, Prince Sattva had to hurl himself from a precipice so that the mother tiger could lap up his blood. Or there was King Shibi, who, in order to save a dove, stripped all the flesh from his body despite the tears and protests of his family. And then there was a Moonlight King who willingly did what that evil Brahmin wanted, whether being pierced with a thousand nails or cutting off his flesh to light a thousand lamps. Of course, all of this was later proven to be trials by Indra. But in the end all the wounds are healed, and they all

---

6. Sandro Botticelli (c. 1445–1510) was an Italian painter during the Early Renaissance, best known for his work of *The Birth of Venus*.

revert to their initial happiness. Can this really be called a trial? Upon
seeing their broken bones and torn flesh, would their families not wish
to end their own grief and anger in death? Is the life of a family member
less important than that of a tiger or a dove? In offering themselves to a
tiger or stripping their flesh for a dove, wouldn't they be afraid of harming
their own family by sacrificing themselves? Of course these are extreme
cases, but they are meant to promote the spirit of Buddhism. But I could
never praise such sacrifices, because the recipient is not worth it . . ."

"So you wouldn't become a Buddha."

"But the worst is the story of how Shakyamuni got Ananda to become
a monk. It was pure coercion. He would stoop to any underhanded
means. It was a complete violation of his human rights. But the love
Ananda felt for his wife was something really worth admiring!"

Zhang Shu couldn't help but laugh.

On his first day there, he too had seen the story of how Ananda became
a monk depicted in a painting on a cave wall. It was in Cave 254, a work
from the Northern Wei dynasty. Ananda was Shakyamuni's own brother.
He had a beautiful wife and was unwilling to become monk. Shakyamuni
took him on a tour of Heaven to look at the goddesses and then to Hell
to witness the punishments such as boiling criminals alive. Only by doing
this a number of times did Ananda concentrate on the Buddha Dharma[7]
and become an arhat, one who has attained enlightenment.

"You have to be careful and watch what you say here lest you suffer the
Buddha's retribution and find yourself in the part of Hell where they cut
your tongue out!" Seeing her so serious, he couldn't resist teasing her.

"It's not that I have anything against Shakyamuni Buddha." The tone
of her voice seemed to indicate that she sided with Shakyamuni. "This
story, like the Jataka tales about his earlier incarnations, is nothing more
than legend. Prince Siddhartha, the historical Buddha, is still great; the
key here is that those who followed and explained his ideas had problems.
Of all the Jataka tales, I feel only the one about the nine-colored deer
is beautiful, because not only does it trumpet good deeds, but it also

---

7. Dharma: the teachings of the Buddha.

promotes rules for being on guard against evil and for doing good deeds. Hypocrisy is the inevitable result of humanity's stubborn pursuit of good and denial of evil. People would be better off just acknowledging the existence of evil. Good and evil are twins and develop together; killing one will only result in the twisting of the human character. Preserving the integrity of the human character is the greatest beauty, and also the most difficult thing to accomplish. Actually, didn't Siddhartha himself fail to finish the torment of six years of self-denial and mortification? If that shepherd girl hadn't saved him with deer milk, he too would have died and could not have attained enlightenment under the Bodhi tree. If eating and drinking are not forbidden, then love should not be forbidden. Shakyamuni didn't love his wife and became a monk, but Ananda loved his wife and shouldn't have been a monk. Not loving his wife, Shakyamuni didn't really sacrifice anything by leaving her. Staying would have been a distortion of human nature. But Ananda loved his wife, and Shakyamuni forced him to leave her and become a monk. Don't you think that's a distortion of human nature?"

The more she spoke, the more her speech bordered on becoming like a tongue twister. He couldn't help but laugh. Rarely did he laugh with such happiness. As he laughed he considered the girl's rare intelligence.

"It would appear that you will never be able to enter the way of the Buddha." Smiling, he said, "You are too deeply attached to this world; your six sense organs are impure."

"You couldn't be more wrong. Free from delusion, my mind is the Buddha mind, that's the real truth. Burning incense and bowing are all useless. Look at all those monks and nuns. How many have become Buddhas?"

"You have a point." He grew silent. Suddenly he thought of his wife, who would burn some incense, worship the Buddha, and select a fortune stick whenever she found herself at a temple. She wouldn't leave until she got the best one. It had become a pattern with her. And the so-called best fortune stick was simply the one most vulgarly desired by ordinary folk. It made one think of the old woman in *The Story of the Fisherman and the Goldfish*, whose greed was never satisfied.

"Why did you come to Dunhuang?" she suddenly asked, their brilliant conversation of a moment ago, vast and sweeping, cooling off.

"Your question lacks Zen. There is no 'why.' I felt like coming, so I came," he replied.

"There's always a reason." She cocked her head and thought. "But perhaps you're not willing to tell me the reason. Chinese don't do things for no reason."

Her sensitivity surprised him, but he maintained his silence.

"What about you? Do you have a 'why?'"

"Of course I do." Her eyes, black as lacquer, flashed. He liked this hidden haughtiness of hers; it made her seem like an argumentative child, which he found amusing.

"I've dreamed of Dunhuang for twenty years."

"Twenty years? How old are you?"

Paying him no notice, she continued, "I have always been mysteriously attracted to this place. It's Buddhist territory. In addition to being a treasured place imbued with the glory of heroes, it is also China's mysterious and enigmatic "Bermuda triangle."

"You could write fiction."

"You experienced no fear as you crossed the Hexi Corridor?"

"No."

"You're strange."

"You're the one who's strange. This is the first time I ever heard that there was something frightening about the Hexi Corridor . . ."

"You mean you've never heard how accidents often occur there and people are swallowed up?"

"Sure, I've heard about accidents, but there are reasons such as the weather or the skill of the driver . . ."

"Enough!" she hastily cut him short. Normally he could not stand being interrupted, but this time he was not upset and actually hoped to spend some time arguing with her. In fact, he hoped to stay there with her.

"In all your life, you've never encountered anything mysterious?" She asked, her two large eyes, like black jewels, challenging him.

7

Zhang Shu arrived at Dunhuang on a windy night. The first thing he did was find a place to stay. He didn't have much money, so staying in a hotel was out of the question. With a tip from the locals, he ended up at the guesthouse with two rows of simple rooms at the foot of Sanwei Mountain. The manager was a wrinkle-faced old man who treated him somewhat coldly. He carried his bags into his room, which didn't even have cold water. He asked the old man for half an ear of corn to gnaw on, but fell asleep before he finished eating.

He slept soundly the entire night. Only on the following day did he look at his face in the mirror from which the silver backing was peeling. He looked like a cornered beast that had escaped from the desert. He wondered why the old man hadn't taken him for a ghost the previous night.

Later he went to look at some of the caves that were open to the public, and, like Xiao Xingxing, saw some of the Jataka tales but had not reacted to them as intensely as she had. Before coming, he had heard that a folktale expert by the name of Chen Qing lived there. He really wanted to meet him. Perhaps he would obtain something unexpected from him. Later, he noticed Cave 73, which was missing one of its frescoes.

While having supper, Zhang Shu had somewhat sullenly asked the old manager for a cheap glass of heated wine. Actually the old man liked to talk and told him that he had seen the bathing goddess painting in Cave 73. It was painted by a famous Tang dynasty painter, a monk by the name of Yu-Chi Yiseng. It had been stolen a short time ago. The cave had been closed until just recently, but he had no idea why it was suddenly open again.

It was unusually quiet that night. The silence swallowed everything, including the darkness.

As Zhang Shu lay a bit tipsy on his simple plank bed, he heard someone knocking.

Someone was knocking. Coming out of his alcohol-induced euphoria, he suddenly thought of *Strange Tales from a Chinese Studio* and the fox fairies—spirits that take on the form of a young woman and who come in the middle of the night—or the budding beauties who were in fact ghosts. No place could have been better than this remote place for the appearance of ghosts and fox fairies.

He opened the door. A strange-looking monk was standing before him. He was wearing a red cloth robe and was rather shapeless—the places that should have protruded were woefully sunken and vice versa. His shape seemed to change, like a bag of flour when kicked.

"Are you . . . Zhang Shu? His voice was rather direct, as if he were about to belt out a couple of opera notes.

"And who might you be, venerable sir?"

"I am Dayejisi, the abbot of Sanwei Temple."

"You are not Han Chinese,[8] then?"

"I am of the Yugur nationality.[9] He joined his palms, bowed, and smiled. "No one has stayed in this place in ages. Why did you decide to stay here?"

Zhang Shu was upset by such prying. "I don't have any money, so I didn't have any choice. Does that bother you, venerable sir?"

The monk shook his head repeatedly and continued to smile. "Your disciple finds that Mr. Zhang has a good face. I came especially to give you a physiognomy reading."

"A reading? I don't need one," said Zhang Shu indifferently. He didn't offer the monk a seat, as if the monk were nothing.

"The way I see it, you have a good face." Dayejisi was unconcerned and kept speaking with assurance. "The *Mayi Physiognomy* says, 'Man is a combination of Yin and Yang, shaped by Heaven and Earth, and endowed by the five elemental phases. He is the soul of the ten thousand things. Thus, his head resembles Heaven and his feet the Earth; his eyes resemble the sun and moon, his voice thunder; his blood vessels resemble

8. Han Chinese are an ethnic group. Ninety-two percent of the population in China are Han Chinese.

9. Yugurs are one of China's fifty-six officially recognized nationalities. Most live in Gansu Province of China.

rivers and his bones metal and stone; his nose and forehead resemble lofty mountains, his hair, the grass and vegetation. The sky must be high and the earth thick; the sun and moon must be bright, and thunder must be resonant; the rivers must flow and the metal and stone must be solid; lofty mountains must be precipitous and grass and vegetation must be fine.' Therefore, the best physiognomy tends toward completeness. The top of Mr. Zhang's head is round and thick. Your front and back are fully grown, your forehead is fresh and square, your ears are round like wheels, your nose straight like a gallbladder, there is clear distinction between the whites of your eyes and your pupils, your eyebrows are fine and long, your nose vigorously prominent, the 'three portions' of your face are harmonious, your looks are imposing and you will certainly have a long life, rarely be ill, and you will be happy and prosperous. In addition, your eyes are clear and your gaze unwavering, your countenance limpid, your bearing broad. Seen from afar, you are grand like the autumn sun shining in a frosty sky; seen up close, you are imposing like a gentle breeze moving spring flowers. When confronting something, you are firm and resolute like a wild beast pacing in the mountains; you are outstanding and unfettered, like a red phoenix soaring on its path of clouds; seated you are as immovable as a boundary stone; reclining you are as still as a perching crow; walking you are like a smooth flowing river; speaking you are as majestic as a towering peak. You are circumspect in speech, deliberate in action, unmoved by joy or anger, and undisturbed by honor or insult. You are unperturbed in the face of anything. Therefore, you have an abundance of spirit, as in the saying, 'He who has an abundance of spirit is a man of distinction; he will never be caught in a calamity and forever enjoy the happiness to the end.'"

"Am I that good? I think you exaggerate, venerable sir." Although Zhang Shu's voice was still a bit cold, he was beginning to find the monk absorbing. There was something special about him, thought Zhang Shu.

"It's just that you have a small mole at the corner of your eye. The Palace of Wives and Concubines, the twelfth palace in the *Mayi Physiognomy,* is located at this point. Coincidentally, your mole is located above the 'door of betrayal,' which means that relations between husband and wife will not be harmonious. This indicates there will be bickering, especially with regard to outside relationships. In addition your Hall of Wealth and Golden Horse display a 'floating red,' which indicates unexpected calamity. It is not advisable to reside away from home for very long."

Zhang Shu looked up suddenly. The monk was still smiling. His face seemed familiar to him at once.

"Didn't you just say that calamity will never fall upon me? And now you say that I will suffer from unexpected calamity. Aren't you contradicting yourself?"

"You are wrong, Mr. Zhang. What I just spoke of is innate physiognomy. But 'where there is mind and no marks, the marks follow as the mind grows; where there are marks but no mind, the marks follow as the mind perishes.' The marks—in other words, the looks, clothed by good or bad luck are not predetermined by Heaven. If one loses the spirit Heaven has endowed one with, one's phoenix eyes will gradually become dim and confused and one will accomplish nothing in one's life. What's more, one's spirit is concealed in the five elements, visible in his outward form but without leaving trace. It's hard to stop any unforeseen misfortune!"

Zhang Shu's heart gave a thump.

"So, venerable sir, you came here just to tell me this? Okay. Now I know. You can go now, please." He managed to maintain a cold and proper restraint.

The monk waddled away, looking like a bag of flour. Still he was all smiles, and his smile seemed strangely carved on his face, frighteningly mysterious. It made one think of a mask on which a smile was stamped.

"We are neighbors. If Mr. Zhang cares to favor me with his advice, your humble servant awaits." The monk looked around in the dark. Zhang Shu shut the door.

At once he realized why the monk's face seemed so familiar. He was the spitting image of the polychrome statue of Ananda, the emissary, standing before the stolen *Lakshmi Bathing* painting which had been located in Cave 73. Had Ananda just manifested his own soul?!

He broke into a cold sweat. After a long while he awakened from his bemused state. That dirty wall covered with spiderwebs was still stood before him.

Suddenly it seemed that everything that had just occurred had been a dream.

The monk never reappeared and nothing else disturbed him. The guesthouse was crude and old. He couldn't figure out why a famous painter such as Xiao Xingxing would stay there too.

8

As a result, Zhang Shu began to constantly ask Xiao Xingxing about Yu-chi Yiseng, the Tang dynasty painter.

"He is representative of the Yutian School of painting in Tang dynasty. He was pretty famous," said Xiao Xingxing, sewing up a button, as she kept her eyes on the pot sitting on the hot plate. "His paintings are fairly unique in the way in which 'figures seem to come out of the wall as well as his even blending of colors.' The scholar Dou Meng says, 'he applied his brush with sharp, vigorous strokes as if he were bending wire.' His technique and method stimulated the styles of the schools of the Central Plains. He was esteemed by the emperor at the time, Tang Taizong."

"Tang Taizong? He was . . ."

"He once visited the Central Plains during the Zhenguan reign period of the Tang dynasty.[10] King Yutian personally recommended him to Tang Taizong . . ."

"What did he paint?"

"Mostly Buddhist images. He must have been a devout Buddhist. The *Xuanhe Register of Paintings* records his Buddhist paintings, which probably included *Maitreya, The Buddha and His Followers, Great Compassion, The Prayer Mat,* among others. His frescos can be seen in many places including Ci'en Temple, Feng'en Temple, and Puxian Temple in Chang'an. You've never seen his work before?"

---

10. The Tang dynasty (618–907 AD), covering a period of 289 years, is considered the greatest dynasty of ancient China.

Zhang Shu shook his head. He was wearing a black T-shirt and uniform shorts, from which extended his hairy legs. In the past when summer came around, he didn't know where to hide his legs, but hairy legs like his had become a symbol of masculine beauty. A little reserved, he sat across from Xiao Xingxing, in the only chair in the room, so Xiao Xingxing sat on the edge of the bed. He saw a cord stretched across the room on which hung a number of things, most likely women's underwear and such. For that reason he tried to avoid looking in that direction. A small hot plate stood in one corner, which he had helped her set up. On the hot plate sat a bubbling stainless steel pot.

"How long do you plan to stay?" he asked.

"I haven't decided. Perhaps I'll leave in a few days, or maybe I'll stay the rest of my life."

He smiled and then stood up to say good-bye.

"Why don't I come with you tomorrow to see Cave Seventy-three? I think I'd like to look at that empty space."

He hesitated a bit before nodding. He didn't know why he preferred to examine the caves alone on his own.

"Why are you so interested in Yu-Chi Yiseng? Would you like to see a painting of his?"

"What did you say? What painting?"

"I brought several books on painting with me. In one of them is a picture of his *Lakshmi Bathing*—a fresco at Dandan Temple in Hotan, Xinjiang."

9

It was the first time he had seen the *Lakshmi Bathing*; his response was almost imperceptible, the Buddha's compensation for his devotion.

He found it almost inconceivable that 1,300 years earlier someone could have painted such a beautiful human figure. No, this painting was nothing like the one in his dream. The goddess bathing in the lotus pool was naked save for one leaf covering her buttocks and some ornaments on her neck and arms. Beside her was a chubby little boy, also entirely naked.

One arm of the goddess was pressed against her belly, the other cradled her breasts. Owing to the painter's technique of combining a dizzying palette and sharp delineation, you could almost see the flesh and flowing blood beneath her skin (it should be admitted that the printing of the book was of a high quality). But what was most startling was her lifelike expression. Her modest charm and affection were real enough to set one's head spinning. He suspected Yu-Chi Yiseng had a nude model; otherwise he couldn't have painted such a lifelike goddess.

Zhang Shu also noticed Yiseng's profound interest in the woman. Yiseng was without a doubt a sensualist. He imagined when Yiseng painted those two half-concealed breasts, he must have been aroused. He smiled at his own wild conjectures.

He focused on examining her eyes—only those eyes corresponded to his dream. They were big and dazed, startled and evil—the eyes of a living person.

10

The old manager showed up.

He never knocked. On account of this, Xiao Xingxing had become annoyed with him a couple of times.

His other problem is that he liked to drink. He wasn't choosy; he'd gladly take a couple of swigs of anything. When he drank, he didn't eat. He'd drink out of a large glass jar, gulping it down as if it were water.

"How many times have I told you not to use a hot plate?" he scolded her loudly.

"The food here is awful. If I don't cook on a hot plate, what am I supposed to eat?" In such situations, Xingxing wasn't the brightest in dealing with others.

Zhang Shu took a small bottle of wine from his shoulder bag. The bottle cost only eighty three *fen* and held only five or six cups, but the man received it like a treasure.

"It's not that I won't listen to reason," said the old man swigging a mouthful. "What are you doing here? I wonder. You city folks are used to enjoying the good life. But you don't stay in a good hotel, no, you insist on this place . . ."

"Uncle, this is a Buddhist land of immortal caves. Why did Shakyamuni cast aside his princely rank and practice the difficult Way?"

The old man screwed his mouth into a crooked smile. "This girl's got a good head on her shoulders. How long do you two plan to stay here?"

The old man had referred to them as "you two." They both wanted to protest this inappropriate address, but for some reason, they didn't bother to explain.

Zhang Shu told the old man that he had come here to collect folktales and that Xiao Xingxing had come in search of artistic inspiration.

"Collect folktales? Then why don't you contact Chen Qing, the folktale expert in these parts?"

Zhang Shu said that he had heard of the famous Chen Qing, but figured someone so well known would be difficult to see. Hearing this, the old man laughed like a child.

"What? Chen Qing—that's me! I am Chen Qing!" he exclaimed.

II

That night was the first time Chen Qing told them a story.

Legend has it that in ancient times there were no caves here. There was a river that swelled in spring, on the desolate banks of which grew tamarisk, parasol trees, and sacsaouls.

Later, a monk by the name of Le Zun came from the east, accompanied by three disciples. They were headed west to worship the Buddha, acquire sutras, and search for paradise. At the time, it was the height of summer and scorching hot. Their thirst was unbearable, so Zhi Qin, the third disciple, went in search of water. The sun was about to fall behind the mountains and shone on Sanwei Mountain, forming a myriad golden rays, in the midst of which sat a huge Miatreya Buddha, surrounded by millions of bodhisattvas with their myriad appearances, smiling as they conversed freely amid magnificent buildings in a purplish atmosphere. There were also countless fairy maidens playing musical instruments and dancing.

Looking at the scene, Zhi Qin was stupefied. He decided then and there to paint the spectacular scene and sculpt the Buddha and bodhisattvas. And so he took up hammer and chisel and began carving out the first cave . . .

But why is it written on the stele that Le Zun carved out the first cave? Legend has it that Zhi Qin had the merit of digging the first cave and his master held him in high esteem. His fellow disciples, being jealous of him, wrote that Le Zun was the first to see the light . . .

Whoever sees the Buddha's light on Sanwei Mountain is destined to become an illustrious person.

12

Someone says I have an illustrious physiognomy," said Zhang Shu.

"Who said that?"

"Dayejisi, the abbot of Sanwei Mountain Temple."

"Him? You saw him? What else did he say?" For some reason Chen Qing seemed frightened.

"He said that although I have an illustrious visage, I will suffer a disaster shortly and that it's not good to be away from home for very long. He encouraged me to leave soon."

"He'll let you go? Then you had better go, leave, leave."

To Zhang Shu, Chen Qing seemed to have aged at once. Xiao Xingxing was snoring regularly nearby.

"Why? Does he have a lot of power around here?"

Chen Qing took one last swig of wine and said, "Young man, don't ask so many questions. Do whatever he told you to do. Don't make trouble for yourself."

"Does one fear ghosts in the realm of the Buddha? All the more so when there are no ghosts."

"Young man, you are raving! I have been here for decades, and would know if there are ghosts or not!"

"Is Dayejisi a Yugur?"

"Yugur! He's Han Chinese! His wife is Yugur! If he tells you to go, you'd better go; do whatever he told you to do . . ." The old man was long-winded. He stood up. At that moment the first light of dawn shone through the thin curtains. Zhang Shu pulled back the curtains. All he could see was the golden light on Sanwei Mountain and cloud upon cloud. The solemnity infused with a profound light made an unusual impression. The lower clouds were covered with light and shadow. It was as if a will composed of bright music was controlling dark and shifting passions.

"Hurry Xingxing! Look at the Buddha's light on Sanwei Mountain."

Unfortunately, Xingxing was still sound asleep and didn't see it.

13

The following day, Xiao Xingxing, who was determined to have Zhang Shu accompany her to Cave 73 to see what, if anything, remained of the fresco *Lakshmi Bathing,* knocked on his door, waking the soundly sleeping Zhang. There was nothing he could do but take her on his old creaking bike.

Xiao Xingxing sat on the back. As he got on his bike, he had a strange feeling. The previous night, Xingxing had slept, nestled against his shoulder like a timid and lovable little woman. There was an angel's purity about her face. She wasn't a woman, but a girl. He thought that there were women who would never grow up. A soft warm breeze blew across her face, making it itch. Her hair was lifted on the wind like willow catkins fluttering over his nose. He remained absolutely still lest he startle her like a small bird. Cave 73 was closed. They stood in front of the door for a long time. Few people remained in the area. A woman wearing a gray head scarf walked alone slowly. She was dressed in a long, black high-collared gown with a gray vest. Colorful embroidery highlighted the collar, sleeves, and front of her garment, but it wasn't all that pretty because her clothes looked dirty. Clearly she was a minority woman, but they couldn't tell from which ethnic group.

Afterward they decided to visit the Great Southern Buddha and the Great Northern Buddha.

14

I admit there is one mistake that Zhang Shu helped me rectify.

It was with regard to an issue concerning the image of Maitreya. Like most people I believed that Maitreya was that fat, smiling monk, which was a mistake.

It turned out that the robust fellow was called the "bag monk," who, according to *The General Historical Record of the Buddha* and other sources, was called Xie Bi and also known as Changtingzi, a monk from the Five Dynasties. Legend has it that he was fat and often carried a cloth bag when he went begging and was also good at foretelling good and bad luck and when it would rain or be clear. Before he died, he recited a gatha: "Maitreya, the real Maitreya divided himself into billions; he often manifests himself to people, but people don't recognize him." From then on, people assumed he was the incarnation of Maitreya. But in fact, he was just one of billions.

But the real Maitreya, or Mi Le in Chinese, who was named Ajita, was born into a Brahmin household and later became a disciple of the Shakyamuni. He died before Shakyamuni and was reborn in the Tusita Heaven. Billions of years after Shakyamuni passed away, 5,670,000,000 years to be exact, Maitreya will be reborn in the world of men and became a Buddha under a dragon-flower tree in the Hualin Garden. He will teach and save countless beings, carrying forward Shakyamuni's Way by becoming the Buddhist Messiah.

The Dunhuang sculpture of Maitreya, which is thirty-three meters in height, was produced during the second year of the Yanzai reign period when Empress Wu Zetian ruled. Its face is calm, dignified, and beautiful. It is said that originally there was a priceless ruby inlayed above his nose between his eyebrows. The sculpture was the spitting image of Wu Zetian herself.

Zhang Shu said that the locals later called the statue the Great Northern Buddha. It was also known as the "White Buddha" and echoed the seated Maitreya, which was twenty-six meters in height, in Cave 130, and referred to as the Great Southern Buddha and also known as the "Black Buddha." It is said that the Black and White Buddhas are the instigators of all the mysterious disturbances at Dunhuang. That's what Chen Qing later told him.

15

The calm dignity of the White Buddha stood in sharp contrast to the cold magnificence of the Black Buddha.

The first time Xiao Xingxing saw the Black Buddha, Zhang Shu noticed that she trembled all over. In the dark, he saw her face go white, and on the way back she didn't speak a word.

The gilt had come off from around the corners of the Black Buddha's mouth and jaw, exposing the reddish color beneath, which resembled oozing blood.

"It looks like blood, doesn't it? There is a story!" Old Chen Qing was in high spirits because Xiao Xingxing bought him a bottle of Jiannanchun.

"During the October Revolution, Lenin forced the White Russians into exile, some of whom came to our Thousand Buddhist Caves. One young White Russian lad wanted to scrape some of the gold off the Black Buddha, but couldn't reach that high, so in his impatience, he fired a gun. Ping! Blood began to flow from the seven apertures in the Black Buddha's head! Outside, the wind raged and lightning flashed. The Black Buddha reached out and with a flick of his horsetail whisk froze all the Whites Russians to death on the Qilian Mountains . . ."

Seeing Xiao Xingxing's increasing fright, Zhang Shu wanted to prevent Chen Qing from continuing his story.

"There is also a story about the White Buddha," said Chen Qing, drinking happily. "At the time, carving the White Buddha was a big deal. The red spot on top of the Buddha's head, which represented the auspicious Buddha's light, had to be executed in a striking fashion. Later, a monk from the western regions learned of this, so made a long journey to offer a huge ruby, which was placed in the crown of the Buddha's head. Many, many years later, when the scripture cave was discovered, a lot of westerners showed up and made off with all kinds of precious objects and scriptures. One westerner discovered the red spot on top of the White Buddha's head. He could see that it was a precious stone. So one night, by the light of the stars, he climbed the nine-storey tower, tied one end of a rope to one of the big beams, and fastened the other end around his waist. He then leaped on top of the Buddha's head and chipped at the stone with a steel chisel. Flames shot up all around and the ruby cracked. The following day, the monks found a corpse with a rope around its waist in the Main Hall of the Nine-Storey Tower. Later an elderly monk placed a ball of red glass on the crown of the White Buddha's head. Never again did its dazzling luster appear."

That day, Zhang Shu and Chen Qing talked late into the night. Xiao Xingxing did not feel well, so she went back to her room to rest. Around midnight, a rainstorm occurred. Amid the wind and rain, the two men could clearly hear the sound of human weeping. Chen Qing sobered up, and Zhang Shu's hair stood on end.

"Did you hear it, lad? Another disturbance!" Chen Qing staggered out the door, pushing aside the raincoat Zhang Shu offered him. "I shouldn't talk about the Buddhas. I wonder if the White one is angry or the Black one? Tomorrow I will have to offer incense and add oil to the lamps."

Muttering, the old man disappeared into the darkness as the sound of weeping drifted more clearly through the rain.

Zhang Shu pulled on his raincoat and took a flashlight to trace the sound of the weeping. He couldn't believe it, but the sound led him to Xiao Xingxing's window. Could it be the perpetually happy girl who was crying? Staring at her dark window, all he wanted to do was go in and find out.

16

Xiao Xingxing couldn't sleep.

For years she had been afraid of the sight of blood, even if it was fake, imaginary, or symbolic.

When her period came each month, she would fall ill.

She had been frightened as a child. Many things frightened her;

almost everything frightened her. The illusionary frightened her, but the real even more. At times she would make a scene, but it was in order to suppress her fears. "As a child I was afraid of old women, totally afraid. As a child my eyes always detected something frightening about them. I first experienced this feeling with my maternal grandmother." So Xiao Xingxing wrote many years later in her autobiography, which she wrote for herself. "My grandmother was a Buddhist and had a large Buddhist shrine standing in her bedroom. It was covered with glass and capped with a red cloth. Inside the glass case was a black Shakyamuni. I often fell asleep under the gaze of that black Buddhist image amid the scent of incense and the rhythmic tapping of the wooden fish. Actually, I went to another world, a black world, which was filled with all sorts of strange and frightening dreams."

Sometimes, however, her grandmother was quite sweet. For example, her grandmother took her to play at the Puji Temple, which was a holiday for her. On such occasions, her grandmother, who was normally so mean, would become gentle and happy. She would greet everyone with a smile, and others would smile back and call her "Lay Buddhist Rong." Xingxing never forgot a young woman, also a lay Buddhist, who slipped her a couple of plums, a bright, sensuous red like rubies. She was stupefied. She clutched them in her sleep for several nights and refused to throw them away long after they shriveled up. Another person who fascinated Xingxing was "Lay Buddhist Lin" whose tasty vegetarian food— vegetarian chicken, fish, meat, and gluten—was Xingxing's favorite as a child, even though it was all made of soy. Then there were those magnificent Buddhist ceremonies when a number of monks in red *kasayas* knelt on their straw mats intoning the sutras as the incense swirled round the altar and several monks who led the recitation rhythmically beat the wooden fish. Xingxing also had a straw mat on which she sat rather than knelt. In fact, she sat facing the opposite direction, quietly hugging her knees and watching as the group of bald heads rose and fell, like moons, in unison above their red *kasayas*.

In today's parlance, Xingxing was a child who suffered from extreme introversion. She practically lived within the confines of her own little world. At night, as her grandmother snored, she would climb the altar and undo the frightful red cloth and speak on her own with the black Shakyamuni. In the shifting light and shadow, she would have the illusion that the Buddhist image would raise its eyes or display a profound smile. Each time this happened, she would feel an indescribable joy, and her heart would throb as if it would leap from her throat.

As a result, she became accustomed from an early age to talking to herself. Often she was assailed by many doubts and unhappiness at night; then, as if by divine revelation, she would know what she had to do after talking with herself.

Her mother and grandmother called her a "little demon" and didn't much care for her. She knew how to please them, but could never control her facial expressions. She often gave a look that was exactly the opposite of what the situation called for. But even worse, each time she made a face, a voice within her would say: fake. Thus, she'd want to laugh, but later she'd want to cry. After she grew up, her laughter would shine and her crying would be glorious. Most people felt she was broadminded and outspoken. She delighted in this appraisal, but she always feared that people would see through her. In short, hers was a solitude that was incompatible with others.

Yes, it happened one morning over ten years ago, you could say something from a previous age, and therefore never clear. She woke early with the presentiment that something was going to happen. She went to her older sister's room. Her slender sister always slept comfortably, her blanket pulled tight around her. It was a sign of chastity. By contrast, Xiao Xingxing's mother always scolded for the way she slept. She would throw off her blanket and sleep with her legs apart or she would squeeze the blanket between her legs. In short, she wasn't the sort of girl people liked. Besides, she was another girl in the family, and so no one regarded her birth as an important matter.

Her father was the only exception. At the time, her father was preoccupied with carrying out a political campaign aimed at the members of the Communist Party in the early 1950s. He didn't even look at her until ten or more days after she was born, but that one look was decisive in that her father gave her a lifetime of love. To him, she was a beautiful baby. But because her father never expressed his feelings for her, she harbored a sense of inferiority for a long time. She sometimes thought her feelings of inferiority stemmed from her slender sister, Xiao Yueyue, who was so gentle and refined. Xiao Xingxing, however, felt that her breasts and butt were too big, her waist too narrow, and her legs too thick. Everything was wrong.

That morning was like any other. Xiao Xingxing dawdled around at home until the last minute, and then amid the mutterings of her mother and grandmother, rolled out the door like a gust of wind. Her book bag, gloves, surgical mask, and scarf cut a colorful figure in the cold wind. She rushed to the subway entrance—that was when the first subway line had started running—looking at her watch and chewing the last bite of *mantou* as usual. On the platform, she suddenly heard a noise sweep toward her and before she could turn around, she felt a violent blow on her shoulder that nearly sent her over the white warning line. She saw the gazes of the other passengers freeze as several young men pounced on a young man wearing a suit and carrying a briefcase, who was running very fast. The heavy thuds of the men's boots echoed throughout the subway. Then a shrill voice, like metal on glass, shrieked: "Catch the counterrevolutionary! Catch the counterrevolutionary!" In the end, the young man had been flung down and beaten senseless at the subway exit. His eyes, which had moments before been bright and shining, were now a bloody pulp. Xingxing covered her face with her hands. At that moment, she caught a faint glimpse of the cold light from a pair of handcuffs, the sight of which pierced her to the heart. Three trains passed and still she trembled.

From then on, whenever she saw that viscous dark red color, she would feel like vomiting. It was a color followed by death. She felt that the color concealed a mysterious omen. Sure enough, three days later, she saw the notice at a bend in a desolate street, the far-off notice that she'd never forget.

She once again felt as if everything had been blotted out by that dark red nightmare.

17

Xingxing woke up very late.

The first thing she did upon getting out of bed was to look in the mirror. Her eyes were swollen. Her entire face looked pale and puffy.

"What's Weiwei up to? And Mousheng?" She filled her bowl with leftover porridge, took a couple of pieces of Yunnan rutabaga, and ate without much of an appetite. She felt it strange that she thought of her husband and son only during the day, in the morning just after getting out of bed. But night belonged solely to the past, to her secrets.

Mousheng had counseled her many times not to go: "If you have to go, at least wait till I'm on vacation so that we can go together. I'll have no peace of mind if you go alone." "If the two of us go, what about the child? I'm a painter; I have to get out." When Mousheng put her on the train, he said, "If you decide you don't like it, just come home. Don't be too thrifty. If you need money, I'll send it. Away from home, things are not that sanitary. Be careful what you eat. Write often . . . don't worry about the boy . . . have a good time and enjoy yourself."

Sometimes Mousheng was so caring and solicitous. Xingxing knew that many women envied her, but they didn't know the real Mousheng. She consoled herself with the thought that no marriage was perfect. She really feared every day becoming the same. She felt the frightening triviality of routine slowly eating away at her soul, increasing her inertia. She began to put on weight and was incapable of painting for a long time. One day, as Mousheng asked the same question he asked every day with his usual zest, "Xingxing, what are we having for dinner tonight?" she blew up for no apparent reason.

Man is not an emotional or rational creature, but rather a creature of habit. How terrible it was to be a creature of habit!

"Dear Mousheng, How are you?" she sat down and wrote. Picking up her pen, she felt a profound fatigue. She wrote "Dear Mousheng, How are you?" several times, and each time tore up the letter she was writing. But then Weiwei's plump, grinning face appeared before her.

Dear Mousheng, How are you?

Being in Dunhuang is like being in a Buddhist land. My old mental haze seems to have dissipated somewhat, only to be replaced by a new kind. But one thing is for sure: when I get back, I'll paint things that will surprise you. How is Weiwei? Is he still picky about his food? I hear there is a new medicine called "male dragon for healthy bones," which is good for children. Why not give him some? Don't keep him covered all the time. His cough comes from being covered, not from the cold.

Do you miss me? A kiss for you. Kiss Weiwei for me.

Xingxing July 9

When she finished the letter, she felt as if she had fulfilled some obligation. She heaved a sigh.

18

At lunchtime, Zhang Shu showed up with a live fish and two Yellow River melons.

The fish Xingxing cooked was delicious, and Zhang Shu ate three bowls of rice. As he ate, he kept his eyes fixed on her. She noticed but paid no attention.

"Xingxing."

"Huh?"

"I was wondering who was lucky enough to be your husband." Zhang Shu did his best to make it sound like a joke, but his awkwardness only confirmed that he was serious.

"My husband is just an ordinary guy."

"What does he do?"

"He teaches management in a university."

"That puts him in a favored position today. Why doesn't he go into business? Don't people say these days that nine out of ten million people are failures here and the other one million leave the country on business?"

Xingxing laughed. "Maybe he'll go into business. What about your wife? What does she do?"

"She's the director of PR at a big company."

"Now that's really the job of the moment," said Xingxing, regaining some of her liveliness. "She must be very pretty."

"People say she's pretty."

"What do you mean 'people say'?"

". . . everyone's appreciation of beauty is different. What I mean is when a husband and wife have been together for a time, looks don't really matter."

"Do you have any children?"

"A son. He's nine."

"That's it. There's no way for us to become in-laws."

"You have a son, too?" he said, startled.

"Yes, and he might become your son's rival in love someday!" She laughed, which wiped away her inner unhappiness.

"Can I ask how old you are?" He couldn't believe she was already a mother, but he didn't want to be presumptuous by asking a woman's age, so he tried to make it sound like a joke.

"I'm thirty; a little on the old side, right?" She smiled, taking a bite of melon.

19

Xiao Xingxing was far more shaken by Sanwei Mountain Temple than she was by the Thousand Buddhist Caves.

Zhang Shu had taken her for a camel ride with the idea of spending a long, carefree evening at Yueya Spring to relax completely.

Dusk at Yueya Spring possessed an intoxicating beauty, filled with a romantic atmosphere. Zhang Shu looked at Xingxing from behind as she rode the camel and felt an emotional upwelling. Her silhouette was pretty and full. At dusk, her short hair turned gold, and her flowery skirt was lifted by the breeze, as if some heavenly maiden were scattering flower petals. He couldn't believe she was thirty and had a four-year-old son.

He wanted to say something to her, today, here, at the Yueya Spring.

But Xiao Xingxing insisted upon going to Sanwei Mountain Temple. She was set upon locating that monk who looked like Ananda. Her recalcitrance made Zhang Shu angry.

"He might know something about Lakshmi!" In the end, Xingxing played her trump card and had her way.

20

Dayejisi didn't necessarily have a smile pasted on his face the way Zhang Shu had described. He treated Xiao Xingxing coldly.

"From ancient times, those who are particular about fortune-telling tell only the fortunes of men." He sat on a mat next to a Buddhist table. It was very dark inside. As per the rules, Xiao Xingxing burnt incense sticks and worshiped the Buddha. Zhang Shu accompanied her but said nothing.

"Why tell the fortunes of men and not women?" Xingxing seemed so anxious that she wanted to grab the stick for tapping the wooden fish from his hands and hurl it away.

"The fate of woman is unfathomable," said Dayejisi haughtily, bringing his palms together without really even looking at her.

"It's my fault. I told her about your ability to tell fortunes, sir," said Zhang Shu in a low, muffled voice. "Since we are here, I entreat you, sir, to please tell her fortune, good or bad."

"May I ask what relation this female benefactor is to Zhang Shu?"

"She's a relative of mine," said Zhang Shu, without thinking. Xiao Xingxing almost burst out laughing. She thought it amusing that Zhang Shu, who was normally so serious, could lie with so much composure.

"I will do as Zhang Shu wishes." Dayejisi stood up, smiled, and fixed his eyes on Xiao Xingxing's face.

"This female benefactor's face is quite strange!" He suddenly exclaimed as if in a Shanxi Opera.

"In what way?" Zhang Shu seemed more nervous than Xingxing.

"In looking at this female benefactor's face, I see she has delicate and pretty features as well as a white and good complexion. Her hands are small and squarish, and she should belong to the element of metal. But her pupils are black as lacquer, indicating she is intelligent, lively, and likeable, also belonging to the element of water. Though this female benefactor's form is incomplete, still there is harmony in her bones and flesh. The *Mayi Physiognomy* says: 'One's bones determine one's ups and downs in life. You don't want to be too fat or too thin. When too fat, Yin overcomes Yang; when too thin, Yang overcomes Yin. In their complementarity, Yin and Yang form a single whole. Moreover, her breath is long and leisurely. A mountain shines when there is jade in the rocks; river charms when there is gold in the sands.' This is the best treasure. I heard her voice a moment ago and it is pleasing, the so-called sound of flowing water, the cries of flying jade birds, and the playing of stringed music. It's just, it's just . . ." Dayejisi hesitated for a moment, the trace of a sneer on his lips. "It's just that the mole at her hairline on the left of her forehead is not very auspicious. I'm afraid she will dominate her loved ones."

Xingxing's heart thumped. "Venerable sir, by loved ones, do you mean my husband?"

Dayejisi smiled surreptitiously. "I am a monk, and it is not a good idea to discuss mundane affairs. When she was eighteen, the female benefactress encountered difficulty, depriving her of a loved one. And twelve years later, the same thing will occur, unless you rein in at the last moment and resolutely retreat posthaste."

"In twelve years. That means this year!" cried Xingxing.

"That's why I want you to retreat while you can," said Dayejisi as he took up her hand to look at her palm. "The female benefactress's palm is actually quite good, showing both prosperity and long life. Moreover, your internal organs and physiological functions are extremely young—at least ten years younger than your actual age. Such good qualities are worth protecting. I urge the two of you to leave here before you regret it."

"Venerable sir, I'd like your advice on something," said Zhang Shu, seeing that Dayejisi was about to leave. He stepped forward. "Venerable sir, you are from these parts and have seen a lot. I was wondering if you know about the painting *Lakshmi Bathing* in Cave Seventy-three . . ."

Before Zhang Shu could finish, Dayejisi waved both hands and looked irritated. Zhang Shu noticed how sensitive he was with regard to the matter and his evasiveness.

"Was he very accurate?" Zhang Shu asked Xingxing. He was dying to know who the "loved one" was when she was eighteen.

"Not bad," said Xingxing, who had wanted to say that he was too accurate. Then she suddenly remembered that she lost Xiaojun when she was seventeen and not eighteen. She didn't know why, but she was unwilling to tell Zhang Shu about these past events. For some reason she felt Zhang Shu was self-centered. He was treating her so well because of the distance between them, but as soon as she got close to him or she threw herself at him, he would very quickly tire of her.

She had known quite a few men, and for this reason she had them pegged within a matter of moments.

21

Xiao Xingxing locked herself in her room and painted.

When Zhang Shu went to visit her, he discovered that she had painted a lot of strange lines, some of which resembled fish or birds.

"Are you all right, Xingxing?" he asked with concern.

She smiled sadly and said, "The reason I came here was to verify a dream."

"Verify a dream?"

"Yes. Since I was very little, I've often had dreams, strange dreams. But the oddest thing is that my strange dreams have a way of coming true. Once they come true, I no longer have them. The dream of the last two years is especially strange . . . In the dream . . . I see myself coming to a large cave covered inside with frescoes. I can vaguely make out what appear to be painted asaras, bodhisattvas, heavenly kings, and muscular men . . . I knew it was the Mogao Caves. But in one of the caves is a huge pool of water in the middle of which is standing a person . . ."

"A person?"

"Yeah, a young person. You could say a boy. He looks seventeen or eighteen, tall, thin, broad, and square-shouldered . . . oh, the boy slashes his wrist with a small knife and the blood spurts out. He is standing like a ramrod in the middle of the water like a fountain of blood. The water soon turns red. The frescoes around him soon turn red as well. But the strange thing is that boy's expression. He seems to be smiling. His face . . . it gradually becomes transparent like a piece of transparent paper. What's more, he becomes thinner before my eyes and looks unreal . . ."

"Are you okay?" he asked, alarmed at seeing how pale she had become. She smiled wanly, as if all the vitality had vanished from her body. "It's nothing. I have an old ailment—when I see blood, I feel dizzy and sick. Sometimes I can't even think. It must be a reflex."

"Well, let's not talk about it."

"I've already done so. At this point in my dream, I wake up in alarm. This is followed by dizziness and nausea, and sometimes I even throw up."

"Why don't you see a doctor?"

"There's no point . . . the medicine doesn't work on me."

She stood there, her face pallid. She looked alone and helpless. Her dark eyes were filled with a childlike tenderness.

"I've noticed that you really look like—"

"What?"

"Nothing," he said, blushing. "You look like a little girl."

"I'm someone's mother."

"I mean . . . your eyes. You'd see such eyes ten years ago, but you don't see them today. Do you know what I mean?"

She looked up at him with tenderness, then quickly lowered her eyes. His heart felt constricted, touched by some inexpressible feeling. He softly stroked her hair. Then quickly controlling himself, he hastily left.

II.

Lakshmi

I

Lakshmi was a goddess in the Hindu pantheon. She deals with fate, wealth, and beauty. She first appeared in the *Rig Veda* and was personalized in the *Atharvaveda*.[1] She was produced when the devas and asuras stirred the Sea of Milk. She is also known as the Girl of the Sea of Milk. The Buddhists assimilated her as a protector of Dharmadeva. She was the younger sister of Vaisravana and had great merit among the people and was once called Gongdetian, the Goddess of Luck. In Tibetan Buddhism, she is considered the goddess of wealth.

Such was the background on Lakshmi that Zhang Shu was able to piece together; strangely, none of the descriptions matched what was depicted in the frescoes. Not one of the descriptions mentioned her beauty. At most they mentioned her "large, long eyes and calm mien." Was the painter Yu-Chi Yiseng too partial to her? If so, where did his feelings come from?

The only thing that was certain was that she was a deity in Brahmanism, Hinduism, Buddhism, and Tibetan Buddhism. There were very few such deities. In today's terms she would be a female spy with the additional quality possessing dual citizenship or more than one passport.

It didn't seem to matter whether she was Vaisravana's wife or sister. But the most amusing thing is that her husband, or her brother, evolved into a Chinese man named Li, the deva king who holds a pagoda in his palm, who had three sons, the most famous of whom, Nezha, followed him into the Central Plains, adapting the Western to China and becoming an immortal. This represents not just the exchange of the talented persons

---

1. A sacred text of Hinduism..

between Buddhism and Daoism, but it can be said that like Prince Nezha, who battled the Handsome Monkey King, he was a real foreigner. What would the real Nezha of Buddhism think if he saw how the Chinese modeled him in clay as a boy? Zhang Shu concluded that it was Nezha at the side of Lakshmi in the bathing pool.

But he couldn't explain why according to Tibetan Buddhism, Lakshmi wore the skin of her son.

How had the beautiful Lakshmi, as painted by Yu-Chi Yiseng, become the demon of Tibetan Buddhism? When the answer dawned on him, he felt terrified.

2

Zhang Shu was unable to control his curiosity about Lakshmi. One day he mixed with a Japanese tour group to get a look at one of the caves opened for special visitors, usually not open to the general public (back then China just opened its door to let foreign tourists visit), hoping to learn something. But he was discovered.

It was a woman who discovered him. She wore a large gray scarf and was dressed in a long black robe with a dirty vest. It was the very same minority woman he had seen when he was with Xiao Xingxing, the one shuffling along alone at Cave 73.

Zhang Shu was escorted to the Dunhuang Cultural Administrative Office. Dusk had fallen and the faces shone darkly by the light in the office. A tall, heavyset, middle-aged woman stood under the light. Her hair was cut short and her bangs, which hung rather unsuitably over her forehead, couldn't conceal her age, which was evident from the soft, fleshy folds of her neck. Her neck was white but slack. Her chin quivered with every move she made.

"May I see some ID?" The woman spoke softly but clearly, as if each syllable emanated from her diaphragm.

"I'm sorry, but I don't have any ID on me." Zhang Shu looked directly at her. As she moved and sat down under the light, he got a good look at her face. She looked like Guanyin, a goddess of mercy, filled with compassion for people. Her eyes looked upon him with pity. That pitying look infuriated him.

"Don't be so quick to say you didn't bring it. Have a look," her voice softly sounded again. Zhang Shu watched her as she spoke and saw that her lips scarcely moved, as if she were afraid that moving them might create wrinkles at the corners of her mouth. Her face was the kind that was taken good care of to an excessive degree. Her lips were extremely sensuous. He suddenly fancied that this Guanyin could swallow a doe by scarcely moving her lips.

He turned his canvas backpack upside down.

A small ID fell on the desk.

He suddenly recalled that it was his father-in-law's high-ranking cadre medical ID. Before leaving, he had accompanied the old man to see the doctor, but he couldn't say why he had stuck the ID in his bag.

The woman snatched up the ID, her eyebrows raised in amazement.

"What is your relationship to Secretary Wang?" She looked up, her eyes still filled with pity.

"I'm . . . his daughter's husband," he said unwillingly after a moment of silence. This strange reply caught her off guard.

"Oh, you are his son-in-law." With a feeble wave of her hand, she indicated that he should take a seat. But he continued to stand without moving.

"What business brings you here?"

"I'm interested . . . in local folktales and thought I would collect some . . . ," he stuttered.

Curious, she tilted her head to one side.

"How is Secretary Wang?"

"He's fine."

"What's your wife's name?"

"Wang Xiyi. Uh, how do you know—"

"I know Secretary Wang. He has always shown a good deal of concern for us. Several years ago he came to the Mogao Caves and even favored us with his personal instruction." A faint smile played over her sensuous lips. She pressed a buzzer and a young made-up female clerk appeared.

"Your name is Zhang Shu, correct? Little Ma, would you see to it that you prepare a special visitor's pass for this gentleman, so that he can look at any cave he wishes. Of course, you have to obey the rules." She smiled, but he felt in her words there was actually an iron hand in a velvet glove. She's no doubt a sharp woman, he thought.

She tore a page from her desk calendar and swiftly wrote a few words and said, "If you are looking for folktales, you can contact this person. He'll assist you. If you need anything else, feel free to call me at any time. My number is 431542. My name is Pan Sumin . . . you can go now."

She rose to her feet somewhat indolently and gestured as if to see off a visitor.

He unfolded the piece of paper and saw written there the name Chen Qing.

3

"You mean you met Bodhisattva Pan?"

Zhang Shu was displeased by the abject terror Chen Qing showed at the mention of Pan Sumin.

"We all call her Bodhisattva, which is a wise and compassionate being in Buddhism. Don't you think she looks like Guanyin, the goddess of mercy?" As the old man spoke, all the wrinkles on his face seemed to move.

"Does she have a lot of power and influence here?"

The old man evaded the question and said, "She seems to have taken a liking to you, so I can be frank with you. Come here and listen up, lad."

Zhang Shu could feel the hot liquor on his foul breath.

"In a couple of days, there's going to be a big Buddhist ceremony up at Sanwei Mountain Temple. At that time, I'll figure out a way to get the key to Cave Seventy-three for you. You want to have a look at the Lakshmi cave, don't you?" The old man whispered mysteriously.

Zhang Shu felt a shock deep within.

"Really?"

"Why would I lie to you?"

"Is it okay if I take Xiao Xingxing?"

The old man shook his head. "I give an inch and you want to take a mile. Aren't you afraid of ruining your luck by taking a woman there in the evening?"

Zhang Shu didn't insist. When he went to see Xiao Xingxing, as he usually did after eating, he found her light out and her door locked.

4

Zhang Shu stood absentmindedly in front of the unlocked wooden door of Cave 73 before approaching it with determination. The door creaked as he pushed it open. The cave was black as pitch inside. He cautiously turned on his flashlight before closing the door behind him.

It was a world unto itself. Almost unconsciously his flashlight first swept over the image of the emissary Ananda, which smiled as usual. Its secretive smile was so strikingly similar to Dayejisi's smile carved out of wood that he wondered if he wasn't posing as that polychrome sculpture. He felt like kicking it to see if it would crumble like a half bag of flour into a heap.

He pulled his eyes away from the statue to look at that empty space. It was the same as ever, not a single hue had been added for his evening visit. He could only vaguely discern the remnant of a lotus petal, half of a plump white foot with reddish toes, and a bunch of pearls. He squatted, nearly pressing his face against the wall, persisting in his search. He seemed to smell an unusual scent, a delicate fragrance like that of tree resin.

Later a ray of bright light—ten times stronger than his flashlight—shot in from behind him. He looked back, but the bright light forced him to close his eyes. All he could make out were silver filaments of light.

"Who's there?" His shout sounded feeble even to himself.

"I'm the protective deity of this sanctuary."

He heard a woman's voice. It was not a young voice and it had a northwestern accent. He blocked the strong light with his hand hoping to get a good look at the woman.

"Do you think I'd let you see me? Ha-ha-ha . . ." Her laughter was hearty, as if she had grown up herding and shouting at cattle and sheep on the plains. She stubbornly shone a huge flashlight, much stronger than his, into his face. Her laughter seemed to bring everything in the dark cave to life, as if both Kasyapa and Ananda were mocking him in the darkness.

"Put down your flashlight and listen to what I have to say." He had a sudden inspiration and thought of that woman who looked like Guanyin. Right or wrong, he had to play this card.

"I have a special visitor's pass signed by Pan Sumin. If you don't believe me, you can call her."

His words seemed to have the effect of a prayer on the iron hoop of the Monkey King. A moment of silence followed before the light moved upward like a torch, shining on the ceiling of the cave. He immediately turned his light on her. It was the face of a fifty-year-old woman, her head in a gray scarf, from which several white hairs protruded. Her black robe and gray vest were dark. Her eyes, like a dead man's, were fixed on him. It was that same minority woman.

"Oh, so it's you. So you are Chief Pan's guest?" The voice remained skeptical.

"Yes."

"Let me see your papers."

She took the special visitor's pass and scrutinized it, pressing it close to her eyes, as if she were smelling it.

"What are you doing here in the middle of the night? Didn't you see enough during the day?"

"No."

"What is it that you wish to see?"

"This painting." He used his flashlight to point at the empty space.

She swayed a bit. "What is it that you are up to?"

". . . I'm researching this."

"Oh, so you are engaged in research on the frescoes? Are you from Beijing?"

"Yep."

She seemed to heave a sigh of relief. "Why didn't you say so? It's easy to examine this painting. Although it was stolen, I still have the original in my possession."

"What do you mean by original?"

"This painting dates from the late Tang dynasty and is a copy. The original was painted by Yu-Chi Yiseng."

"You're saying that you have Yu-Chi Yiseng's original work?" Zhang Shu's throat seemed to contract.

"It's not mine." The woman didn't seem to understand what he meant by original work.

"You have it?"

"Yes."

"Can I see it?" He said in a low and anxious tone of voice. He felt a pang of fear that she might refuse him.

"Why not?" replied the woman, as unconcerned as if someone wanted to borrow a rag.

He was speechless.

"I'd like to know why you are so interested in this particular painting," said the woman, suddenly raising her head. In the light, the wrinkles on her forehead resembled cart tracks. Zhang Shu recalled how she walked alone outside Cave 73. He was suddenly filled with fear.

"I'm . . . very interested . . . in . . . Lakshmi. I . . . think . . . Yiseng's painting . . . isn't of the real goddess."

"Oh! Ha-ha-ha," the woman laughed madly again. "The real goddess Lakshmi? You tell me . . ."

"Lakshmi is described differently in Hinduism, Brahmanism, and Buddhism, and Tibetan Buddhism depicted her as a fierce demon. What was her original form? Why is she a goddess to so many religions?"

"You are very observant," laughed the woman, mocking him. "Why so many 'whys'?" she said, placing emphasis on the word *why*, imitating him. "The Goddess Gongdetian was married to the Deva King of the North! The Deva King could do whatever he liked with her. What's so hard to understand about that? Do you know about the Deva King?"

"I know about him, Deva King Vaisravana of the North, one of four deva kings."

"Did you know that the four great deva kings are also referred to as the four vajras? They are the heavenly spirits who hold vajra staffs and protect the Dharma. They are also yakshas. Are they fierce looking? Take a look at the four corners of this cave." She raised her large flashlight and shined it at the ceiling. The four deva kings were painted at the four corners.

The flashlight played over the blue faces and fangs like a spotlight on a stage. Shadows floated above the colorful statues. Zhang Shu felt a shiver down his spine.

"Do you know about China's Two Generals of Hengha?" The woman removed her scarf releasing a disheveled mass of dirty gray hair. "Actually they were vajra demigods. At one time there was only one vajra demigod, who was called Dharma-mati. But in China it is said that divine status was conferred upon the Two Generals of Hengha after the deaths of Zheng Lun and Chen Qi, but there is no mention of this in the Buddhist scriptures."

"Of course there isn't—that's from *The Investiture of the Gods*."

The woman laughed grimly. "You know a lot. That classical novel of heroes and gods says that the four great deva kings were generals of Mara, the Destroyer. They were sent west by Jiang Taigong to serve as the deva kings. I suppose you know about that, too?"

"There's nothing strange about that, after all the Chinese sinicized Buddhism. Didn't Vaisravana later become Deva Li Who Holds a Stupa?"

"You don't know crap." The woman blinked her eyes continuously as she spoke, as if she were proud of her own Buddhist knowledge. "That happened in the Song dynasty. By the Yuan dynasty, they were in charge of good weather for crops, and even the implements used in worship had changed!"

Zhang Shu said nothing more and instead adopted the respectful air of a subordinate receiving orders.

"Are you in your fifties?"

"Huh? . . . More than fifty." He laughed to himself. His stubbly beard must certainly have been enough to frighten anyone in the darkness of the cave.

"More than fifty and doing research on frescoes. Do you know when Buddhism was transmitted to the Kingdom of Khotan?"

"I haven't read that much, but I recall that in the *Record of a Journey to the Kingdom of Khotan* it says that it was two hundred years after Shakyamuni entered nirvana. The King, Yu-Chi Sheng reigned, and Buddhism began to flourish in Khotan . . .

"A little knowledge and away you go. I can see how much you know. Khotan was established two hundred thirty-four years after the Buddha entered nirvana; King Yu-Chi Sheng sat on the throne one hundred sixty-five years after the country was founded. Not bad, you had Buddhism flourishing one hundred years earlier in the Kingdom of Khotan."

"I'm ignorant and ill-informed," said Zhang Shu, fed up. "But I don't have the slightest idea of what all this has to do with Lakshmi."

Once again the woman laughed grimly. "Such a common fellow! Listen up and I'll tell you. At first the king of Khotan did not believe in Buddhism. Later, a bhikshu by the name of Vairocan visited him and told him that the Tathagata had sent him. He said if you build a sunken relief for him, he'd let you rule forever. The king of Khotan replied that if he showed him the Buddha, he'd naturally do as he was told. Vairocan rang a bell and asked the Buddha to appear. The Buddha sent Rahula in the form of the Tathagata, manifesting his face in the sky. Henceforth, the king of Khotan believed in Buddhism. Do you know who Rahula is?"

"The eldest son of Shakyamuni."

"I didn't ask you whose son he was." The woman had a quick and explosive temper. "He later became an Arhat. After the king of Khotan became a believer, the entire royal clan followed suit. Yu-Chi Yiseng, of course, was a member of the royal clan and an outstanding painter. During the Zhenguan reign period, the Emperor Taizong was uneasy about the Gansu Corridor and sent a massive force to guard the region. He also invited a number of members of the royal clan to the Central Plains—in fact, they were actually hostages. It was in those days that Yiseng came to the Central Plains. At that time the only paintings from the Central Plains that the emperor really liked were those by Yan Liben.

But after Yiseng arrived, the emperor was crazy about his paintings. He did that painting of Lakshmi bathing."

Zhang Shu didn't utter a word; he marveled silently at how wondrous it all was. He never expected that such a coarse-looking woman, one who appeared to have no education, would know so much about the history of Dunhuang and Buddhism.

"But from the Zhenguan reign period to today is about thirteen hundred years. How was Yiseng's painting preserved to this day? And how did it end up in your hands?"

"Good question." Eyes lowered, she continued, "My mother left it to me. In the five prefectures of the Gansu Corridor, the only person surnamed Yu-Chi was my mother."

"Then you mean to say that you are a descendant of Yu-Chi Yiseng? From Xinjiang? You're so pleased to agree to let me see it, aren't you afraid that I'll want to keep it?" Zhang Shu continued to remain skeptical.

The woman looked up quickly. "No, I'm not afraid. I've looked after this place for thirty years. Good and bad, I've seen it all. It's just—"

"It's just what?"

"It's just that the painting is in bad shape. My mother said that when I was too little to know what I was doing, I poked out one of Lakshmi's eyes."

"Poking out a Buddha's eyes means bad karma," joked Zhang Shu to dispel the frightening atmosphere.

"It sure does. Take a look," she said, as she removed her right eye. Her eyelid shrank back leaving a dark cavern. Zhang Shu was shocked.

"My daughter paid for this glass one." The woman seemed unaffected as usual, as if her eye were worth no more than a marble. Deciding he had had enough talk, Zhang Shu stood up. He was scared out of his wits and wanted to get away as quickly as possible.

"If you'd like to see the painting, come up to the peak of Mingsha Mountain tomorrow night between eleven and one in the morning and get it."

That was the last thing he heard as he left the cave, following which he looked up and saw the stars twinkling in the black sky above.

5

Just as Zhang Shu was having his first romantic experience after arriving in Dunhuang, a young man knocked on Xiao Xingxing's door.

He was a student traveling from Beijing. He loved to travel to far-off places as cheaply as possible. He was now hungry and thirsty and had come to this cheap place on the recommendation of others. Who could have seen foreseen that only one light would have been on in the entire place? Who knows where Chen Qing had gone to have a drink? As a result, only Xiao Xingxing's light was still burning.

6

Xiao Xingxing suddenly found herself assailed by the introversion of her youth, and for two days she was unwilling to see anyone. She couldn't complete any task, and her mind was troubled by some nameless anxiety. All of this occurred after Zhang Shu had expressed his special feelings for her.

It ought to be said that she did have a good impression of him; in fact, she actually liked him at the beginning. She found him quite masculine in a sexy sort of way. After a few days of contact, she did reveal her charms to him. The more passionate she became, the stronger she expressed herself. She liked the way he looked at her and was pleased that she could attract the interest of such a splendid man. Subconsciously it was as if she wanted something to happen and she wanted him to express himself. She enjoyed hearing confessions of love. She had heard all sorts of confessions, but none like those she had read in fiction.

But after hearing them, she felt afraid. It's the same with an actress who wins the hearts of her audience and then is afraid of losing them. She wants to do what is most pleasing to the audience, but not necessarily what is most pleasing to herself. In addition to fear, she also feels tired on account of this. She doesn't know if taking off her dress and ornaments and lying naked on a bed like a slattern would make the men like her or not.

She knew what a man like Zhang Shu would expect from the woman he loved. Most of them are aesthetes, who only too quickly grew disappointed in the object of their love. It was precisely this loss of interest that she couldn't tolerate. Her only choice, then, was to flee.

But at her age, wasn't fleeing like a tiring old drama? She just wanted to try it for all she was worth, just once, regardless of the outcome, to experience the beauty of loving and being loved, just once.

But the moment she began to think this way, the experience frightfully soon lost its beauty. This was perhaps the reason she would never be genuinely happy.

7

He appeared before her eyes as if he had fallen from Heaven.

It was very quiet that night so the knocking came gently. When she opened the door, he was there, the calm light flowing over him. She saw that he was tall and thin, with broad square shoulders. She stepped back as if she had seen a ghost. As a result, her hair was outlined in the light, a quivering golden light. Then he seemed to see the fear appear in her eyes.

Her fears were an old story that arose between her dreams and how they came true. They had come true several times already, but not quite in this way, as the person in her dreams materialized, especially on such a peaceful night.

Several years later, Xiao Xingxing described her feelings at that time to me in this way: "I thought I would go on having that dream. I thought the blood would soon come spurting out of his wrist. I wanted to run, to flee from that scarlet nightmare."

Later events in fact confirm that she did flee, but he didn't.

8

"Can I . . . can I have a drink of water?" he asked. His voice was so hoarse that he could scarcely be heard. His skin was dark and scaly, blood oozed from his lips, his Adam's apple bobbed, and he looked as if he were going to faint.

"Of course . . ." she muttered.

What happened then seemed a matter of course. He drank the water, but so quickly he almost burst into tears. Seeing his Adam's apple bob, she suddenly felt sorry for him. It was like a scene repeated from her past. As he stood there awkwardly holding the glass, she heated water for him to take a bath. She used the small hot plate that Zhang Shu had hooked up for her.

Next she roasted some corn on the hot plate. Turning the corn slowly, its aroma filled the small room. The splashing of bathwater was heard behind the tightly shut bathroom door. The sound gave her a warm feeling of security on that quiet night. She sat there lazily listening to the water and smelling the aroma of the roasting corn. Warm, she felt she would drift off to sleep if she closed her eyes.

The young man finally came out, dripping wet. His wet hair stood up in spikes like sisal cord. He put on a clean T-shirt and shorts, both of which were old but looked very comfortable. He was a handsome young man. The young man in her dream was always shrouded in mist; this young man stood before her in shining clarity under the light. She could even make out the down above his lip.

But his eyes seemed to be covered with a mist of sorts. She knew he only had to shut his long lashes and he'd go right off to sleep. He was exhausted. She knew he would be lovely to look upon as he slept.

"There's no way you'll find a place tonight, so you'll just have to make do with sleeping here tonight," she said rather flatly. As she spoke, though, her heart was pounding. She bent over and divided the bedding in half and then improvised a bed on the floor, following which she sat down cross-legged as if it were the most natural thing.

"No, no . . . how will this ever do?" His eyelids remained tenaciously open, though they looked as if they were going to stick together. He remained standing, his embarrassed smile at once grateful and apologetic. "I'll sleep on the floor. I'm really putting you out . . ."

He had a lovely voice with a perfect pitch. But his voice was filled with exhaustion. From the very first she could see that he was pretty stubborn, which was only confirmed later as they interacted. But she always vacillated. This was the pattern established on their very first meeting and one that never changed.

Naturally the stubborn person had his way. The exhausted young man collapsed on the floor amid the aroma of roasting corn. He slept soundly, snoring ever so softly. To the best of her recollection, no member of the opposite sex ever slept so soundly. Even her four-year-old son would grind his teeth in his sleep.

As always, she lay back with both hands behind her head. But the aroma of the roasted corn and his rhythmic breathing rose like a vapor, a vapor replete with seduction. Later, she simply turned on the light and looked at his face as he slept soundly.

9

Many years before there had been another young man like this. Thin and tall, whose shoulders were broad and square, but whose hair was different. In those days all the young men kept their hair cut short; a little longer and people would see them as "troublemakers." But he was more intelligent than most, and therefore more skeptical and more stubborn.

Only occasionally did that far-off young man enter her life. One day, she went to see a friend, where she met that man. There was something different about him. He had a pair of limpid eyes; his pupils seemed golden and especially beautiful. More than a decade later she read about those eyes in a cheap book on physiognomy. The book called those eyes tiger eyes, which portended a prosperous future. But there must have been some other feature on his face to contradict this; otherwise, he wouldn't have ended up so badly.

His name was Xiaojun.

10

Zhang Shu knocked excitedly on Xiao Xingxing's door. The young man had just arisen from his makeshift bed on the floor.

Xiao Xingxing was still lying quietly in bed and seemed unaware that anyone had entered. Zhang Shu called to her once. She looked over at him with a strange look

The young man gave him a pleasant look and began gnawing on an ear of corn.

For a moment, Zhang Shu almost thought he had entered the wrong room.

Yellow kernels of crushed corn were reduced to yellow liquid, which made Zhang Shu's mouth tingle when he saw it. He looked over at the small pot on the hot plate and saw steam rising.

"Are you going for a walk? The weather's great today," he said, looking at the hot plate.

"She's not feeling well; she didn't get much sleep last night," said the young man, also looking at the hot plate.

Xingxing stared silently at the ceiling. A circle of light shone on the ceiling in which motes of dust slowly sank.

"Xingxing, I have something to say to you," said Zhang Shu, weakly as never before.

Only then did Xingxing look over. She seemed to have just awakened. This was the way she really looked, not in the least dissembling. Her beauty was actually quite moving.

"Oh, it's you . . . I'm sorry," she said, unsure why her face flushed. "I didn't sleep well last night. I'm very tired and don't feel like getting up."

Alarmed and bewildered, she didn't know what she was saying. Long after, she continued to regret her reply. "I didn't sleep well and I don't feel like getting up." Her words provided too much food for thought, especially for a man who had just become interested in her, someone who watched her every move.

Zhang Shu threw an unhappy glance at the young man and departed.

He didn't want to appear upset, lest it give the young man airs.

The weather was really fine. The sky was unusually blue, the air clear and not too dry, the same as the morning they had met.

II

Zhang Shu's heart ached.

When he saw that young man get up from his makeshift bed on the floor, he was shocked speechless. His pride demanded that he leave at once, but that same pride also made him refuse to admit defeat.

Besides, Xingxing's appearance of having just awakened was quite moving. That image remained fixed in his mind. Her disheveled hair, flushed cheeks, and two dreamy eyes formed the picture of a slovenly angel.

He wanted to do everything possible to dilute that image with another face. He felt it odd that when he was far from home he often forgot his wife's looks. Just after he had returned to Beijing, he went to a get-together at the house of an old classmate. His classmate had gone to work at a carpet factory where he made good monthly wages. He didn't know many of the people there. There were eleven or twelve. Later a slender and graceful woman showed up. His classmate introduced her as Wang Xiyi, a decent pianist. The woman elegantly took a seat at the piano, which was old and shabby, and began playing. It was the song on everyone's lips titled "For Alice." She did play well, and the familiar tune made him feel sad but excited. They began seeing each other. One autumn day, as they sat on a park bench, she told him she was the daughter of the provincial party secretary. After sitting quietly for some time, he suddenly blurted out, "I thought you came from an intellectual family. Your name sounds as if it were chosen by a bookworm." Then he suddenly felt her thrust his hand into a warm, soft place. He wanted to pull his hand back, but was too late. That was the first time he had touched a woman's privates. It was true, many people said his wife was beautiful, but he never thought her so. He didn't find his wife's face, which was of a standard beauty, to be lovely, and as soon as they were apart, her face became wan and lacking in features. Unfortunately, it was true, but he never told anyone. He hated himself for it. He found all sorts of reasons to prove his wife's superiority and his own inferiority. If it hadn't been for his wife's audacity, he probably never would have married. He was always hesitant when it came to women and always took a carefully observant, wait-and-see attitude. The first few times they made love, he felt a vague revulsion for her, because it did not conform to his aesthetic sense. After the mystery and the excitement had entirely vanished, all that remained for him was a feeling of having been cheated.

But his feelings were completely different for his son. When he carried that small life home from the maternity hospital, he treated it as if it were part of his own life. The baby only weighed 3 *jin* at birth and didn't even have the strength to cry. It could only produce some weak inarticulate sounds of "gugu," so they gave him the nickname Gugu and his actual name was similar: Zhang Gu. He was probably familiar with all the pediatric clinics by the time his son was three. Upon seeing him, all the doctors would frown. At three years of age—and with some difficulty— he finally managed to get him into a kindergarten. On the second day, one of the women working there called and said Zhang Gu had a fever and a stomachache, and wouldn't eat. After that they were never off the phone. They were never off the phone. Slowly he learned to slip ration coupons to the women and give them a calendar or other things at New Year to be on the good side of them. As a result the women took care of his son and the phone calls decreased. But the child was unusually scrawny, so every day after work he had to stop at the free market to pick up some things that the child liked to eat. In addition, he was always buying illustrated magazines to satisfy the child's spiritual needs. But the leader at the scientific lab where he worked was not so pleased with his image as a "good father," because maintaining such an image necessarily affected his performance at work. Of course, in the eyes of his boss, he was the most unpromising and least ambitious despite performing some very successful experiments. To make matters worse, he didn't have a diploma. His wife constantly reminded him of this until it became quite tiresome. One day his wife shouted at him, "I have no idea what you are thinking about from morning to night."

In fact, he was thinking absolutely nothing. He simply felt that was the way life ought to be. Moreover, he felt responsible for his son. He always figured when the child grew older, he would have a little companion. But the very first complete sentence his son uttered was, "I don't like my father, he's bad."

In his son's eyes, he was the person who disciplined him and who was strict with him. When he was nine, Zhang Shu caught him in a lie and whipped him. Later, he saw the following words in his son's notebook: "Father beats people like the Japanese. When I'm big and strong, I'm going to beat him to a pulp."

Only then did he realize how his son saw him.

12

That day, Xiao Xingxing didn't raise her head until quite late and said, "You ought to be going."

The young man nodded and collected his washed clothes.

"My clothes aren't all dry," he said.

"What?"

"My clothes aren't all dry," he stubbornly repeated, looking at her.

"Come back for them in a couple of days," she said dryly without looking at him.

He began to collect his things. His fingers were long and nimble and he did things quickly. He quickly gathered together his pitifully few possessions and put them in his bag, following which he naturally began to straighten up the room.

"Leave it. Don't bother," she said, still without turning to look at him. She propped herself up only after she heard the door open. The young man looked straight at her, tenderly and confused, his lips pressed tightly together. His Adam's apple bobbed the way it had done the night before as he gulped down the water. There was a stone on the little table by the door. In the light streaming in through a crack in the drapes, it looked like a beautiful crystal.

"Don't forget your things," she said, looking away.

"It's for you. I found it at an antique stand."

His voice was in a way touching. She sat up.

"I . . . I don't want to leave," he said, biting his lip as if he had made a momentous decision. "You aren't feeling well and you need someone to look after you. I'll leave when you get better."

The last few words were spoken resolutely and decisively. She looked at him, surprised. After a long while, she was enveloped by a warmth she hadn't felt in ages.

"Can you look after anyone?" she asked as coldly as possible.

"Of course. I'm a medical student." He had already taken a seat on the floor, his long legs pulled up with his head with his spiky hair between them.

"You study medicine? What field?"

"Chinese medicine."

"A . . . a future Chinese medicine doctor," she smiled. He saw it as a sarcastic smile. "So that's the reason for the great humanitarian spirit."

"Can I take your pulse?" He seemed very earnest, which only made her sarcastic smile meaningless.

Before she could answer, the young man was already on his feet. He firmly grasped her wrist without so much as looking at her.

"Your pulse is quite sunken, an evil heat has blocked up your stomach, what we call a 'lily disease' in Chinese medicine. Because your emotions are paralyzed, a depressed fire has scorched your Yin to the extent that the qi and blood cannot moisten the hundred vessels, thus afflicting them. Your heart has a Yin deficiency and your mind is absent, so even if you want to lie down and rest, you can't; your bones and joints are weak, so you find it difficult to walk. You suffer from lung vacuity and possess insufficient defensive Yang. You feel hot, but don't have a fever; an evil heat in the stomach can lead to severe vomiting and diarrhea . . ."

As he spoke he didn't look at her, but she quietly examined his wrist. That red in her dreams seemed to flow before her eyes.

"What's wrong?" The young man finally realized that she had become pale as a sheet.

"It's nothing." The sarcastic smile remained on her lips. "You sound like you know what you're talking about. Unfortunately, I have never believed the word of a doctor."

13

In the end the young man stayed.

That was because she suddenly vomited. The thick, smelly liquid wouldn't stop, pouring out continuously like the red liquid in her dream. The bed and the floor were covered with the deep red color of dried blood.

When she woke from total darkness, she saw that the mess was nearly gone. The young man was carefully cleaning the last stains. A wound that had lay concealed in her heart for many years suddenly began to ooze blood. It was very painful and she began to weep.

"Do you still feel sick?" asked the young man, pausing from his work. Since meeting her, he seemed to have contracted some strange illness. When she smiled, he felt like smiling, too; and now, seeing her in tears, he felt like finding someplace to cry.

"What's your name?"

"I'm Xiang Wuye."

"Wuye? Why Wuye?"

"My father chose my name."

"It sounds a little Buddhist."

". , . you need acupuncture treatment for acute gastritis." He didn't seem willing to pursue the line of conversation. After washing his hands, he took acupuncture needles, alcohol, and cotton balls out of his bag and applied needles to her two-sided *neiguan*. Not wishing to hurt her, he was extremely cautious. She looked at his vague shape through her tears. "I'm sorry," she said vaguely.

"Why do you say that?"

"I'm sorry. It's so dirty . . ."

"Didn't you say I have a humanitarian spirit?"

"You like to get even."

"Unbutton please. I have to insert a needle in your *zhongwan*, the middle part of your gastric cavity."

She slowly unbuttoned her clothes. She didn't have a sleeveless undergarment on underneath and tried to cover her brassiere with her clothes. She was suddenly very conscious of her body. She saw a strange hand raise a needle and approach her naked belly. His thin hand moved briskly. Several fine hairs on the back of his hand shone golden in the light.

His hands were just the opposite of hers—heavy with thick joints and chilblained in the winter and very clumsy at work. That other young man who was far away.

14

At night, Mingsha Mountain was shrouded in a steel-blue mist, making it look like a dream world. The pyramid-shaped peak appeared solitary and mysterious. At the foot of the mountain quietly trickled Yueya Spring, the same steel blue in color. The strange color made one think of various pieces of blue metal soldered together.

During the day, Mingsha Mountain was a masterpiece in gold that would knock any sculptor off his feet. But at night, the mountain was impenetrable, even to the most outstanding sculptor. It belonged to the mystery of nature, and to the moon, the stars, and to feminine beauty.

Zhang Shu took off his shoes and went barefoot. His calluses were smoothed by the fine silky sand. The steeper the slope became, the more he resembled a gecko, his hands and feet equally stuck to the mirrorlike surface of the sand. By the light of the steel-blue moon, he could almost make out his twisted form in the mirror's face. The transparent blue resonated with the mysterious sound of a chilly rain dripping on steel. In the cold of night, he ascended to the top of the peak, where, startled, he saw the bluish crescent moon in the ocher sky. It was a crescent moon, but very oddly shaped—it had become a multifaceted diamond. It was suspended over the horizon, imbued with a fragmentary beauty. The countless purplish stars looked dim by comparison. Because they looked so elegant, refined, regular, and scholarly, the entire sky resembled a conspirator's chessboard and the moon looked like a piece of broken glass that a mischievous child, filled with life and vigor, had tossed on the board.

Someone stood beneath the crescent moon. It was a woman. For a moment he mistook her for that protective deity in Cave 73. By the desolate light of the moon he clearly made out a beautiful young woman, if the word *beautiful* existed in this world. Not only was she beautiful, she was also coquettish. Her sexy waist swayed between her ample bosom and backside, reminding one of a rattlesnake. Her skin appeared smooth and slick, and suffused with the bright dark-greenish brown in the moonlight. He was awed by the color of her skin, because he had never encountered such a woman.

Later he could distinguish her face, which was filled with the hue of the western region. Her eyebrows were long and her nose high, two full lips half opened rapaciously disclosing silvery bright teeth. Her eyes seemed very deep, shining with the color transparent amber, and her occasional wink made him wonder if a star hadn't fallen into her eyes.

15

I admit the section about Mingsha Mountain has its fictitious elements.

I have never seen Yu'er, not even a photo. As such, I have no way of determining if she is as beautiful as Zhang Shu claimed. The moment Zhang Shu looked back on this period of time, his otherwise placid attitude became rather confused. He really has nothing from Yu'er. Later, I suspected it was all just a dream. And yet what I just narrated is a dream within a dream.

Men sometimes need such dreams. This is particularly true when they don't know what to do when it comes to reality.

16

Later the young woman took something from behind her and handed it to him. "My mother told me to give this to Mr. Zhang," she said. She had a heavy accent. Zhang Shu trembled as he took the painting from her. He couldn't believe that such an exceptional painting could fall into his hands in such a way. As he trembled, he touched the young woman's fingers. He assumed he had touched her silver ring, but he later discovered that she wore no such ring. He had, in fact, touched her finger. That finger was so cold and hard that it felt like metal. It would ring if he knocked on it. He was shocked.

"Is that woman in Cave Seventy-three your mother?"

"Yes." The young woman sat properly on the peak, her two legs bent in a perfect arch. She looked extremely elegant.

He placed the rolled-up painting on his lap and undid the string to open it. The young woman placed her hand on the string.

"Take it home and look at it. The wind is blowing; if you are not careful, it might tear," she said softly. He redid the string around the painting.

"Tell me, is this painting authentic?" he asked, looking the young woman in the eye.

"Of course it is."

"Why is your mother so trusting of me?"

"We Yugur people are all very trusting." The young woman stared at him, her eyes twinkling in the dark.

"What's your name?"

"Yu'er."

"Where do you work?"

"I'm young and still in school." She tossed her head, swinging her hair to cover her profile. Her innocence and artlessness touched Zhang Shu.

"Where's your . . . father?"

"He's no longer . . ."

"Then it must be hard for you and your mother." He watched as she lowered her lashes. He took out his old plastic wallet. Inside was three hundred yuan. He gave two thirds to her.

A jeering smile passed over her face as she took the money. He didn't understand what it meant until much later.

17

Zhang Shu was the sort who didn't seem to have had a childhood. He was mature for his age. His face had a strange appearance as if his reticence led to a lack of expression and, perhaps on this account, his face had no lines. His was a face that never showed wrinkles. As a youth, he didn't look young; and as the years went by, he didn't seem to age. It is said that fresh blossoms are the most fleeting of things, while an old stump will live to a noble age. Zhang Shu's face was this way. Save for a little beard, Zhang Shu's features remained unchanged. His eyes, though, possessed the stubbornness and skepticism of a middle-aged man.

His mind was the exact opposite of his face; it was rich, sensitive, and, had it been a face, it would have been very wrinkled. No one ever suspected the sorts of wild thoughts he harbored. At times he was a daydreamer. As a child, he belonged to the geology group of the Jingshan Children's Palace, and all he did was dream about mining. He was obsessed with dreams of sapphires. In his obsession to find sapphires, he spent a long time at Mogui City in Xinjiang during the "Great Link-up." Although he never succeeded in finding a sapphire, he did find agates of various colors as well as an exquisite piece of petrified wood with a tortoiseshell pattern. It was an inky stone in five colors, glittering and shining even in its regularly protruding edges. Soon after determining that it was from the Jurassic period, he and his wife had a falling-out. His wife dropped it, shattering it. He was terribly upset. "You look at this damn stone all day long. Do you expect it hatch? Is it valuable? More valuable than me? A stone is worth more in your eyes than I am!" his wife screamed hysterically. He felt strange that his wife, who was normally so gentle and cultivated in an affected way to outsiders, could suddenly become an enraged mother panther. Hair flying, nose running, and tears running down her face, she broke whatever came to hand. He felt it odd that a woman like her could be more practical than him. She was shockingly materialistic. But he wasn't at all like so many men his age in being anxious to replace their wives. Perhaps this was due to the fact that he had lost hope in the institution of marriage itself and was confused and frightened by women in general. After a long period of time, this attitude affected his physiological functions.

His fear of women dissipated only after he met Xiao Xingxing. He thought of her as a girl he had met in his distant youth. He could talk to her about his childhood and other matters of his heart that he had kept to himself.

18

I believe that Zhang Shu's feeling that Xiao Xingxing was an old friend at first sight can be explained by Jung's theory of the anima.

"Every man carries within him an eternal image of the feminine. It is not the form of a specific woman, but rather the clear and unambiguous image of the feminine. The image is unconscious and is the original hereditary key element engraved on the masculine organism. It is the imprint or archetype of the sum total of our ancestor's experience with the feminine, the deposit bestowed by women. Since the image is unconscious, it is often projected onto the beloved and is one of the important factors behind sexual attraction and repulsion.

"Regardless of what reasons a man might have for loving a woman, they are all secondary, because the principal reason resides in his unconscious. A man will try again and again to join with a woman who conflicts with his anima, but will always find that it leads to antagonism and dissatisfaction."

In this regard, Wang Xiyi, no doubt, is the sort of woman who conflicts with Zhang Shu's anima.

If this explanation is too simple and absolute, then how best can it be explained?

According to Jung's theory, Lin Daiyu represents Jia Baoyu's anima, which explains why upon first seeing her he said, "I have seen this sister before."

Therefore, the explanation for the legend of the Spiritual Jade and the Crimson Pearl Plant is not the karma of three lives, but rather the mutual attraction of fusing mental images. Most religious mysteries can be confirmed through modern scientific theory.

Originally, Zhang Shu had wanted to examine the painting with Xiao Xingxing. However, he had seen what he had no desire to see at the lighted window—a strange man applying a silver acupuncture needle to her abdomen. From where he stood he could see nothing else, but he could imagine her exposing her white abdomen to him. He was totally at a loss to explain how the two of them had so quickly become so close and arrived at a tacit understanding. He felt that the needle was not directed at her abdomen but rather at his heart, for he felt a sudden ache there.

Just before dawn, he finally opened the painting. Lakshmi was bathing in a lotus pond; beside her was a plump child. The painting was identical to the one in Dandan Temple in Hotan, Xinjiang, and the brushstrokes were a tad clearer as well. With the piling up of years, the painting had faded so that all that remained were ocher and mineral green hues. Despite having been carefully mounted, the painting appeared extremely fragile as if it would crumble by being touched. One of Lakshmi's terrified and wretched eyes had been gouged out, leaving a terrifying black hole.

He stared in shock at that black hole for a long time.

III.

Ganapati

I

Indian Tantric Buddhism refers to the Joyful Buddha as Ganapati. Ganapati means joyful, hence the name Joyful Buddha.

Joyful Buddhas come in two forms: individual and in couples, referred to as honored pairs. Nandavajra, Jinavajra, and Jichakravajra are usually in couples.

Single or in pairs, the joyful Buddhas are all naked, which symbolizes their separation from the mundane world. In their embrace, the male represents method, the female wisdom, and the accomplishment of both. Together, the male and female represent a complete individual. Through cultivation they arrive at "Happiness," but happiness that symbolizes faith and not debauchery.

The Joyful Buddha, also known as Nandikesvara, or Nandavajra, is the Buddha of Wood in Tantric Buddhism, and depicted as a man and woman in naked embrace. According to the Buddhist sutras, the male is the eldest son of Mahesvara and is called the Spirit of Desolation, who takes delight in doing evil and harming the world. The female is a transformation of the bodhisattva Guanyin. In their embrace she receives his love and keeps him from doing evil, and for this reason is called Nandikesvara. In paintings, the two are depicted as standing in naked embrace, wearing hats and necklaces of skeletons. The male is fierce and robust, the female is tender and charming.

In the *Four Vinayaka Dharmas* a legend is recorded, according to which Guanyin, great pity burning in her heart, used the roots of her great compassion and transformed herself into Vinayaka and went to King Nanda's residence. The king, upon seeing the woman, was inflamed with lust and embraced her. The woman refused him and said, "Although I am like a woman of passion, which hinders enlightenment, I have been concerned with the teachings of the Buddha and have attained a monastic's robe. If you wish to touch me now in lust, can you follow my instructions and protect the Dharma in the future? Can you help me protect the practitioners and not obstruct them? Can you obey me and not do evil in the future? If you can follow my instructions, you can be my bosom friend." "Hearing you speak now, I will follow you. Henceforth, I will do as you say and protect the Dharma." Thus, when Vinayaka smiled and embraced him, he said, "Good, good. Your wish is my command. I will protect the Dharma and will not create obstructions." From this it can be seen that the deva was the bodhisattva Guanyin.

There is yet another explanation: the Joyful Buddha is the six heavens of desire of Buddhism. According to Buddhist belief there are five methods of sexual intercourse in the realm of desire, such as a couple embracing to make love in the ordinary world. "The joy resulting from the kinds of the sexual desire of all sentient beings" is a view related to the ancient Indian worship of the procreative forces. The sect held that all things in the universe came from the replication of the procreative drive of the Genetrix. Therefore, they viewed sex as a way of serving the goddess and of worshiping her.

Master Tsong-ka-pa, in commenting on the unity of the Buddha and sexual union, said, "The enlightened mind is drops of dew poured down from five-color light of the rainbow. Replete with two sexual organs, human beings must visualize a vajra (penis) and a lotus (womb), and imagine a five-colored light filling them."

The union of two beings is "as essential as the two wings of a bird and the two wheels on a cart." It is said that through this practice a man and a woman can more quickly attain the Way and become Buddhas. In this way, the second-rate position of women in Buddhism can be rectified.

2

In her shabby old room, Xingxing painted with the simplest of supplies.

Due to Zhang Shu's influence, Xiao Xingxing paid special attention to the frescoes of Lakshmi, and she did find several, which, though located in secondary places in the caves, were actually eye-catching.

Xiao Xingxing imagined that Lakshmi must have been a sharp woman. For one, she could wrap the intelligent Vaisravana around her little finger. Secondly, she was a central goddess in the pantheons of Hinduism, Brahmism, Buddhism, and Tibetan Tantrism.

Xingxing thus imagined Lakshmi's childhood, youth, and young adulthood. She had to possess the qualities of an international female spy. She wasn't exactly beautiful, nor was she particularly favored. She was born when the asuras were roiling the Sea of Milk and was referred to as the girl from the Sea of Milk. Naturally, she couldn't compare with Venus, who rose to the surface of the sea on a shell. Even though she was born of common parents, she harbored a childish ambition, and her childhood was most certainly anything but common. For a girl to be successful, the first thing she had to do was destroy old notions of chastity, thought Xingxing. Average-looking Lakshmi had to be tricky to win Vaisravana. There are twenty protective deities in Buddhism, and Vaisravana is ranked number three, next to the famous Brahma and Indra, and could be considered the one who possessed real power among the army of protective deities. Lakshmi was ranked eleventh. Biancaitian, who was ranked just ahead of her, was superior to her in all ways, be it in terms of intelligence or skill in debate. Add to this her pleasant voice and lovely countenance, and Lakshmi would have a difficult time besting her. Moreover, it is likely that Gongdetian, as she was called, did not ascend to the throne of a Buddhist protective deity until after she married Vaisravana and was only called Lakshmi in her youth.

As a result, Xingxing completed four paintings.

In the first painting, two white clouds on which stood Vaisravana and

Biancaitian,[1] floated against a backdrop of blue sky. Vaisravana's eyes were fixed on a naked young woman bathing in a lotus pool. Biancaitian was arrayed in the robes of a bodhisattva, her face filled with anger, and ready to go off in a huff. The water in the lotus pool was crystal clear, and several pink lotuses were in full bloom. The naked young woman smiled flirtatiously as she plucked a lotus blossom. Naturally, this was Lakshmi.

In the second painting, Lakshmi, who was dressed for her wedding and looking supremely satisfied, sat with Vaisravana, who looked somewhat repentant. Far off in the distance, Biancaitian stood upon a cloud staring at Vaisravana. The gandharvas,[2] the wind gods, and the asuras[3] made merry with song and dance. The sky was filled with flying flowers and striking colors. Aupapdaka, or transformation, children gamboled in the lotus pool.

In the third painting Lakshmi had become a wife. She sat in dignified silence. In her left hand she held a fly whisk, in her right she held her son. With a flick of her fly whisk, she scattered gold and silver. Below was the mundane world, where countless people kneel to receive the gold and silver. Vaisravana sits to one side, looking regretful. It looks as if Lakshmi, quickly after marrying, controlled the wealth. She had also ascended to become Gongdetian, one of the Buddhist protective deities.

Later, Xingxing decided to add a picture of Lakshmi's childhood in which the asuras who are stirring up the Sea of Milk stare blankly as Lakshmi slowly ascends. Behind her the Buddha light shoots in all directions.

When Xingxing did these paintings, she felt admiration for Lakshmi, because she would never be so resourceful. As such, when people appraised her, they all said her talent far outstripped her fame.

---

1. Biancaitian, Goddess of Learning, Eloquence, Music, Poetry, Speech, Rhetoric, Wealth, Longevity; protects against natural disaster; inventor of Sanskrit; River Goddess.

2. Male nature spirits, husbands of the Apsaras. Some are part animal, usually a bird or horse. They have superb musical skills.

3. Group of power-seeking deities, sometimes referred to as demons or sinful. They were opposed to the Devas.

3

Xingxing often thought she was a bit of an oddball.

For her, sex and love were two separate things. From an early age she began to take an interest in the opposite sex. But it wasn't until the age of twenty-five that she understood what sexual love was.

This was probably due to an inherent deficiency of her generation.

When Xingxing was very young, the male idol she worshiped was the actor in the Polish movie *Mermaid of Warsaw*. She was only five years old at the time, but she wept copious tears when the actor was injured. Later she liked a number of male roles in movies and plays and often wept over their misfortunes. She had a special liking for misfortunate males. At the age of nine, she surreptitiously "read" *Dream of the Red Chamber* at night as her grandmother slept. She wept for Daiyu's plight and death and eventually suffered from weak nerves. The lack of sleep and extreme introversion led her to the brink of death, but it was there that hallucination and intelligence were born. These two qualities nourished her throughout her life and transformed her into a painter who towered above others.

Girls develop much earlier than boys. In light of this, every girl is a little woman. At the start of the Cultural Revolution, all elementary schools closed to pursue "revolution." Chairman Mao buttons had just appeared, and obtaining a good one was as good as and as pleasing as a holiday. One day, an older neighbor boy came over and gave Xingxing a glow-in-the-dark button and pinned it on her chest himself. Jubilant, Xingxing suddenly felt the boy's hand flit like a dragonfly over her breast. The shock nearly knocked her off her feet. That night she dreamed and slept uneasily. From then on, she experienced a vicious cycle and ended up in a shambles over dreams about sex. During the day, she felt disgust for herself and her developing body.

One psychology book on the subject of sex said a small minority of women worldwide experience spontaneous sexual desire. They were intelligent, healthy, and full of energy. Unfortunately, Xingxing belonged to this category; even more unfortunately, she viewed her desires as evil.

As a result, she spent most of her time from morning till night under a cloud of evil. She was ashamed of her thoughts, which were impossible to talk about. Looking at her sister and her thin and elegant body and docile nature, she felt even more inadequate. She liked her sister's flat chest and slim figure. Hiding from her mother and sister, she sewed a tight vest for herself, which was so tight she could hardly breathe, and was soon suffering from prickly heat. Her breasts continued to swell at an alarming rate.

To rid herself of her dreams, she read from morning to night. Half the books she had read in her life she read during that part of her life. In books, she found men different from those she had admired as a child— most of them, though, were stamped from the same mold: Voynych's Gadfly, Chernyshevsky's Rakhmetov, and Turgenev's Insarov. Not only did she weep for the misfortunes of the male characters as she did when she was young, she also imagined herself in the roles of the main female characters. Perhaps she fell in love with Xiaojun at first sight because he was like Rakhmetov, a Chinese equivalent to a member of the December Revolution. At the time he was engaged in the fight against the "Central Cultural Revolution" (later "the Gang of Four"[4]).

In the years after she encountered and lost Xiaojun, she ignored the pangs of sexual awareness and fantasized about a pure and undying love. However, at the age of twenty-five, after fully understanding the nature of sexual love, she felt totally disillusioned. It was then that she started thinking about getting married.

4

Xiaojun didn't smoke, but could drink. Parties in those days weren't really extravagant, and the liquor was usually nondescript. He did like to drink out of a big jar as if there were no other way to demonstrate his masculinity. But in her eyes he was a real man with light golden eyes.

---

4. A leftist political faction with Jiang Qing, Mao Zedong's wife, as the leading figure during the Cultural Revolution (1966–1976) in China.

At times he seemed pretty wise. During the awful years of the Gang of Four, many young people couldn't find anything to do and were depressed and dispirited. Others proposed starting a new people's revolution to overthrow the Gang of Four (of course they weren't known as the Gang of Four then). But Xiaojun said, "When a house is filled with moths that eat clothes, you have to slowly clean them out; you can't burn the house down to get rid of them! Revolution is absolutely not the way."

At other times he was really like a child. The first time he went to Xingxing's house, her parents asked him his name. He flushed red and then recited what sounded like his CV: "My name is Yan Xiaojun. I live at Zhongzhi Xiyuan Office where my parents work. I attend the middle school attached to Qinghua University. I'm seventeen . . ." Xingxing bit her lip and laughed to herself. Later, her mother commented, "He's a good boy."

5

Wuye accompanied Xingxing around Dunhuang collecting rubbings.

Some exquisite rubbings sold for as much as 450 yuan. If Xingxing liked a piece, Wuye had his ways of buying it at a substantially lower price by cutting out the middleman.

One rubbing was actually listed as *Lakshmi Bathing,* but it was done in a vulgar fashion to attract a prurient interest—Lakshmi's breasts spilled over her arms in a disgustingly exaggerated way. But Xingxing didn't bat an eye.

"I'd like a whole bunch of these. Can I talk with your boss?"

The clerk hesitated a moment before taking them to a large room in the back of the shop. The room was gorgeously decorated, a feast for the eyes. An unusual fragrance hung in the air, like some burning aromatic wood. Several animal skins hung on the wall side by side making the room look even more sumptuous. Xingxing was startled by the sight of two women sitting on a sofa in the corner. One of them was that old woman she and Zhang Shu had run into at the door to Cave 73. Shuffling along by herself at the time, she looked like a doddering old woman, but now she appeared to be around fifty. She wore a long red silk gown and a blue and white embroidered vest. Her gray scarf had been replaced with a trumpet-shaped red hat. Her wrinkled visage resembled a chrysanthemum blossom, but her eyes were expressionless. The young woman sitting next to her, though, was as dazzling as a ray of bright light. With the eyes of a professional painter, Xingxing scrutinized every inch of her. She found her, though, to be flawless. It was the first time she had seen such a beautiful young woman. Her first thought at the time was to try to convince her to model for her; of course, the best would be to take her to the art academy so as to do her colleagues a huge favor. The young woman was splendidly attired and wore a round, flat red hat from the top of which hung a large red jade and from inside hung a ring of pearls. Her braided hair was ornamented with colored pearls, pieces of silver, agates, and shells. Two bright eyes like stars glowed amid the precious raiment along with her smooth ochre-colored skin.

So that was Yu'er. Strangely, Xingxing was moved at the sight of Yu'er like Zhang Shu, but Wuye was not. Wuye said the only thing he noticed at the time was the glittering array and that he was examining her dress and ornaments rather than her face. In short, after seeing Yu'er, Xingxing completely forgot her original purpose and asked her straightaway if she would let her paint her portrait. Yu'er consented without the slightest hesitation. But the woman sitting beside Yu'er eyed Xingxing with suspicion. Then she spoke to Yu'er, saying, "How can you let someone paint your portrait, silly girl?"

"Madame, I am a painter," asserted Xingxing, as she took out her ID from the Academy of Art.

"Yugur people do not pose for painters." The old woman sat bolt upright and looked straight ahead. "You'll steal my girl's soul."

That day, despite uttering all manner of niceties, she was unable to gain the confidence of the old woman. Later, Wuye understood what the trouble was. He took out the only bill he had—a fifty-yuan note—and placed it on the table. Only then did her objections cease.

The portrait Xingxing painted of Yu'er still hangs in the gallery of the Central Academy of Fine Art. If judged solely by this painting, then

Yu'er was not a woman whose beauty launched a thousands ships. But it's said that a true beauty cannot be painted nor photographed. The same reason that no great book can be made into a successful film or TV show. Truly brilliant natural objects can only be created once by the creator, and any human copy is doomed to failure. But Xingxing insisted that she had captured Yu'er's expression. She finished the portrait in a matter of two weeks. While Xingxing was painting her portrait, Yu'er wasn't allowed to move and had to be as still as a rooted plant. One day, Xingxing just had to ask her if she could do yoga. She answered in the affirmative. "The Buddha sat in meditation under the Bodhi tree for forty-nine days before realizing perfect enlightenment and becoming a Buddha." Speaking reverently, Yu'er continued, "But I'm not that good. There are a lot of girls who practice yoga here, and I'm not much to speak of."

Yu'er's modest attitude left Xingxing with an even better impression of her. Xingxing began making all sorts of good dishes for her, but Yu'er didn't seem interested in food. This only made Xingxing admire her even more, finding her elegant and refined.

After Yu'er became Xingxing's guest of honor, Wuye moved out. After he moved out, he became even more important to Xingxing. Zhang Shu, on the other hand, visited frequently. As soon as Xingxing picked up her brush, he'd knock at the door, come in and sit quietly watching. Sometimes he would make a comment. Xingxing discovered that as soon as Zhang Shu arrived, Yu'er would look even more beautiful than usual. But she could never detect a thing on Zhang Shu's impassive face.

6

One day, Xingxing said to Zhang Shu, "It wouldn't be hard for me to become a Buddha if I wanted to. Shakyamuni Buddha did nothing but sit and meditate under the Bodhi tree. Some people say he meditated for seven days, others say it was forty-nine days, but that's unimportant. Anyway, the night he became a Buddha he attained knowledge of his former incarnations and those of others as well as attaining knowledge of good and evil early in the evening; in the middle of the night, he obtained divine vision and universal knowledge; late in the evening, he attained supernatural insight into the ending of the stream of transmigration and knowledge of birth and death. Isn't this form of 'samadhi' the same as today's *qigong*? Doesn't *qigong* refer to divine vision or opening the eye of wisdom? But few people today understand Shakyamuni's moral conduct, and despite maintaining outward forms of practice it is difficult to become a Buddha."

"You've always got so many strange ideas," laughed Zhang Shu, "and you remember all this stuff."

"On top of that, I've found that there is always something unusual about the births of great people. Jesus was born of a virgin; as for Shakyamuni, his mother Maya bore him from her right side. As far as I can tell, most of them seemed to lack a mother's love when small—it's an inherent deficiency—otherwise they wouldn't view the opposite sex with such prejudice and enmity."

"That's probably the case and why they became the founders of religions."

"However, I don't think Jesus Christ matches Shakyamuni in terms of wisdom or morality, and is even inferior to our own Confucius and Laozi and so on."

Zhang Shu and Xingxing sat on a stone bench in the courtyard behind the guesthouse. It was four o'clock in the afternoon and the sun was still strong. The shade of the tree covered their heads and the sunlight stretched their shadows out for some distance.

Wuye approached from the distance.

"Is the portrait done?" asked Wuye, smiling politely at Zhang Shu before quickly turning to Xingxing.

"No, I'm taking a break today." Xingxing took her cap from the stone bench, but Wuye didn't take a seat. Instead he leaned against the tree.

"Xingxing was just presenting her informed opinion on why Jesus does not compare to Shakyamuni," said Zhang Shu, smiling.

"Do you really believe that?" asked Wuye, his sleepy eyes suddenly opening wide.

"I'm not the only one. Lots of great people, such as Rousseau and Nietzsche, thought so, too."

"Whoever thinks so is greatly mistaken. They're just downright wrong," said Wuye, somewhat peeved.

"Mistaken in what way?"

"Jesus is far away greater than all these people. In addition to being a philosopher and wise man, he was also a true social reformer. Just read the New Testament and you'll see."

"I've not only read the New Testament, I've read the Old Testament as well," Xingxing replied in a sarcastic tone. "It's probably better not to read it. After reading it, God's holy love amounts to nothing. The Christians say that 'God loves the world, but God's love is not unconditional.' First of all, people must love him; they must become his slaves and sacrificial lambs before he will love them in return. Moreover, that love must be cruelly tested. Think of Job with his sincere faith in God, who, simply because God is bored and makes a bet with Satan, loses family and fortune—his ten children are killed, he suffers from leprosy. Isn't that a little excessive?"

"But in return Jehovah bestows on him even more than he once had along with his fortune and his children."

"The only reason for this is to demonstrate his own power by toying with a person's dignity! How could he be compensated? Property is one thing, but how could he be compensated for his dead children? What is more, can this kind of 'bestowal' and 'love' be placed on par? Jehovah's love of man is clearly a falsehood. His punishments and gifts alike serve only to assert that he is 'God of the omnipotent,' that's all. Buddhism is different. At least it is more real than Christianity. Nietzsche claimed that Buddhism is the only religion in history that is empirically true. There was, in fact, a Shakyamuni, whereas God is a human fabrication!"

"How can you say such a thing?" asked Wuye, flushing. It was the first time he had ever contradicted Xingxing, and from his stammering reply it was obvious that his view was heartfelt. "How can you say that God is a human fabrication? God exists. Thomas Aquinas proved it. First of all, we know already that everything in the world is in motion and every movement has its cause ad infinitum, then God must be the Prime Mover; second, every event in the world is both cause and effect, then . . . then God was the first cause; third, every . . . everything in the world is relative, then . . . then why make such comparisons, because abso . . . absolute truth, goodness, and beauty exist and this . . . this is God.

"Fourth, that which exists not by necessity is comprehensible; but rather, that which exists of necessity is incomprehensible," said Zhang Shu, picking up and reciting for Wuye. Wuye and Xingxing looked at him in surprise. "That which is real is the possible and cannot account for its own existence; whereas the necessary is that to which the possible owes its existence. The first necessary being is God. Fifth, the world is a single marvelous mechanism in which all things act for a purpose. This has to have been created by a superior intelligence, which is God. Right?"

"Yes, yes . . . that's right." Wuye looked at Zhang Shu as if he were his savior. "Actually, many . . . many of the founders of mo . . . modern science were clergymen or priests. Bruno and Roger Bacon, f . . . f . . . for example, were both priests; Pascal was a great mathematician as well . . . well as a pious believer. In fact, one could say that . . . that all the great humanists of the Renaissance were Christians . . ."

"So what of it?" said Xingxing, fanning herself with her cap. "What does that prove? I tell you, Buddhism has more in common with modern science. Let me give you a little example. Take the 'vacuum' in modern physics, for example, which includes an infinite number of particles that are endlessly produced and destroyed. This is identical to the Buddhist concept of 'sunyata.' The world is composed of these particles, but they lack independent physical existence, and the momentary appearance of this vacuum is just as expressed in the Buddhist sutra: 'Form is emptiness; emptiness is form' or as the neo-Confucian Zhang Zai put it in his Correcting Youthful Ignorance, 'The Supreme Vacuity is material-force, then something and nothing . . .'"

"Those are forced analogies . . ."

"The two of you can keep arguing and there'll never be a conclusion," said Zhang Shu slowly. "You'll never see eye to eye. One of you admires totalitarian religion; one of you admires humanistic religion. What I mean by totalitarian religion is that you admit there is an unknowable force dominating the world, which humanity must worship with fear and respect. God is omniscient and omnipotent; man is petty and insignificant. Humanistic religion, on the other hand, emphasizes human powers. Man wishes to understand himself and his relationship with others as well as his place in the universe. Man should realize his ideals and not blindly obey; man wants to exercise his powers and not be submissive. Have I understood it correctly?"

"I've . . . I've never admired a totalitarian religion nor do I believe Christianity is anything of the sort. Jesus Christ himself was from an ordinary family and was always in the company of the lowest stratum of society. He cured their illnesses and helped them overcome their worries and their problems. If you are referring to the Old Testament, then there is a little of the 'totalitarian' there. But . . . but the New Testament says "Love thine enemies,' so how do you explain that? So the blood of Jesus Christ is not as valuable as the deer's milk of Shakyamuni!"

As Wuye was speaking it suddenly occurred to Xingxing and Zhang Shu that Wuye was a Christian.

"It appears that Wuye is a Christian and that Xingxing is a devout Buddhist," said Zhang Shu indolently. Recalling that he was supposed to meet Chen Qing that evening, he wanted to put an end to the conversation.

"I don't believe in Buddhism." So Xingxing was just as pigheaded as Wuye in her unwillingness to not let someone else have the last word. "When beautiful faith becomes a religion, then it has its dark and evil side. I think religion is a kind of spirit, one that can be self-deceiving. There's nothing wrong with that per se. People are different from animals because animals only need deceive others, while people must not only deceive others but themselves as well. That's the source of faith, ideals, and other trifles. Don't you agree?"

Zhang Shu and Wuye both seemed to shiver.

Yu'er arrived. Amid the gray religious dispute appeared a beauty, the flower of creation.

"This is the embodiment of the truth, good, and beauty. What is God?" Xingxing glanced at Wuye triumphantly.

"Are . . . aren't you a bit hasty in your conclusions?" Wuye immediately replied. Xingxing discovered that when Wuye was anxious, he began to stammer and that the clearer he tried to express himself the more unclear he became. In this regard, he was different from Xiaojun, she thought.

7

Zhang Shu and Xingxing were both mistaken. Wuye was the only member of his family who was not a Christian, but he did believe in the "Christian spirit." In this regard, he was unlike most men. Giving made him happy, and he would even give his life for someone he liked. He came from an old distinguished family, one of the top families south of the Yangtze River. Everyone knew the Xiang family. There were many prominent members. Four out of every ten in government service were of the rank of section chief or above; in business, three had already become world-famous traders; those in science or medicine were even more numerous. The only shortcoming in the Xiang family was the regrettable lack of writers and artists. Wuye felt he was the only member of his clan without promise. When he was young he perversely got it into his mind to study painting, but this idea met with unanimous opposition from the clan elders, so he had to give it up. He didn't really want to study medicine. In addition to having the wrong temperament, he also secretly felt that he wouldn't be interested in the girls who studied medicine. He saw them as a bunch of mummies in white coats, or like "wood alcohol" (a homophone in Chinese for "[girls of] false purity").

For some unknown reason, he didn't like the company of girls his age or younger. He felt they were like the wind, without any substance, or like some cheap, glittery trinket or bauble—pretty but without the slightest value. He should have studied art for his aesthetic appreciation was superior to most men. He preferred an unusual, unpretentious face to that of a beauty. When he saw Xiao Xingxing, he was attracted by her vital beauty. Later, he came to know her intelligence and philosophical insight. He had been atremble since the day he noticed her creamy white skin and sumptuous breasts when he treated her with acupuncture. Later still, he had read her palm and discovered that her inner organs were very young. He told her, figuring she would make a big deal of it. Who could have foreseen that she would have calmly replied that Dayejisi of Sanwei Temple had already told her her fortune.

Wuye couldn't ascertain what she really thought of him. He did discover that when it came to having fun, she preferred him; when it came to conversation, she preferred Zhang Shu.

"I've noticed that you are very caring," she said to him.

He felt like saying, "I'm not caring about just anyone." But he held his tongue.

8

Xingxing never would have dreamed that the reason Yu'er had consented to be her model with such alacrity was on account of Zhang Shu. That night on mysterious Mingsha Mountain, Yu'er had taken an immediate liking to Zhang Shu. For several days afterward, she felt like visiting him at the Sanwei Mountain Guesthouse. Yu'er was no longer a virgin; her first boyfriend was a yellow noodle seller. That relationship lasted much longer than those she had with other men later. She was bright but didn't have much education. She felt Zhang Shu was different from other men. First, she didn't want to appear too anxious; second, she couldn't miss this opportunity. Thus, when an opportunity presented itself, she was hard on the heels of fate—she knew that Zhang Shu was staying next door to Xiao Xingxing.

As a result, she saw Zhang Shu several times at Xingxing's, and each time she threw him meaningful looks. But unfortunately, Zhang Shu never noticed. He and Xiao Xingxing talked about those unusual things, and she found it impossible to join the conversation. She found them a bit strange, but that only made him more attractive. Each day when she changed outfits, the fine clothes and jewelry only enhanced her beauty. But the moment she took her assigned seat, the brilliance of the not so pretty Xiao Xingxing overpowered her, making her feel as helpless as the White Snake pinned under the Leifeng Pagoda.

If Xiao Xingxing hadn't changed her mind that day and gone to the Yulin Caves with Wuye, Yu'er might have lost what connection she was fated to have with Zhang Shu.

Zhang Shu returned quite late that day. As usual, the first thing he did upon returning was to examine the painting by Yu-Chi Yiseng. He had made little or no progress in researching Lakshmi, and had started to lose interest in the matter and had considered going home.

But he couldn't find the painting—the place where he kept it was empty. He turned pale with fright and searched thoroughly several times again to no avail. Preoccupied, he sat by the window watching as the stars sank in the curtain of night. Finally, without turning the light on, he climbed into bed without even bothering to wash his feet. It was then that he heard a playful laugh following which he felt a soft, warm body.

At that moment, as the Buddha is his witness, he felt his hair stand on end. He fumbled to turn on the light, almost tripping over his shoes. When he finally managed to turn on the light, he saw Yu'er, as she lay under the blanket, stretching out her beautiful arm and covering her face, her lips slightly protruding as if she were going to smile. She was the epitome of beauty.

"You! What kind of joke is this?" he said, his fear giving way to anger.

Yu'er opened her arms wide and stared at him with her amber-colored eyes, her long lashes fluttering.

"Get out of here! Don't make a fool of yourself!" he roared, pressed by his rising fear, his back to her.

Now, facing the window, he heard a rustle behind him followed by the sound of tired, shuffling footsteps. He saw an uncommonly lovely torso flash by him like a flash of brown light; he saw the curves of an exquisite form—like something on an ancient Greek vase—narrow at the waist and widening at the hips. Her dark, silky brown hair, which hung down to her waist, seemed to emit a fragrance and brushed softly against him like a jellyfish.

That lovely brown vase leaned in the doorway, trembling ever so slightly. In one hand she held a red silk garment that rustled strangely. "What do you have there?" he heard himself say, his words catching in his throat. "I'm taking back the painting. Aren't you sorry to see it go?" he heard her ask tenderly. Desperately he stepped forward and pulled aside the bright red garment, revealing the painting. The moment he grasped the painting, he felt a cold, metallic grip.

9

She grabbed him and wouldn't let go, scarcely giving him a chance to breathe. The moment he touched her body, every thought deserted him, leaving his mind blank, as if by magic.

Her body was smooth and cold like marble. Though she burned with desire, her body remained ice cold. In his confusion she seemed more like some mysterious black eel, a descendant of the fishy tribe, who was at that moment leading him into an evil labyrinth, where he would not be able to find another human being or himself. Everywhere was her reflected light, a brown light as cold as metal. Everywhere he looked he saw a golden woman, a naked, brightly shining woman. Was she a mystic consort or the compassionate Guanyin, the goddess of mercy? He found her mysterious, resembling both a young girl and someone who had lived a thousand years. In fact, she made love cold and impassively without the least hint of feeling, then frightfully she was as unbridled as a wild beast, her body filled with a heavy animal scent. This scent totally demolished Zhang Shu's reason, intelligence, morality, and everything else associated with civilized human beings. At that moment, he even felt that his very soul was stark naked. In that absence of all else, he experienced an immense happiness and freedom—if two such things exist—he had never before encountered them.

That night a fierce wind howled. Zhang Shu heard it but thought it was his own ears ringing. Several years later, when he recalled that night, Zhang Shu's ears would ring.

By midnight, the wind had subsided substantially. He suddenly awoke.

The woman beside him was sleeping soundly, her lips parted greedily, revealing her shiny teeth. Her hair stuck together because of the sweat on her forehead. Looking at her, he was filled with a deep sense of regret.

After dressing, he walked to the window where he lit a cigarette. His legs felt as if they would give way. That cold body filled him with the same fear one might have felt in the presence of a snake or scorpion. He felt that that cold body would suck him dry.

The stars were beginning to fade. He thought of Xingxing next door. What would she think if she knew? Civilization had changed and transformed Xingxing too deeply. It was so difficult for two such civilized people to communicate and love. Then he thought of Xiyi, his wife. Now perhaps they were even. Neither could say anything about the other. Thus, it had always been so easy. He couldn't help but secretly admire Yu'er's resourcefulness and decisiveness. Civilized people appeared so stupid and pitiful before the uncivilized. And so he pondered until his cigarette burned down to his fingers. He suddenly recalled his son—his weak and scrawny little Zhang Gu. He felt he could never be as open as he had been. His son's sharp little eyes would see right through him. Children are always smarter than adults.

10

Wuye dragged Xingxing off to the Yulin Caves so that he could see an old classmate, his best friend from his high school days. His friend was the captain of the basketball team and school chess champion, but the previous year he had gone to Dunhuang and not returned. Only after numerous inquiries was his family able to learn that he had become a monk at the Yulin Caves. His parents had made the long trip and pleaded with him tearfully to return home, all to no avail. For this reason, Wuye was more determined to see him.

However, they had been unable to see him. On the way, a sandstorm overtook them by surprise, preventing them from proceeding. They were on the bus at the time. The sandstorm rose, forming a thick, gray, impenetrable barrier, cutting off all visibility. The bus was jolted.

Xingxing saw many passengers talking—their lips were moving, but she couldn't hear a thing. The storm swallowed all other sounds. As the bus was making the second turn on the mountain switchback road, the bus spun like a top, following which, Xingxing felt herself hurled through the air and slammed to the ground. Just before she lost consciousness, she seemed to see an infinite number of multicolored fragments in the sandstorm.

Later, her head spinning, she seemed to find herself on a camel. Jounced around on the camel's thin, bony back, she felt as if she were being painfully shaken apart. She heard the wind howling in her ears and felt as if she were soaked to the bone by the freezing rain. She wanted to say something or shout but was unable to do so. She was incapable of producing a sound, and try as she might to open her eyes, all she could see was a ghostly black shade. Terribly frightened, she squeezed the camel's back between her legs. The camel suddenly knelt, nearly throwing her to the ground.

Startled, she suddenly glimpsed light in front of her. She could also see that the windblown sand was still obscuring everything. Her clothes had become the same ashen color as the blowing sand. Then she discovered that she was unable to find herself and that she was not riding a camel, but was being carried by Wuye.

Wuye was carrying her on his back! Only the two of them seemed to exist in the vast grayness. She clutched him as if she were clutching her own life. But he knelt. He really did seem to climb like a camel making his way through the gray sand. She wanted him to stop, but she couldn't say a word. She had no other way to express herself except by grasping him. She saw blood in the moving sand beneath her.

It was only later that she learned Wuye had been more severely injured than she. He had lost a lot of blood from his badly scraped knees. The blood made her recall that dream and the far-off young man who had died. Drowsily, she tried her best to keep from vomiting. By the time Wuye had carried her to the bus stop, his face was deathly pale, his body was covered with sand, and his trouser legs were wet with blood. The sight of him left the experienced dispatcher tongue-tied with fright.

Much later, she commented, "I was so moved at that time. Bleeding though you were, you carried me to the bus stop."

"I carried you the way Jesus was forced to carry the cross." Amazed, she examined him. His seriousness, without the slightest trace of humor, made her suddenly recall that day and how, at the sight of all that blood, she had expressed a womanly surprise and concern, which he had stubbornly if not brutally dismissed.

As she recalled it later, the gray day of the sandstorm was forever closely linked to that clear, cold autumn evening seventeen years before. At dusk that autumn day, at a bend in that lonely bluish road, she saw the following announcement, which was colored the same blue by the streetlight:

> The counterrevolutionary Yan Xiaojun, whose every thought was reactionary and who was extremely active, venomously attacked the Central Cultural Revolution Committee and venomously attacked the standard-bearer of the Cultural Revolution during the Great Cultural Revolution. On x day, x month, 19xx, Yan, who illegally possessed a huge quantity of reactionary pamphlets, sought to flee, and the Public Security Bureau gave pursuit. The suspect put up a desperate struggle and was killed at the scene.

She stood for a long time in front of the announcement. Suddenly, blood seemed to spread on that thin piece of paper, staining it purple. The blood began to drip. At the time, she recalled the young man she had seen three days earlier at the station and how his bright eyes had been reduced to a bloody pulp. Died at the scene? How much blood did such a living person have to shed? In that bloody light she vomited a dry purplish . . .

"At twenty-nine, the female benefactress will encounter difficulties and be deprived of a loved one!"

That awful Dayejisi! He was off by one year. She was seventeen and not eighteen. This year, it was twelve years after she was eighteen. No wonder . . . she thought of Wuye, his deathly pallor and his bloody knees, and her heart trembled.

II

But she was already powerless to resist. The night of the accident, Wuye kissed her. It was a brief kiss, but both of them were trembling. Tears welled up in Xiao Xingxing's eyes.

"Xingxing, I think you are very strange."

"What?"

"You're the miraculous combination of the civilized and the natural. You . . . have such a beautiful body and you are so intelligent . . ."

Xingxing looked at him, surprised and bewildered. Such a beautiful body? It was the first time anyone had said that to Xingxing.

"Do you really think I am beautiful?"

It was Wuye's turn to be surprised: "You mean no one ever told you before?"

"Ever since I was very young I have been ashamed of my body." She laughed unconcernedly. "Everything is out of proportion and nothing goes together."

"What do you mean out of proportion? Are proportion and beauty the same thing?" Wuye's eyes were as docile looking as a lamb's. "As far as I am concerned, only the different is beautiful. Those of us who have taken anatomy class are completely familiar with the female body. But only one in ten thousand is different, and she should be the queen of all women."

"You should study painting or art."

"That's right. And if you let me paint my ideal beauty, I'd paint one more distinctive than Picasso or Matisse."

She put her arms around him and pressed her face to his. He was young and his flesh firm. She could feel the hot blood flowing through his veins. Had Heaven returned Xiaojun? Seventeen years earlier, when Xiaojun had embraced her in Miyun Reservoir, she had felt the same flow of hot blood. Unfortunately, she didn't know anything at the time, she didn't understand a thing. She understood now, but it was too late. Eleven years separated them! That was a whole generation! The warmth from his breast enveloped and moved her. She wept. No, she wanted to live one more time and love once more, completely. Who was afraid of a hell of fire?

Shakyamuni had threatened Ananda with such a hell and Ananda had given in, which just showed that Ananda's love for his wife was not deep enough. Perhaps love was no longer suited for the ever changing rhythm of modern society, but true love has its own unique rhythm that struggles free of all others. Disregarding others and letting down one's defenses, one will have no complaints regardless of how one is wounded. Do you want to love? Then you must be brave and take risks and at the same time dispel any illusions regarding a happy ending. There is no end for true love.

"We should go to Sanwei Mountain to watch the sun rise tomorrow," she said.

12

She had never seen the sun this color anyplace else.

The sun was slowly rising over Sanwei Mountain. The sun glowed a feeble white against the light purple backdrop. How strange was Sanwei Mountain. It filtered the golden light of the sun, which tenaciously squeezed through a gap in the mountain, a patch of auspicious Buddha light, and the sun became white like a negative.

A fresh breeze whispered, blowing across their heads and shoulders. She saw his eyes glow with a little golden light.

"I'll take your picture, Wuye."

"Okay."

She raised her camera and he turned to look directly at her. The little gold immediately disappeared from his eyes. It was just reflected from the light of the Buddha and not emitted from his own eyes.

"How's that?"

"Good." She smiled.

"Let me take one of you."

She shook her head resolutely. He gently embraced her. She responded coldly at first then put her arms around his neck. He was burning.

"It's good." He softly kissed her hair.

"What?"

"Everything, everything is good." Tears actually welled up in his eyes.

"If only we could stand like this forever and become two stone statues."

"You're so sentimental," she said, pressing her face to his chest where she could feel the vigorous throb of his heart. Once again she felt the vibrancy of his youth. He was too young. He was hers, but she would soon lose him. She couldn't bear the pain of losing him.

"It's too bad that I'm too old to fall in love," she said, removing her arms and holding herself as if she were cold.

"So love knows age? The fortune-teller said you are ten years younger than your actual age. He also told me that I am ten years older than my actual age. In that way, I'm much older than you." He looked at her tenderly. Her hair had a soft sheen to it; it was parted in the middle revealing her white scalp. He raised her chin and leaned to kiss her. Her eyes appeared misted over and she turned away.

"What's the matter?"

"I don't like this."

"Why?"

"It's too easy for people like you."

"I don't understand."

"That's not my concern."

The tears vanished from Wuye's long eyelashes. She was a labyrinth to him. He wound around for ages only to find himself lost. But he liked labyrinths and the uncertainty. He took it all as an intellectual challenge of sorts.

"Do you think you can separate spiritual love from physical love?" He frowned seriously.

"Yes."

"You're wrong," he countered. "Spirit and flesh basically cannot be separated. There should be no obstacles from spirit to flesh, and from flesh to spirit. Only then is love natural and whole."

"Perhaps. But did you ever think what would happen after realizing complete love? Have you thought about that?"

He looked at her in surprise. He felt that her voice was filled with hopelessness.

"Nothing can be complete. If you realized complete love, then love would perish. The next step is hate, or death. Death is, of course, better than hate."

He didn't protest. His lips were tightly clenched.

"That's the coward's argument," he said after a protracted silence.

There was total silence. The pale sun had risen high above and the golden rays of light had turned white, whiter than the sun itself.

She couldn't believe he contradicted her.

He could hardly believe it himself.

But he seemed as determined as ever. His lips were pressed tightly shut with no sign of backing down.

"You're right," she replied softly after a long pause. Then she turned and walked away.

He was left standing there alone. The wind messed his spiky hair. He became a hollowed-out silhouette, leaving nothing but a long, thin shadow on the ground.

13

For some reason, Chen Qing's stories were no longer that important to Zhang Shu. In his tales, the beautiful was beautiful, the ugly, ugly; the good was good and the evil, evil. Zhang Shu preferred stories in which the beautiful and ugly, the good and the bad were mixed. He liked nothing better than discovering the beautiful in the ugly or the good in the evil. In all likelihood, the reason he was attracted to the story of Lakshmi was because she was never the same—she could take delight in bathing with her son in Yu-Chi Yiseng's painting but wear the skin of her son in a Tibetan painting. Moreover, her overweening competence was displayed by the important roles she played in the pantheons of Brahmanism, Hinduism, Buddhism, and Tantric Buddhism; this alone said it all.

This only served to deepen his fear of women. He thought of Yu'er and that woman called a bodhisattva, and they all seemed to possess chimerical, enigmatic, and ancient qualities. He had more trouble discerning the real Xiao Xingxing, probably because she had so long worn a coat of armor that she was divided against herself.

In days of old, according to legend, Sanwei Mountain did not possess its three peaks and was called Ox Ridge Mountain. It was constantly illumined, by the sun during the day and the moon by night. But suddenly came a day when there was no sun or moon. Everyone inquired everywhere and learned that it was something bad wrought by Sirius, the Heavenly Hound, which had seized the sun and moon and was then going to savor them slowly in its cave.

Everyone was anxious to rescue the sun and moon. There were three brothers by the names of Dawei, Erwei, and Sanwei who were all masters of the martial arts. The three brothers called together all the people in the area and with lanterns and torches they were led by the mountain spirit to the cave of Sirius.

Hearing the exploding fireworks and the banging gongs and drums, Sirius was frightened and trembled. Rushing out of the cave, he was confronted with the sight of hoes, knives, spears, swords, and clubs. So many had come for his hide! Startled, he ran. But Dawei was quick. He lopped off half his tail with his sword. In pain, Sirius tucked what was left of his tail and fled. That's why to this day dogs always tuck their tails when they run.

The sun and moon were saved and Ox Ridge Mountain was constantly illumined. Fearing lest Sirius return to steal the sun and moon, the three brothers took up residence on the mountain to protect the celestial bodies. With the passage of time, the three brothers became the three peaks. In order to memorialize their contribution, the people changed the name of Ox Ridge Mountain to San (meaning three) wei Mountain.

When Chen Qing finished his tale, Zhang Shu recorded it hastily. Xiao Xingxing appeared in the doorway.

Zhang Shu liked to apprise women in silence.

Xiao Xingxing was no different from most women in that she couldn't stand silence. But confronted with silence, she would become talkative, though her speech was not for expression but rather for covering up.

Zhang Shu, though cognizant of this point, didn't know what she was trying to cover.

Xiao Xingxing actually enjoyed playing the role of an elitist character, remote from the masses. On account of Zhang Shu's formidableness, she satisfied herself with playing the naïf. This was one of the reasons she wanted to keep their contact to a minimum.

He always had any number of reasons for coming to her room, but she never had a reason to reciprocate.

Therefore, when she gracefully appeared in the doorway, he was somewhat taken aback.

"I heard you had trouble on the way to the Yulin Caves. Is that true?" he asked, examining her. That day he had gone to see her, but when he arrived at her door and heard Wuye, he turned around and left.

"That's right," she said, smiling unconcernedly. "We were lucky and not swallowed by the 'Bermuda' of Dunhuang."

"Ha, so you have a new theory with which to explain things. Did you see the Three-eyed Buddha at the Yulin Caves?"

"What Three-eyed Buddha? The bus rolled over on the mountain switchback. We never made it!"

Chen Qing narrowed his eyes and fixed his gaze on her. "What do you know, young lady?" Then he began to speak ever so slowly:

"The great Buddha at the Yulin Caves has a big, jet-black eye in the middle of his forehead—that's why he is called the Three-eyed Buddha. When the statue was being carved, the benefactor paying for the statue asked the carver to add an eye to the Buddha's forehead, making things extremely difficult for the carver. He thought and thought but didn't know where to get the eye and so decided to pluck out his own. As this thought popped into his head, the small stream beside him began to gurgle. He looked over and saw a large clam, its shell opened, revealing a large shiny pearl. The carver was overjoyed. Carrying the pearl in both hands, he ran to the cave. It's strange, before that the wind always blew and the cave was filled with dust, but after the Buddha received his third eye, dust never blew into the cave. For this reason, our ancestors referred to the pearl as the 'dust-dispelling pearl.' When the Buddha is happy to see folks, the weather is clear, but when he isn't in the mood, the wind blows, kicking up the dust. You went on a day when the Buddha was in a bad mood. I bet someone on the bus had bad luck."

"Do I look like someone who has back luck," said Xingxing mischievously, throwing Zhang Shu a glance.

Chen Qing snorted and said, "Not you, but that young fellow, the one called Wuye or whatever. His name is awkward sounding! He looks dangerous to me. Haven't you told him to go to see Abbot Dayejisi to have his fortune told?"

Xingxing suddenly grew worried. Chen Qing and Dayejisi were, with regard to the importance of reading a person's fortune, the same. So was she really going to bring bad luck to Wuye? If that was the case, she had to leave him immediately and forever.

14

It was a gloomy day. The air was filled with a frigid mist beginning in the morning. The moment she opened the door, a foul air entered her room. She suddenly had a bad premonition.

In the mist Wuye was leaning on the rickety old bike that belonged to Zhang Shu.

"Going?"

"Let's go."

"Isn't Zhang Shu going?"

"He said he had something to do." Wuye took her backpack from her shoulders and went to hang it on the bicycle. "If you had asked, he would have come."

"Nonsense."

The bag was too big to hang on the bicycle, so she took it back, put it on her shoulders again, and sat on the back of the bicycle. They set off.

The rickety old bicycle creaked.

"This bag is a pain. My shoulders are about to break." She felt the two narrow straps cut into her flesh.

The creaking suddenly came to a halt as he braked and put his feet on the ground. He turned around. His movements and his look of tenderness all seemed so familiar to her. Her heart thumped.

He got off the bike and took the bag from her shoulders and placed it on the back of the bike. "I told you not to carry it, why try to show off?" Suddenly he seemed more like an older brother. Without saying a word, he put her on the bar in front of him. "This won't do." She flushed red. His arms were like steel walls on either side of her. She felt his breath on her and felt herself melting in his warm embrace. She was powerless to resist. As she was thrust against the arms around her by the bouncing bike, she seemed to feel an electric current pass through her to her most secret place. She hadn't felt anything like it for a long, long time. She closed her eyes and felt dizzy. She felt like dying at such a moment.

"What's the matter?" he asked, looking down at her. He could feel her trembling.

"Let's not go. I have a premonition . . ."

"Don't be so superstitious. Nothing will happen with me here." He was once again a little boy. With a self-confident wave of his hand, he pedaled harder, making the bike fly.

15

The first thing they saw was the small shop.

The small shop stood alone on the mountainside. Two yellow dogs stared at them listlessly without making a sound.

"Hey, why don't the dogs bark?"

"Perhaps they're incarnations of the Buddha," he laughed.

"You're always so blaspheming of anything spiritual. Retribution will come."

"I've already escaped beyond the three realms and have transcended the five elements." Wuye then ran off to play with one of the dogs. The dog was unresponsive, its ears drooping. She snapped several pictures.

At that moment, a frail-looking young woman appeared in the door of the shop.

In the mist, her hair took on a seductive color. She was dressed in tight-fitting gray clothes and stood straight as a knife blade, harsh and beautiful.

She said something that neither one of them understood. Xingxing smiled at her, but she ignored her. The two of them set off for the entrance to the caves when suddenly she was there behind them, screeching at them. To Xingxing it was like steel on glass. She was scared out of her wits.

16

The Tantric cave was darker than the others. The cave, which was usually closed, was open for them. She praised Wuye, and he seemed proud of the way things had succeeded in opening for them. The appearance of the Buddhist images was not as mysterious as it was said to be. She felt they were of no importance at all, but what was important was the form of cultivation, which was mysterious. She noticed that while they were naked, they had not forgotten to wear their crowns or their long strands of bone beads. Perhaps it was just a sign of theirs. The appearance of the Buddha was conceived by man. Did this form of adornment have its origins with some clan in ancient India? She stood transfixed, praising the incomparable colors. But years later what remained fixed in her mind was the deep ocher and bright mineral green. She didn't find the mineral-green Plague Spirit or the mineral-green goddess perched on him like a lizard at all aesthetically pleasing. That skinny ocher reptilian goddess that clung so tightly couldn't be called beautiful. Good and evil, Yin and Yang, were inseparable, pressed close together. Once more she thought of the Taiji diagram. Yes, this was probably ancient India's equivalent to the Taiji diagram. Although a man and a woman were embracing, there was nothing lascivious about it. This, then, was the mysterious sign of ancient India's Taiji diagram. All the ancients were great dialecticians and long understood the unity of opposites and the principle of I in thou and thou in I. In the white part of the ancient Chinese black-and-white Taiji diagram, there was a black spot and in the black part, a white spot. The dancing deity Vaspa was even more mysterious and praiseworthy. His body was that of a man, but he had two faces—one was the ferocious face of a male deity, the other that of a charming female deity. Together, they actually formed a harmonious whole. It appeared as if the old topic of one divided into two parts and the joining of the duality into a single whole had been discussed and resolved by the ancient Indians. She recalled how the idea of one dividing into two and two joining to form one caused a great debate that led to revolution that took so many lives. It was all so funny! Yes, the moderns thought they were superior in understanding, but the ancients possessed even greater understanding. But that was normal. It was just like the younger generation being unable to believe in the experience of their parents' generation. One couldn't take the philosophy of the ancients on faith until one experienced its like and opposite principle.

However, it was more frightening to come to arrive at a principle that was neither the same as nor the opposite of an earlier one.

Xiao Xingxing stared at the complex of color composed of deep ocher and mineral green. She thought of how she often found herself between a rock and a hard place: she could choose between the bright mineral green and the deep ocher.

That skinny, lizardlike goddess perched on the Plague Spirit was painted in a lifelike fashion by a Chinese artisan.

It was the goddess localized.

When the Joyful Buddha lived in his own land, he certainly bore no resemblance, of this she was certain.

Later, when she had stopped dreaming of the young man who slit his wrists, she started dreaming a new dream in which she saw herself pacing back and forth in a strange land. The sunlight was so bright that all those walking became transparent shadows. The statues of that strange city, though sculpted out of bright light, were heavy and black. They were many pairs of bronze men and women making love under the sunshine.

Wuye had been ignored for an hour and a half. His attention was focused entirely on her. Her silhouette was graceful and full. Her hair, which was as stiff as wire, was puffed and shining. In the darkness of the cave her white T-shirt shone with a glow of moonlight. The nails of her fingers touching the wall of the cave became pink shells in a sea of mineral green. She only saw ocher and mineral green, but he saw pure white, which was her color, between those two colors. Standing there, she melted into the vast fresco and seemed to become a spirit in the human world to link good and evil.

"It's strange," she said.

"What?"

"I said it's strange," she said as if waking from a dream. He was much taller than her and was standing close by. For that reason all he could make out was her protruding lashes and delicate nose.

"Are you talking about this painting?"

She didn't utter a word. She thought of Zhang Shu's interest in Lakshmi. Beautiful Lakshmi had become something ferocious and frightening in this cave. Strangely, she found the ferocity more appealing than the beauty. Later in her dream about foreign carvings of the Buddha, the Buddha always possessed a ferocious mien.

Wuye held the flashlight for her and his arm was tired, but seeing her so obsessed, he continued to hold the light for her, changing hands as he shifted his feet.

"Actually, I know how to remove that fresco," he said.

In the vastness of the cave, his voice sounded disembodied. She turned to look at him as if she didn't know what he was saying.

"It's very simple. You use the resin from a special tree, that's how the foreigners stole frescoes in the past. A relatively intact one can still be seen in the Brussels Museum."

"What gave you such a strange idea all of a sudden?" she said, smiling, as if she had just understood what he was saying.

"You like it so much," he said, turning his eyes away. "I can see you're crazy about it."

17

What happened next was certainly a mistake. Xiao Xingxing, for the life of her, couldn't figure out from where those people had suddenly appeared. Perhaps they had been concealed in the cave all along. Whatever the case may be, they shouted at the top of their lungs, shattering her eardrums. She saw that thin woman, who looked like she was carrying a knife, grab Wuye by the wrist. Wuye was pretty strong, but he suddenly seemed pitifully weak. He struggled, but as fruitlessly as a child. The woman was expressionless, but her eyes were cold though sharp. Xingxing knew it was a mistake. She approached the woman and smiled amiably and gestured to her trying to explain that the young man was a good person and that his talk of applying gum to the fresco was just a joke, but the thin woman was unmoved. The thin woman's face shone with a thin but healthy beauty in the dark. Only then did she see the group of people behind her, a group of strong men. In the dark she could make out six or seven pairs of fierce green eyes. She could see that Wuye's face had taken on an ashen pallor.

Wuye would remember that frightening moment the rest of his life. He believed that the thin young woman was the embodiment of Death, because only Death could have such a cold, metallic grip. Her hand was like a steel trap at which he dared not glance for fear lest it be that of a skeleton's. The black shapes of the men turned out to be nothing. He assumed they were just her bodyguards and that she was the real threat.

He heard Xingxing earnestly entreating the thin young woman, earnestly entreating her without stopping. But it seemed as if no one understood what she was saying. Xingxing kept smiling patiently. When the men pushed him to take him away, she shouted angrily. She pulled the big men's arms and cursed the thin young woman with venomous words. But they appeared as if they hadn't heard her, as if they didn't take her seriously.

Xingxing saw Wuye's ashen face. She rushed toward him and one of the big men pushed her away. She staggered and almost fell. She saw Wuye's ashen lips move, but she couldn't make out what he was saying. Suddenly the thin young woman laughed grimly. Then she pulled a knife from her gray clothes and thrust it rapidly at Xingxing's heart. She felt as if bluish drops of dew were glittering at dusk. Strangely the thin young woman raised her eyebrows as if pleased with herself, then slowly pulled the knife toward herself. It took a while before she realized that the thin young woman had no intention of stabbing her or herself and that she was simply gesturing. The scabbard of the knife was a bronze green in color and seemed to be decorated with a skeleton. What did her thrusts with the knife mean? Was it satisfaction, a threat, or a kind of rite?

The knife flashed in an arc and returned to its scabbard. In a moment everyone vanished without a trace.

Xingxing watched as the last ray of light vanished behind Sanwei Mountain.

IV.

Guanyin

I

Guanshiyin is the most important bodhisattva among Buddhists. Her fame and impact among common people is as great as Shakyamuni's. She is second only to the Buddha and is referred to as a Mahasattva. The meanings of the word *bodhisattva* include "conscious beings of enlightenment" and "beings with a mind for the truth," and their duties are to help the Buddha save all beings, solve all worries, and preserve eternal happiness.

Guanshiyin, the primary bodhisattva among Buddhists, is also known as Guanzizai and Mahasattva Guanyin. Her name has also been translated using different Chinese characters. In order to avoid conflict with the name of the Taizong Emperor of the Tang dynasty, Li Shiming, the character *shi* was dropped from her name and she became known simply as Guanyin. The name "Guanshiyin" means "perceiver of the world's sounds" because when those who are suffering recite her name, she "hears" their voice and immediately delivers them. The name "Guanshiyin" itself is indicative of the bodhisattva's boundless powers.

A Chinese version goes like this. It is said that the King Miao Zhuang had three daughters, the eldest two of which married without a hitch. Only the youngest daughter, Miao Shan, who was beautiful beyond compare, was determined to become a nun. King Miao Zhuang waxed wroth and drove her from home. Miao Shan cultivated herself in right practice and attained the perfect reward. Later, King Miao Zhuang became gravely ill and in peril of his life. It was determined that he would recover only if one of his children offered up their hands and eyes. Unfortunately, the two oldest daughters were unwilling. Miao Shan, the third daughter, transformed herself into the fairy of Incense Mountain and cut off her arms and put out her eyes. Only after King Miao Zhuang took these and recovered did he learn that the fairy was actually his daughter Miao Shan. Thus, he appealed to Heaven and Earth, pleading that the Buddha might allow his daughter to produce arms and eyes anew. Later Miao Shan grew a thousand arms and a thousand eyes and became the Guanyin of a thousand arms and a thousand eyes. King Miao Zhuang also took refuge in the Buddhist precepts.

Another version has it that King Miao Zhuang was actually King Chu Zhuang of the Spring and Autumn Period. After his daughter saved him with her arms and eyes, the king ordered that a temple be constructed and for her image to be carved with her arms and eyes intact. Those attending misunderstood and ordered a thousand arms and eyes. As a result, a Guanyin of a thousand arms and a thousand eyes was produced.

At any rate the various forms that Guanyin took was just a way of confusing people, thought Zhang Shu.

In the fiftieth chapter of *Dream of the Red Chamber,* titled "Lantern Riddles in the Spring in Winter Room," there is a passage in which Li Wan says, "Guanyin lacks a biography. The answer is a phrase from the *Four Books.*" To which Daiyu replies, ". . . though good, yet having no evidence." This means that there is no reliable biography of Guanshiyin.

In fact, the two horse child deities, the son of a chakravati, or the daughter of King Miao Zhuang, are all nothing but legends. Even the gender of the real Guanyin cannot be determined much less his or her biography verified.

2

Xingxing lost her way on that dark and windy night.

The thick clouds in the sky seemed to be continually descending, melding with Sanwei Mountain, making everything black as ink. The distant outlines of the trees whistled liked strange beasts, as if something cold and heavy were going to pounce on her. She suddenly felt naked and that an animal's cold nose was right on her heels. She could scarcely breathe. She flew. She saw the same two dispirited dogs staring at her, looking like ghosts and goblins.

She suddenly recalled the *Dharani of the Future Life*.

It was related to something that had happened many years before. When her maternal grandfather died, her grandmother said to her mother that she was going to recite the *Dharani of the Future Life* to see his spirit across to the other world. Her grandmother knelt on a mat before the altar niche and recited it all night long.

She had learned about the *Dharani of the Future Life* from her grandmother and could even recite a few lines of it. The sacred *Dharani of the Future Life* was the magic spell used as the last resort for anyone on death's door. If her grandmother knew what she thought, she'd turn over in her grave.

But the *Dharani* was very effective. By the time she had repeated it sixty times, she could detect that the clouds had lost some of their inky darkness and were growing light around the edges. She could almost see a golden light streaming through the lowering clouds. She recalled the story her grandmother had told of the opening of Heaven's door. Once each year, the Buddha shows himself, usually on a day in the seventh lunar month. Or it was in the middle of the seventh month now . . .

The Buddha rode in a golden chariot. To his left was Samantabhadra and to his right was Maitreya. Why did the Buddha and the Apollo both ride in golden chariots? But Apollo was unaccompanied, perhaps because it was easier for him to pursue whatever goddess had taken his fancy. In what way did the Buddha appear? In his spiritual body, in his body of bliss, or in his body of incarnation?

It is said that in ages past, the Buddha never appeared. His features could not be fixed, because, according to the early Buddhism, he had transcended human form. During the time of King Asoka in India, just a few men showed their desire to become monks by worshiping the Buddha's footprints. When the Buddha began to be represented in art, it was symbolically through visual metaphors of the Wheel of the Law, a throne, or the Bodhi tree.

The actual image of the Buddha appeared only during the Gandhara period.[1]

She felt that beginning then, the Buddha had lost legitimacy. When she thought of the Buddha now, she would rather think of him as a Bodhi tree, a lotus flower, even a sea or even imagine him as a pure and innocent newborn baby.

3

Later a friendly voice was heard in the darkness.

A black car pulled up silently alongside her. She remembered the car and a shiver still ran down her back as if a cold, black beetle crawled there. The feeling was soon displaced by the friendly voice. A woman stuck her head out, and in the light reflected from the headlights, Xingxing could see the kind, broad face and the not altogether bad-looking double chin. The eyes were long and narrow and the eyebrows sparse. She couldn't clearly make out her expression, but she felt the face was restrained and dignified, as if Guanyin herself had appeared in the flesh.

"Where are you going?"

It must have been the third time the woman asked. Xingxing stepped over to the car window without taking the distance into account and suddenly found herself within inches of the woman. She felt ashamed but did not show it and stepped back a bit, but the woman laughed without concern.

"I . . . I'm going back to the Sanwei Mountain Guesthouse," she replied, nearly whispering in the woman's ear. It was then that she noticed the stately dignity in the woman's eyes.

The car door opened and she stepped in. She saw that there was another man in the car in addition to the driver. He sat with his back to

---

1. Gandhara is the name of an ancient kingdom located in northern Pakistan and eastern Afghanistan. The Kingdom of Gandhara lasted from early first millennium BC to the eleventh century AD.

her, looking out the window. From behind, he looked extremely familiar, but she couldn't place him.

"The Sanwei Mountain Guesthouse," the woman softly ordered in a nasal tone. She felt that the woman had a very nasal tone of voice, but no one else, not even Wuye would notice. This was a key difference in the way they observed people.

The black car sped silently toward the Sanwei Guesthouse. The man in the front seat seemed to be snoring softly. Xingxing parted the curtains in the car and saw that the thick clouds around Sanwei Mountain were still tinted red. Was it morning or evening? She couldn't resist looking at this disciple of Buddha who seemed to be looking at her. Their eyes met, so she had to say something.

"Thank you . . . thank you so much."

Lips parted in a smile, she shook her head as if she meant to say that something so insignificant wasn't worth mentioning. Her style only strengthened her impression that she was dealing with a person of importance. Therefore, she simply made small talk and began asking some innocent questions.

"What should I call you?"

The disciple of Buddha continued smiling without saying a word. She noticed that she was wearing a silver-gray coat under which she could see the striped collar of her clothes. She looked at the folds on her neck and was certain she was in her fifties, but she only had a few very faint crow's-feet on her face, and she was whiter complexioned than most people. Her cheeks were pink as if they had been rouged, and her long narrow eyes were watery and appeared sympathetic, though they did contain a certain dignity.

"What . . . what do you do?" continued Xingxing.

The woman had her completely confused.

The disciple of Buddha glanced at Xingxing and smiled again as if she were not planning on answering any questions. The car arrived at the foot of Sanwei Mountain. Xingxing seemed to awaken; she thought of Wuye and of that frightening scene that had just occurred. Was the woman in front of her really Great Merciful Guanyin come to save her from her troubles? She could not let her go.

"Noble lady," she said to the woman.

The woman looked at her somewhat amazed.

"Noble lady," she insisted. "Since you don't want to reveal your name, let me call you Bodhisattva. You really look like the Bodhisattva Guanyin."

Her smile frozen on her lips, she looked at Xingxing without flinching.

"Bodhisattva, I'm sure you can help me. She placed special emphasis on the word *can*. She became extremely excited, but the woman maintained her indifferent gaze.

"I have a good friend . . . a young man . . . today we went to look at the Tantric Caves, but . . . but . . ." She began to stammer. "But he was taken away by a group of people. Tell me what do you think I should do?"

The bodhisattva's thin, sparse eyebrows twitched. Then she spoke slowly and evenly in her nasal voice that Xingxing found so touching. She asked about everything that had happened as well as about Xiang Wuye and his kidnapping.

"Can . . . can you help me?" she pleaded. She could see that even if the woman before her was not Guanyin, she still could play a decisive role, that she was someone who had immense power in the area. "If not, then I'll just have to report a crime."

"Don't worry. Your friend will be well treated . . ." The bodhisattva frowned and lowered her head. "In any event, there is no need to report a crime—that would only make matters worse. Okay, here is the guesthouse. See you later."

Xiao Xingxing watched as the black car sped off silently into the darkness. Just as the car was on the point of being swallowed by the darkness, she saw the man sleeping in front raise his head. It was Dayejisi! She wanted to shout. The neon clouds around Sanwei Mountain had already vanished, or perhaps she had been hallucinating.

4

Zhang Shu was startled by Yu'er's outward passion and her inward cool. She came often. But it was always as if it were to hold a ceremony. She always arrived splendidly dressed and smelling just bathed. She lit a burner full of ambergris incense and amid the heady, stupefying smoke she calmly and unhurriedly undressed, as deliberately as if she were working out some difficult mathematical equation. She began to move methodically. Her brownish hair hung down, covering her body. Amid her luxurious hair, he felt he had stepped into a bright golden palace in which a female Buddha was opening her red lips toward him.

Amid those insatiably repeated movements, he realized that this woman with cold fingers didn't really love him. Men are not always as stupid as women think. Yes, the moment Zhang Shu realized that she didn't love him, he began to take an interest in her.

Exhausted, he lay by her side, watching with half-open eyes as she dressed, how she sat, and how she began to embroider. Yu'er was quite adept at embroidery and weaving carpets. She was good at embroidering all sorts of devas and her work sold well. When she came, she always brought her embroidery basket. After the "ceremony," she would begin embroidering.

"Yu'er."

"Hmm."

"That painting . . . your mother doesn't want it back, does she?"

"No," Yu'er said, looking up from the red sleeve covered with devas that she was embroidering. "What do you actually want to do with that painting?"

"Nothing," he said, lazily cradling his head in his arms. "I'm just curious. I'm trying to figure out why Yiseng painted Lakshmi as such a beauty."

Yu'er tittered and ran the embroidery needle through her hair a couple of times. Zhang Shu felt the needle became as golden as her hair.

"Silly, why are you trying to figure that out? Why don't you just ask me?"

"Do you know?"

"Do I know? Just listen: Yu-Chi Yiseng was a member of King Yutian's clan. He could paint Buddhas, bodhisattvas, all manner of foreigners, and deities . . ."

"I know all that."

"He fell in love with his cousin at a young age."

"His cousin?"

"Yeah. Her childhood name was Guonu, and she was a princess of Yutian. Legend has it that she was a born beauty and intelligent too. She was good at calligraphy and embroidery. And like Yiseng, she was a Buddhist. During the Wude reign—618 to 626—of the Tang dynasty, Emperor Gaozu established the five prefectures west of the river, including Liang, Gan, Gua, Su, and Sha. Our Dunhuang was originally Gua Prefecture. In those days, the eastern part of Lanzhou and the Gansu Corridor set up a separatist regime to oppose the great Tang Dynasty. During the Zhenguan reign period—627 to 649—the communications between east and west were not up to the Sui dynasty, the one preceding the Tang dynasty. This was an intolerable state of affairs for Emperor Taizong, and he quickly sent the army to clean up the Silk Road. He also sent members of royal clans including the Tujue, Yutian, and Dayue to the Central Plains as hostages. In the thirteenth year of the Zhenguan reign period, both Yiseng and his cousin were sent to the Central Plains. Emperor Taizong was an intelligent man and highly valued Yiseng. In those days everyone said that Yan Liben was the best painter in the Central Plains. The only painter of the Yutian clan in the west was Yiseng. He painted a lot and his large frescoes can still be seen today in the Ci'en Temple and the Feng'en Temple. These are probably the earliest oil paintings. Once, Emperor Taizong went to see Yiseng paint. He was never so startled to see such beauty as that possessed by Yiseng's cousin because in all Emperor Taizong's harem there was no beauty to compare with the princess of Yutian."

"That's just more conjecture on your part, right?"

"Right away, Emperor Taizong adopted Guonu as his daughter. Yiseng's family on the Central Plains rose in his esteem. But the situation in the Gansu Corridor grew tense in the first year of the Shenlong reign period, 705 AD. The emperor sent experienced troops to guard the area. In order to placate the troops, he married Guonu off to one of the generals guarding the Gansu Corridor. That's how the Yutian princess ended up here at our Gua Prefecture. Before she left, Yiseng painted his *Lakshmi Bathing* painting and gave it to Guonu. People say that that Lakshmi is the likeness of Guonu. Guonu brought the painting with her to Gua Prefecture. Later, the artisans of the thousands of caves copied the painting in Cave Seventy-three."

Zhang Shu remained silent for a long time. Then he suddenly asked, "Was it your mother who told you all of this?"

"Who else?" said Yu'er as she put down her embroidery. Her tiger jade eyes glowed. "My mother's childhood name was Guonu, the same as the Yutian princess. As a matter of fact, my mother is also of the Yutian race. Our Yugur people were originally from Xinjiang and later we migrated to the Gansu Corridor. Do you know what it means to migrate? Oh, you know. In her youth my mom was so beautiful that she looked like a fairy descended from Heaven. Everyone said that she was the reincarnation of the Yutian princess. If you don't believe me, ask Chen Qing, who is an old friend of my mom's. He knows everything about my mom."

Zhang Shu was stunned. So Chen Qing was Yu'er's mother's lover. It was beyond belief.

"How did your mother lose her eye?"

"How did she lose her eye?" Yu'er was taken aback. "She plucked it out herself."

Zhang Shu was stunned again.

"She was mad at my father . . . she didn't want my father close to her, so she plucked it out."

"What did your father do?"

Yu'er blinked her long black lashes and said, "I can't really say what he did. My dad was my mom's second man. My mom said she couldn't forget her dead husband and so couldn't live with my dad with her whole heart. After she had me, she sent him packing."

"Did your mother have a child with her first husband?"

Yu'er closed her eyes and spoke as if preferring not and said, "She had a daughter. She's my older sister."

"Is she here, too?"

"Yes, she meddles around here. I don't see eye to eye with her."

"Does your mom have anything to do with her?"

"Not much, but a few years ago, she saw her every day. As soon as my mom made a little money, she ran off to see her. My sister was shameless. She said she didn't need anything and then swore at Mom and forced her to leave. Mom has cooled toward her in the last two years and doesn't visit her anymore . . ."

5

Zhang Shu for the life of him couldn't imagine that the woman guarding Cave 73 had ever once been beautiful. To find out more, he went to see Chen Qing. In no uncertain terms, the old man said it was true, and without batting an eye said, "You think Yu'er is beautiful? Well, she couldn't hold a candle to even one of her mom's fingers."

These words left Zhang Shu indignant. He didn't know much about Yu'er's background and didn't really want to pursue the matter, nor did he have any hope that the mysterious girl would love him. But there was one thing of which he was certain: she was beautiful. She was ravishingly beautiful, blindingly beautiful. It sent him back to himself and made him realize that he was just an average guy. Xiao Xingxing's beauty was capricious by comparison. He realized why some men could become enslaved by beautiful women. Beauty really had its own power to subjugate.

Each time before leaving, Yu'er would wash and brush her hair. Her head of shimmering black hair, full and alive, contained a certain warmth. It was as bright as gold. She'd brush her hair, change it around, braid it into a golden snake, pile it up, and use a dozen golden hairpins to make it in the style of an ancient Greek sculpture. Then she would apply the greenish juice of a plant to her body. That fragrance reminded him of Beijing in May. Her jewelry, the heavy coral and shell, was polished to a high sheen with that juice. In the middle of her coral necklace was a huge silver pearl that shone between her breasts, like a huge star between two moons. She applied perfume to her entire body and pasted two strangely shaped leaves to the skin by her belly button. She did all of this in a skillful manner to perfection, which Zhang Shu found, in addition to being beautiful, also a bit exotic.

He couldn't think of anything more lovely than this rare beauty.

"You don't believe me?" Chen Qing continued stubbornly, "Just look at their skin. Yu'er's is bronze while her mother's—when she was young— was as white as white 'mutton-fat' jade!"

"Beauty is in the eye of the beholder." Zhang Shu couldn't resist the joke at the old man's expense. But unexpectedly the old man took him seriously and flushed red.

"Lad!" He smiled with embarrassment. "I was nothing. Guonu had plenty of admirers, and when my turn came, I was nothing but a shepherd, and Guonu was the reincarnation of the Yutian princess! In any event, if she had been mine, those unfortunate events never would have happened. But as they say, the fate of a beauty is a difficult one. Alas!"

Later, Chen Qing told him a story about Yu'er's mother, Guonu. The story was so dramatic in places that Zhang Shu was certain portions of it were exaggerated. Guonu was a beautiful and accomplished young woman. In addition to being a famous beauty in the Dunhuang area, she was also a pious Buddhist. Her mother's side of the family was surnamed Yu-Chi and it was widely believed that she was a descendant of Yu-Chi Sheng, the king of Yutian. At twenty she married a young Tibetan, the son of a powerful, noble clan in Lhasa. His name was Zhaxi Lunba, and he was well educated and of good character. He was also a Buddhist. In order to do the research on Dunhuang, he settled here and ended up working in the Dunhuang Cultural Research Institute. The two of them were quite happy together. Later Guonu became pregnant and had a daughter, after which Zhaxi doted on his wife even more. But the good times didn't last. In the mid-'60s, two years before the Cultural Revolution, their relationship suddenly became strained, and according to the neighbors, they argued all night long and sometimes even came to blows. It was then that Guonu once again became pregnant, but unlike the happy first time, she was always in tears. Those who knew her commented on how quickly she aged until one day Zhaxi was killed when his car rolled over on the road from Dunhuang to Zhangye. Guonu insisted that someone was behind it and caused a scene, but finally it came to an end for lack of proof. But what no one expected occurred a year later. Guonu married a Lama from the Tibetan border area and took her two daughters to live with him. Of course, he wasn't a Lama then.

"Is the lama still alive?"

"Yes," said Chen Qing as he began to stare off into space.

"Was he good to Yu'er's mother?

"Yes, yes," he sneered as he tilted back his head and drained what was left in his bottle.

6

Zhang Shu didn't hear about Wuye until three days after the event.

Anxiously, he went and knocked on Xingxing's door. The room was a mess, and Xingxing sat looking at a picture book without really taking anything in.

He sat down opposite her.

"Why not go report the crime?"

"No," she replied hurriedly. "He'll come back."

"Since you are so sure, why are you troubling yourself?"

She didn't protest. The picture book had been flipped through so many times it was on the point of falling apart.

Then Zhang Shu tried to rouse her to go out and get some yellow noodles, which were a specialty of the area and made according to a secret recipe. And just watching the noodles being made was a show in and of itself. A ball of dough, seven or eight *jin* in weight, had to be pulled into noodles as fine as silk. It was all the skill of the master chef. They weren't that great to eat; one ate and enjoyed the skill in making the noodles more than anything. Shortly after her arrival Xingxing was determined to try the yellow noodles and had searched all over Dunhuang without finding a yellow noodle stand and had yet to fulfill her wishes.

Finally, she was convinced, but she really doubted there was a yellow noodle stand to be found. She didn't have much of an appetite either, but seeing Zhang Shu that way she didn't have the heart to say no.

Unexpectedly, they did happen upon a noodle stand with authentic yellow noodles. They were shiny and yellow and firm to the touch like yellow jade. The noodle maker was as thin as a twig. Who knows where his strength came from to sling around twelve heavy strands of yellow dough, one minute looking like fried dough twists, the next minute like a whirling dragon. It was delightful to watch. Forty or fifty people stood around the stand watching as the twelve strands suddenly became 192 strands. Each time the number of noodles increased exponentially. The shiny, yellow noodles appeared one by one. The noodle maker's wife grabbed handfuls and tossed them in a pot of boiling water. They were ready in a matter of moments. Several customers hurriedly handed over the money and after adding condiments, they stood beside the stand slurping down the noodles.

Zhang Shu hurriedly thrust the money into the woman's hand. After adding chopped green onion, crushed garlic, sesame paste, salt, and MSG, he handed the bowl to Xingxing. To his own bowl he added a spoonful of hot pepper. He ate, breaking into a sweat. He looked at Xingxing and, although she wasn't eating with great relish, she was moving her chopsticks.

"How do you make these noodles?" Zhang Shu asked the woman, looking up.

The woman beamed with joy but didn't say a word. One of those sitting nearby answered before she could open her mouth and said that they buried some sort of plant ash where it aged for several months to make one of the ingredients. The woman ignored him and continued smiling, her yellow teeth showing. Zhang Shu had never been interested in the origins of yellow noodles, but wanted to distract Xingxing. She still looked like a sleepwalker, so he didn't pursue the matter.

The two of them walked back by the fading light of the setting sun.

7

"Can I ask you something, Xingxing?"

"Sure."

"Had you met Wuye before?"

"No."

"So you met him after you met me?"

"Uh-huh."

"Then . . ." Zhang Shu kept his doubts to himself. He felt it strange that a mature woman like Xingxing could like such a young guy. In was inexplicable.

"Do you think it's strange?" she asked, turning her bright eyes toward him. "He reminds me of a friend of mine from a long time ago. I confuse one for the other."

"A form of empathy, right?"

"Somewhat, but not entirely. He is cute . . . can I come over to your room and sit?"

She found Zhang Shu's room brighter than her own. People seemed to be much more alert in such a bright room. Zhang Shu poured what coffee was left into a cup, but she didn't want any.

"I never drink coffee."

"Tea?"

"No. I don't touch any stimulants. Wuye knows."

He remained silent.

Wuye knows. From her words he realized how close they were. Wuye knows. She didn't say her husband knows. It was clear that she was telling him he was left out.

"Doesn't your loved one object to you being away from home so long?" he asked, changing the topic.

"I don't have a loved one; I have a husband."

"Why so bitter and hateful?"

"Aren't you in the same boat?"

He laughed bitterly. "It's strange. When I left home, I was fed up. All I wanted then was to be free. Now I'm trying to escape again . . . people are just fickle."

"Do you want to go home?"

"I haven't decided. What about you?"

"I haven't experienced freedom yet to decide if I want to escape from it."

"That's where we are different," said Zhang Shu, placing corn in a pot and turning on the hot plate. "My wife is one of those women who are always doted upon. You can't neglect her for a minute. But I'm not the type of guy who goes out of his way to play up to a woman, so . . ."

"Actually, it has nothing to do with 'playing up to.' Chinese guys are just not very gentlemanly. Making a woman feel comfortable is a virtue. There are probably two types of Chinese guys. On the one hand, you have eunuchs, guys who are even half women. They can't even grow a proper beard. Then there are the superficial macho guys, who are, in fact, like dried preserved cabbage—totally bland. They act tough, but they just tire everyone. There is a third type, of course, but that is the rarest of the rare . . ."

"Then you certainly must have met this rare breed, haven't you?"

"Don't be jealous. I know what you're implying."

"And what's that?"

"I'm sure you're thinking that this third type I mentioned doesn't exist, that all guys are pretty much the same and it's the women who categorize them."

"Don't you think it's just a way of deceiving yourselves?"

"Of course it is—the ways people deceive themselves are all different. But no one is strong enough not to deceive himself."

"I am," he replied somewhat disdainfully.

"Forget it. So what is it you had to come to Dunhuang to do? You could have stayed in Beijing and looked after your wife and son. Why all the interest in Lakshmi?"

His expression changed.

"You're right. It's my own way of deceiving myself," he replied, depressed, kicking an empty box that was lying on the floor after some time.

8

A letter from Mousheng arrived. It contained a few words written by Weiwei. They were round, just like him: "Mommy, I miss you."

This had to have been engineered by Mousheng. The words were like an all-powerful atomic bomb to her, as Mousheng certainly knew they would be.

Her cute little Weiwei, an angel, a little daring, he was so mischievous and had turned a somersault in her belly so that when she was about to give birth, he had turned himself upside down. The doctors busied themselves preparing obstetric forceps, suction unit, and oxytocin. She felt herself tied down with many tubes. It was a painful, frightening, petrifying moment. Even now she couldn't bear to recall it.

It was a stormy night. The unbearable pain she experienced cut her off from the world around her. She made an effort to recall the familiar faces of her friends and relatives but found it impossible to do so. She didn't know what the birth of the child meant for her, but a voice deep inside her began to speak, "One can only thoroughly understand life by marrying and having children."

The voice became louder. She finally recalled who it was that said this, him and his golden "tiger eyes." When he said this, he was still a child, but his expression at the time was very serious. It was at dusk at the Miyun Reservoir. They came ashore after swimming and everyone sat in a circle leisurely drinking cheap wine and eating bread and fried chicken. At times such as those, Xiaojun always had to express some shocking opinions.

He contradicted what she had just said. She said, "A true artist can't have kids or marry."

To this day she didn't know who was right. The problem was that so many things in life were paradoxical. No one could imagine what something was like from a position of inexperience, and once one had experience, they could never return to a position of inexperience.

There was a downpour that day they went swimming. She wasn't a good swimmer, and when the sky and the water merged and she couldn't get her bearings, she became quite agitated. She began flailing with her arms and legs and she felt very heavy. Before she could shout, her mouth was filled with dirty water. When she was certain she was going to die, a hand reached from behind and held her tight. At the time she felt like shouting the chant "Namu Guanshiyin bodhisattva" the way her grandmother had taught her. But she soon realized that it was no Buddha or bodhisattva. It was Xiaojun. Xiaojun had been watching out for her from behind. As he swam using one arm, he clutched her with the other and made his way toward a boat anchored in that vast whiteness. To this day she could remember his steel-like grip and the heat of his breast that penetrated her thin swimsuit and her frigid body. It was the first time in her life that she had been embraced by the opposite sex. But the struggle for life overpowered everything else. She forgot her embarrassment and clung to him tightly. Even after they were on the boat, she refused to let go of him. It was then that she became aware of his strength and the pounding of his warm heart. Ten years later, when she told all of this to her sister, her sister smiled as if it were nothing and said, "These are the feelings all women experience. It was much simpler for him. He got to squeeze a nearly naked beauty, that's all. In your eyes Xiaojun is sacred, but he was nothing more than any other guy."

She was not disappointed by these words. But after thinking about it, her face grew hot and prickly. A nearly naked beauty? She blushed and looked down at her breasts. Immediately she thought of that young man with his pure, clear eyes. At the time he embraced her somewhat embarrassed and nervously. As they sat in the boat, neither one of them said a word. Finally, he lowered his head and said that he had broken up with his girlfriend.

No one could bring back that purity of emotion, that vagueness, that beauty, even with one's life.

She shed a few tears. Then she wrote, "Dear Mousheng." But this time she was smart and didn't waste paper. On one sheet of letter paper she proceeded to repeat the same words over and over again. Then she crumpled that sheet of paper into a ball and threw it out the window.

It was then that she saw two people whispering under the bright blue sky to the northwest. One was the old man Chen Qing; the other was that old woman she had seen hobbling alone outside Cave 73.

9

That evening Yu'er had a big row with her mother. She had no idea who had a rotten big mouth and had come and told her mother about what she had been doing. Trembling with anger, her mother stood pointing at her for a while before uttering a word.

"You worthless thing! No one is good enough for you but a Han Chinese we know nothing about. Although he is a guest of Bodhisattva Pan, it was enough to simply loan him the painting. But you have to go and offer yourself!"

"Who is being nice to him? I wanted to practice tantric yoga with him," replied Yu'er in tears.

"Nonsense! Has he been consecrated? Is he a yoga adept? Practicing tantric yoga with a common person, you really have some nerve to even say such a thing!" Guonu had even more energy than her daughter.

"Father says he has the face of a respectable person and that he'll eventually become a Buddhist. What's wrong with initiating him to the Tantric path?"

"Shameless! Didn't that bastard of a father of yours tell you that you will end up in hell by practicing tantric yoga with someone who has not been consecrated?"

Yu'er softened her tone and said, "Then . . . then can Father consecrate him?"

"Don't do him any harm. Hasn't that bastard, your father, harmed enough people? He's a guest of Bodhisattva Pan's. Treating him well and seeing him off is a merit and a virtue. Don't get any bad ideas!" Guonu raised her cane and shouted, "Foolish girl! I'm telling you that I'm going to have a word with your uncle, Chen Qing, and if you go running over there again, I'll break your legs."

Yu'er pressed her lips together and threw a furious glance at her mother and put her golden snakelike braid across her chest. Her mother would be true to her word, but she wasn't afraid. All her life, her mom hated no one more than the Han Chinese because Yu'er's father is Han. Her mother said that her father played the part of a lama and then a monk, but in neither case was it her dad's forte. "Your daddy is an evil demon," said her mother. "His true appearance was seen in the 'transparent tablet,' and he'll soon be called back by the guardian deity."

But Yu'er didn't hate her father in the least. Her daddy doted on her and was always giving her money and pretty clothes and jewelry. Her daddy said that he made money by teaching the Five-part Vajra Dharma when he was a lama. The living Buddhas and headmen in Tibet all had countless treasures.

When she was twelve, at one time her father went to the Yulin Caves to teach yoga. Yu'er wanted to go and cried and made a scene until her father relented and took her, but not without setting many rules.

Yu'er could never forget how, burning with curiosity, as dusk settled, she quietly followed her father to a Buddhist temple deep in the Yulin Caves. It was dark by then and at the back of the temple there was a lustrous black curtain. A well-dressed young man knelt in front of the curtain, his eyes closed and his face glowing with piety. It was then that she suddenly heard voices from behind the curtain.

She quietly stepped from the Guanyin of a Thousand Hands and a Thousand Eyes behind the curtain. It was stifled with panting and moaning. She saw a naked man and a naked woman intertwined. The woman was so white she looked like a ray of light in the dark of night; the man looked like a dark cloud that was extinguishing the light.

She was transfixed. At that moment, the man looked around—it was her daddy! Her father pointed with one finger and as if under a spell, she retreated without a fuss. She sat down beside a red column with gold filigree and cried.

Later, her father found her and comforted her with tender words. He told her it was a superior form of yoga, the highest form transmitted from Tibet. That day, her father told her many things, about the vajra, the lotus, enlightenment, meditation, and the male and female bodhi minds, and other things. She didn't understand a word; the only thing that made an impression on her was the last thing he told her, which was about the consecration ceremony. "In Lhasa, I served as a Vajra master." Her father's face was bathed in a yellow light. There wasn't a wrinkle on his face; he was extremely youthful. "This place is nothing. In those days I taught the Five-part Great Vajra Dharma in which the consecration ceremony was held before a mandala. One had to bathe and be very clean. I held a bottle of sacred water and I would sprinkle water on the head of the one who was to be consecrated. Then he would drink highland barley wine from a *duobala,* or a bowl made from a human cranium. He would have to drain it at one go. Then I would lead him to choose a specific Buddha. After this he could begin cultivation. This is the initial consecration ceremony, which was very colorful and filled with burning incense. It was extremely solemn."

"Daddy, I want to be consecrated too and practice tantric yoga!" Yu'er said sweetly.

"Nonsense! Children are not consecrated. You are intelligent. Later I will teach you general yoga, which is good for the health. Under no circumstances are you to study Five-part Vajra Dharma, even if someone approaches you, no way!"

Thinking even now about her father's expression as he spoke left her soul stirred.

Later, the young acolyte—the one who had been kneeling in front of the curtain—came out from behind the columns, approached and bowed many times, and respectfully said, "Master, your student has practiced the secret method."

She looked back and chanced to meet his eyes. He was fair-skinned and handsome with a pair of lively, bright eyes. Later she learned that he sold yellow noodles in Dunhuang. Sometime later they began to practice unsurpassed tantric yoga. Starting then, Yu'er became a "female yoga adept."

Eventually her father found out about it. He beat the noodle seller and almost killed him. Yu'er never had any idea of what sort of crime he had committed. As a result, all her later tantric practice was conducted in absolute secrecy so that her father wouldn't find out.

Shortly thereafter, her father did in fact shave his head and go off to Sanwei Mountain to be a monk. The night before he left, he kneeled in front of a statue of Shakyamuni Buddha and wept, confessing his various sins and that he was willing to practice even in the next life. It was the first time she had seen her father cry. But her mother stood there watching scornfully without saying a word.

10

Many things are determined in a brief moment.

Perhaps there was something about Xiao Xingxing in those days that touched people, or perhaps Zhang Shu had some sudden inexplicable urge to express himself, or perhaps it was something else altogether. In any event, Zhang Shu took the painting out of some secret place—that painting he had sworn not to show another living soul.

However, later when Zhang Shu recalled this, he told me that he had shown the painting to Xiao Xingxing in order to alter her mood and cheer her up. After Wuye disappeared, she had been rushing with great purpose here and there and had lost a lot of weight. Zhang Shu was afraid she'd have a breakdown.

Zhang Shu's fingers trembled as if he had encountered something extremely fragile that would break at the merest contact. When the painting was entirely unrolled under the lamp, he used four shiny stones he had obtained at the antique stalls as paperweights to hold the painting in place so that Xingxing could savor it.

Lakshmi was as beautiful as ever. Yiseng had certainly captured the fearful and tragic look in his cousin Guonu's eyes. Her leaving her cousin must have been a heart-wrenching scene. The fear such a beautiful woman must have felt about the road ahead must have been deeply moving. Too bad one of the eyes was missing. Why had the living Guonu also lost an eye? Could there be some mysterious connection linked with something that had occurred over a thousand years before?

He saw a perfunctory smile appear on Xingxing's lips.

"It's a lovely painting—too bad it's a fake," said Xingxing as she lifted her head after examining the painting for a while.

Zhang Shu looked at her anxiously.

"That's impossible."

"Well, then, just forget it," smiled Xingxing. "You can take it and ask an expert."

"How do you know . . . ?"

"Of course, I know. Before entering the Art Academy, I spent two years working at the Forbidden City copying classical paintings. To tell you the truth, I could do a better job. They haven't got the ancient style right."

He was silent. He knew she wasn't joking.

Then who was having a joke on him?

"Where did you get the painting?"

He shook his head to indicate that he was not at liberty to say. He tried to stay aloof, but he was beginning to feel angry.

"How's Wuye, do you have any news?" he replied in a whisper after a while.

She shook her head, "I have a bad feeling about this. Do you remember what Dayejisi said?" She looked up and her eyes were filled with sadness. "What he said about the one in the past was right, but he was off by only a year. By his reckoning, twelve years after the fact at twenty-nine would make it this year. No wonder Wuye . . ."

Zhang Shu stared at her. She suddenly fell silent because she realized she had made an indiscreet remark, but he understood everything from her words. He no longer had to doubt anything. Previously, the motherly tone she adopted whenever she mentioned Wuye was just a form of self-deception.

"I've been wanting to ask you," he said, as he poured a glass of juice for her. "That friend of yours, the one in the past, how did he die?"

She stared blankly and sighed. "That was more than ten years ago. There's nothing to say, really. You wouldn't understand anyway. People in those days were too idealistic and set too much store in 'isms.' During the Cultural Revolution his parents were killed. He had no brothers or sisters. In the midst of such cruelty one was supposed to keep their mind on participating in the world revolution. Isn't that a joke?"

"No, I was the same way at the time."

"In the early '70s, he and some friends decided to cross the Honghe River to Vietnam to resist America and support Vietnam. Only one out of seven succeeded in crossing the river." She bit her lip and tears welled up in her eyes. "I just pity his genius and his zeal to sacrifice himself. This all belongs to the last generation. It doesn't exist any longer . . ."

Zhang Shu was silent. He couldn't bear to see her tearful eyes because he wouldn't be able to restrain himself from taking her in his arms and kissing her. But he had no desire to make such a mistake again.

She always made him think of his childhood and remember that departed age. It was heartbreaking to think about it.

II

Yu'er arrived very late.

She floated in like a red cloud. She was dressed entirely in bright red, which served to accentuate the golden nature of her skin.

She had just bathed and smelled good. Her hair was bright and shiny, and she left her bangs over her forehead, which appeared high and bright. The middle of her forehead just above the bridge of her nose was especially pronounced in the light, not to mention her high nose and long eyebrows. Zhang Shu wondered what kind of fortune Dayejisi would read in her face.

Yu'er stripped off her red coat in her practiced fashion, revealing her clinging garments which were made in the old way, painstakingly embroidered by the Yugur people. A black goat was embroidered on the front and back of her top because it was either an auspicious animal or a magic charm. The vest was so short that the lower part of her breasts shown out from the bottom, which was certainly more dazzling than wearing nothing at all.

Zhang Shu lay on the bed and fanned himself with a rush fan without so much as glancing at her.

When he felt the warmth of her body, he wanted to say something but held his tongue. She pressed her soft, warm lips to his. The long kiss made him feel dizzy.

He opened his eyes to be dazzled by her golden skin. He pushed her away as she blocked a ray of light, which left him in the dark.

"What's wrong?" came her surprised voice.

He was silent as the light continued to play before his eyes.

"What's the matter with you?" she said tearfully as if feeling wronged.

He looked up and saw her sobbing, her chin quivering. The tears came quickly. He looked down at her breasts and saw her chest was heaving dramatically. Each time she sobbed, the lower half of her breasts would shudder. He was suddenly filled with a strong desire. He wanted to hear her cry in a different way; see a different expression of pain appear on her face; see her bathed in different tears. He suddenly turned brutal, pinning her arms behind her back and gripping them with one hand while mercilessly grabbing her hair with his other hand and yanking as if he were going to pull it out by the roots. Her golden hair blinded him like a banner of the sun rays. In the course of struggling she began to feel the desire to be dominated, which was more pleasant than sexual desire. He suddenly smelled an unusual fragrance and one that worked like a hallucinogen, his body sank, shattered, and melted in the delicate fragrance. The stars seemed to shine on her shoulders like specks of crystal, then an orange moon appeared, illuminating her shoulders. He felt her, but touched nothing. "You're a demon," he struggled to say. Her eyes flashed. Only then did he realize it was her eyes.

12

Yu'er came to and the first thing she heard was, "Go away. And don't come back again."

She opened her eyes. Her body was still moving rhythmically like a torrent rising and falling over a sand hill. Through the fog of confusion she saw that face, as cold and barren as a salt flat on which nothing would grow. She opened her mouth, but no sound came out.

"Do you understand what I said?"

Yes, she understood. Her eyebrows arched, then formed a black mass. Her eyes, as bright as the moon and stars, suddenly darkened into two deep, dark wells beyond the light, reflecting nothing back at him save a chilling cold.

"If you understand, then go and don't come back again!" he repeated again, exhausted.

She was stunned for a while and then suddenly she swung her head, laughing madly, as her golden hair danced Medusalike. Zhang Shu felt as if a thousand whips had lashed his face, the pain of which woke him. Her laughter at once reminded him of the old woman at Cave 73. It was the sound of someone herding animals on the plains.

"You mean Han Chinese! My mom was right! There are no good Han Chinese. I tell you, I never loved you, never! My dad says you have splendid look, so I came to you to practice tantric yoga."

"Your dad? Didn't you say your dad had passed away?" Zhang Su eyed her coldly.

"What do you mean? He's alive and kicking. I fooled you. You think you're so smart, but you fell for it. Don't you feel stupid?"

He sneered, "I know you have been lying to me—even the painting is a fake. The one that was stolen from Cave Seventy-three is the real one. Here, here's your painting!" He threw the painting in her lap. That golden Medusa's head suddenly ceased moving like a dead snake and hung, covering half her bright golden face in darkness. One big pitch dark eye could be seen staring at him from beneath her long lashes.

Many years later when recalling that moment, he still felt its falsity. Its falsity stemmed from its drama, the artificiality of the drama. It was as if two fine performers were asked to act in a second-rate play. Although the two might perform well, they still could not overcome a certain rigid structure, no doubt because the spark of imagination was lacking.

She slapped his face. She lashed out because there was nothing left to say. By striking him so viciously, she felt she was continuing some sexually abusive game. He felt as if he had been struck by cold, hard steel. From the time they had first started making love, he had suspected that her hands weren't human and had avoided her touch. And now he found himself entirely enveloped by that cold, metallic feeling.

It was the first time in his life that he had been slapped so, and it was by a woman. For the longest time, all he felt was that cold, metallic sensation. When that red cloud lifted, he had no idea.

13

That night, Chen Qing told a story about the "transparent tablet."

A black and shiny jade tablet is located in the Thousand Buddhist Caves. But a long time ago it was snow white and as transparent as a mirror. According to legend, this piece of jade was brought to the Thousand Buddhist Caves when the King of Yutian and the Tang princess were married. To show his gratitude, the old monk of the cave had the artisans paint the King of Yutians portrat in the cave and had the jade carved into a tablet and installed on the right wall on the south side of the Nine-Story Pagoda. When people from all quarters came to visit the Thousand Buddhist Caves and stood before the tablet, an animal shape would be reflected in the tablet. It was very odd. When someone stood there, the reflection would appear; when nobody stood there, no reflection appeared. Later it was said that the animal reflected in the tablet was in fact the original appearance of the person! Everyone was intrigued by this phenomenon, so people came to stand before the tablet to see their original shape.

In the days when the Red Army was on the rise, there was a bandit here in our northwest by the name of Ma Bufang, who thought very highly of himself. He came here to see his original shape, expecting to see a dragon, a phoenix, or some such noble beast, but what he saw was a black ass. He had his wife and son and daughter come and stand before the tablet. Huh! They were all jackasses!

In a fit of rage, Ma Bufang had the tablet burned. When the fire burned out, the tablet was found unharmed, but had unfortunately turned black, and therefore unable to reflect.

14

Zhang Shu had a hard time falling asleep that night. Later he heard someone crying nearby. It was a deep, hoarse sound, like that of an old woman. First, he covered his head with his blanket, but the sound still penetrated like some sharp metal instrument, slowly grating on his nerves. It floated in the stubborn darkness, faintly discernible, as if it were coming one moment from miles away and from inches away the next. He slowly sat up.

The sound was coming from Chen Qing's room!

That night Zhang Shu played the thief. He pressed against the grimy window to see what he could see. Directly opposite to him was Chen Qing, whose old face was a bit vague under the dim light. An old woman sat with her back to him, but her silhouette looked very familiar.

The sound of weeping continued.

". . . Don't be too upset, it's fate!" Chen Qing's lips suddenly moved.

"If it's not fate, what is it?" came the woman's voice. Zhang Shu's heart skipped a beat—it was Yu'er's mother. He pressed his ear against a crack in the window to hear more clearly. "But that painting was handed down by my ancestors! It has been handed down for so many generations and I've lost it. I'm sure it was Dayejisi who slipped me the fake."

Chen Qing timidly lowered his head and said, "Be careful. Dayejisi is a powerful person. If you're wrong, you'll pay with your life."

"Sooner or later it is bound to come to an end. Life has no meaning anyway. One daughter won't have anything to do with me and the other is no good. Why bother to go on living?"

Chen Qing tried to comfort her. "You have to go on living even if life has no meaning. Why these tears at your age? Stop crying. I feel awful when you cry."

Zhang Shu could see tears streaming from Chen Qing's eyes.

It was clear that they hadn't done it, but who had?

A convention of cheap mystery novels suddenly occurred to Zhang Shu: the most unlikely suspect was usually guilty. The experienced detectives always said, "One has to watch out for the darkness beneath the lantern."

Then an image slowly rose before his mind's eye, followed by another, both of which gradually merged.

"What marvelous partners," he thought.

15

Wuye returned at dusk on the fifth day.

He appeared silently out of nowhere. Xingxing, who was sitting by the window, stood up and stared calmly at him.

She said nothing nor did she cry. As if in a dream, she repeated those warm, honeyed words capable of reducing one to tears over and over again to herself. Each time she repeated them, tears trickled from her eyes. Xiao Xingxing was easily moved to tears. But in life, she rarely resorted to tears and she seldom cried in front of others, even if she was sad.

Perhaps the tears she shed in public had all been shed twelve years before.

Wuye was much thinner and he appeared distracted, as if he had just returned from the dead and was still unaccustomed to his surroundings. Xingxing hugged him tightly and closed her eyes. She could feel the warmth of her body as it flowed away. She wished she could pass all of her warmth to him. He accepted her attentions stiffly. His ten cold fingernails began to sink into her flesh, deeper and deeper. She grit her teeth to bear the pain and she nearly burst out screaming several times—more out of fear than pain. She sensed he was a man who had just escaped from the lair of a beast; his body was covered with the cold scent of it. The whole day she cared for him as if he were a baby. She got him out of his clothes, heated a bath for him, and bathed him with Imperial Crown Bath Gel. The silvery soap bubbles wreathed his pallid face. His blank eyes gradually filled with warmth and gratitude.

Strangely, when she undressed him, she didn't feel in the least bit embarrassed, as if she were the Holy Mother bathing the Holy Infant. She gently rubbed his entire body and washed the dirty, soapy water from him. Then she proceeded to wrap him in a clean, white sheet. He lay there like a baby in swaddling clothes, falling to sleep amid the sound of her hushed lullaby.

Why did his eyelashes continue to twitch even after he had drifted off to sleep? She thought of the distant young man, who had the same long and sensitive eyelashes. That corn-scented night and those many scarlet evenings from the past merged together. She had no idea if he was the reincarnation of that distant young man. She didn't know where they came from, but she was frightened by returning spirits.

She felt warm and damp in that steamy little room. At dusk, when Zhang Shu came over to borrow her thermos, he saw Wuye. It was precisely at that moment when Wuye woke. Through his narrowly opened eyes, he saw Zhang Shu's blue shaved face; it was in fact a handsome face, very masculine.

16

Xingxing did not like to kiss. Whenever anyone tried to kiss her, she would turn away. This included her husband, Mousheng. Kissing never made her happy. She didn't know why, but perhaps it was because all men had bad breath. She knew that this morbid preoccupation with cleanliness, this pursuit of perfection, was an obstacle to her happiness. That distant young man was no exception. She gave him much more, but it amounted to a spiritual love. She couldn't squarely face her own physical needs. They existed and charmed. Once after bathing, she came out from behind that heavy purplish-red velvet curtain that was in his house opposite to which stood a mirror. She saw the momentary matchless glory of the moon and the sun that had risen at the same time before the heavy curtain and she was shock by this glory. She knew that Xiaojun's room was next to hers and she actually wanted to walk in leisurely. No, she didn't want to do anything except let him see her, see her unadorned. She regretted not having done so; she regretted it all her life, for he left this world before ever having really seen her.

Narcissism is the last refuge for anyone seeking the perfect man or woman, because perfection does not exist in the world. Some famous person once said that the first love and the last love is narcissism.

17

Wuye talked as he slowly exhaled the steam from the hot glutinous millet porridge.

He said he had been taken to a large room by that group of people. It was a beautifully decorated room, like a tastefully decorated office. He was tied up because he kept struggling. The thin cords cut into his flesh. He found that skinny woman very strange for her lack of feminine compassion and the way she spit, berated him, and shouted at him. Everyone disappeared, and he was left tied there, where he trembled like an abandoned child. The silence was oppressive. He spent the entire night with his eyes wide open; every time he heard a noise, he would quake with fear. Several times he screamed just to hear the echo. Later he heard the window creak and it appeared to open a crack. He thought that someone had used a scaling ladder like in the movie *Robin Hood* and had come to rescue him. But he finally realized that it was just the wind that was rattling the door and windows.

He thought of Xingxing and when he did so, his heart ached. He thought of how she had smiled and pleaded with those people on his behalf, which must have been difficult for her. She had done it all for him. She was thrust alone into the darkness. How would she get back? She had a poor sense of direction.

He wept for Xingxing and for himself. Although he had been born into a big Christian family, no one really showed any concern for him. His mother and father were both engaged in geographical research. Less than a month after he was born, his mother had left him to accompany his father to the northwest. He was weak from the start and it was a distant female relative who had raised him. The strange old spinster punished him in a variety of ways. At the height of winter, she had punished him by making him stand by the door, as a result of which he developed a bad case of the flu that nearly claimed his young life. Later, in his youth, the old woman often let him go without eating. When he was so hungry he couldn't stand it any longer, he went and ate table scraps at a restaurant. It is said that a child who grows up in a loveless household will turn into a wolf, but he was an exception. Even after such a terrible childhood, he became even more refined and sensitive. He wanted to store up all of his feelings and offer them to one person. In twenty-some years he had not once encountered a woman who moved him, so he developed an interest in traveling. He never expected to meet Xingxing, who became the star of his life, in the northwest.

He valued feelings because of all he had suffered. He found a woman like Xingxing to be a goddess. He loved and respected her. At his age, such selfless passions are common. He felt that if Xingxing was able to shed a few tears for him, he could die for her.

A small purple patch of sky peeked through the dark curtains. These thoughts filled his mind as he looked at the purple light.

18

Eventually that oppressive silence was broken by a voice. It was already light outside when a key turned in the lock of the door. A woman with a kindhearted face opened the door and stepped in. Her dark clothing made her oval face with arched, clear brows look particularly white. She had large, beautiful eyes. Her tender lips, when tightly shut, produced a dimple to the right of her mouth. He couldn't determine her age and had never been much good at guessing a woman's age. She did bear a striking resemblance to the Bodhisattva Guanyin, the gentle one from Cave 259, and not the fierce Horse-headed type. He felt his chance had come.

"Good morning," he said, as he got to his feet and made an effort to be as respectful as possible.

"Good morning." The woman smiled, indicating he should sit down.

"Is . . . is this your office? Yesterday a group of people escorted me here . . ."

With a wave of her hand she silenced him. At the same time she nodded toward the door and a young woman entered carrying a serving tray.

"Have some breakfast, young man," she said indifferently. On the tray were two pieces of dim sum, a glass of milk, and a couple of small dishes of pickles. Everything was nicely prepared. Wuye was famished and when he saw that the woman had no bad intentions, he wolfed it all down. The woman smiled as she watched him.

The woman's smile was fixed, or, perhaps more accurately, only her lips were smiling, while her eyes expressed pity. Later, Wuye discovered that her eyelids drooped. But there was a cool and detached air behind those pitying eyes. Even when she smiled, that cool detachment never varied.

After breakfast, the woman asked him his name, age, and other facts with apparent indifference. Then she smiled and said that she hadn't been able to come earlier to investigate because she had been rather busy and so he had to suffer the inconvenience of remaining in custody there for two days. Not waiting for him to reply, she led him to the room next door. The strange color of the room immediately cowed him. He was blinded for a moment and felt as if his entire body had been soaked through with scarlet. Yes, the principal color of the room was between a deep red and scarlet, a deep color that put a person to sleep. Amid all the red hung copies of many frescoes, including Buddhist Jataka tales, legends, and stories from the scriptures. They were marvelously accurate and could almost pass for the real thing. Wuye sank into a dark red world.

By the time the key sounded in the lock again, he discovered that the red world was tantalizing and seductive. Out of the bloody red shone the naked breasts and thighs of devas. The color of old blood was oppressive. After making several turns around the room like a caged beast, his heart was pounding. Clenching his head in his hands, he squatted and closed his eyes, but that red managed to seep into his eyes and seemed to poison his blood.

When Wuye was once again with Xingxing, he understood why she wanted to vomit when she saw scarlet.

19

At noon Wuye was wakened by a gentle voice followed by the scent of a heavy fragrance something like Red Flower Oil. Then someone placed a serving tray before him. Never had he ever seen such a sumptuous lunch of four dishes and a soup. He recognized drunken shrimp and shark's fin soup, which were exquisitely prepared. They were served with snow-white steamed bread. Without hesitating he wolfed down this tray of food as well, the aroma of which lingered long. Later he began to vomit. As he did so, he felt that aroma penetrate his empty stomach.

When he awoke, it was already dark. Two red floor lamps went on at the same time and then the door opened, through which a large shadow fell. With some difficulty, he opened his eyes and saw that kindly woman. In the red light, her face appeared snow white. She stood there, light and shadow perfect, as magnificent as a court painting by Velasquez.

"I heard you were not feeling well, Wuye." Her voice, though pleasant to the ear, was cool and detached. "Was it indigestion? Will you have some rice porridge this evening?"

She personally handed him a bowl of rice porridge, a jar of fermented bean curd, a small dish of ham, and stuffed bean cake. She carefully handed him a spoon for the porridge, and his heart melted at once. At that moment, the only person he felt he could trust was that woman.

"May I ask . . . your name?" he asked somewhat feebly, holding the bowl of porridge.

The woman smiled again. "No questions please. Eat up. Your situation will be resolved today."

He grew excited at the last comment, prompting him to gulp down the porridge in just a few mouthfuls. He then tried some of the fermented bean curd and found it even more delicious than champagne and a Western meal. The woman smiled as he ate. Her smile was soothing.

"Okay, young man, finish up so we can chat." She sat down beside him in a friendly way, closer than usual. She exuded a faint fragrance, something like tree sap.

"I know everything. You and your friend entered the Tantric Cave that day without permission. Not only that but you also planned to steal a fresco. Is that what happened?"

"No, no . . . ," said Wuye, the blood rushing to his face. "Nothing of the sort happened. I was just joking."

"Come on. It's best just to confess. Your words were recorded, and there are witnesses. Based on this, if a report is filed with the authorities, you'll be convicted." The woman went on speaking without blinking an eye. "But we are taking your age into consideration and want to help you."

His heart began to pound; his chest felt tight so he was unable to speak.

"This could be a big matter or a small matter—it's up to you." The woman's voice was increasingly tender. "Tell me where is the *Lakshmi Bathing* fresco from Cave Seventy-three?"

Like a bolt from the blue he was going to faint.

"The method utilized by the culprits in Cave Seventy-three is identical to the one you mentioned. All you have to do is confess and the entire matter can be settled. You seem like a bright boy, and you should be smart about this matter."

"No! No! I've never ever touched the fresco in Cave Seventy-three. Someone is framing me." He finally lost his temper and shouted angrily, "I was just joking around that day. I've never ever touched that painting!"

His shouts echoed. He felt he was being held in a blood-red cave as only stone walls could echo in such a manner.

It was all a fraud, a fraud, a fraud!

The woman remained as kind as ever, looking at him with pity and compassion, without the slightest impatience.

"Sit down, Wuye, you are becoming overexcited. Calm down. Listen to me and calm down."

He stared blankly at her. The woman was hypnotic. She was controlling him.

"All right, rest for a while. Lie down on the sofa and rest. That's right, relax, starting from your toes. Do your toes feel warm? Okay, we'll take it slowly. Do you feel the soles of your feet becoming warm? The warmth will spread upward to *san yinjiao* acupoint, to your *huantiao* point, to your *zusanli* point . . ."

Her voice put him to sleep. He did feel relaxed. He stared quietly at the ceiling. A red mist appeared before his eyes, growing thicker and then dissipating.

20

Later, how much later he couldn't say, he heard a voice through his sleep saying, "Repeat after me, repeat after me, I stole the painting in Cave Seventy-three . . ."

He wanted to keep repeating himself, but he was very sensitive at the mention of Cave 73. He didn't do as she asked. After three days in the red, sexually suggestive room, he felt himself wasting away, and on numerous occasions he felt like a spider suspended on the wall with one filament sufficient to hang him up. On the fourth day, the same program was repeated. The woman who looked like Guanyin was even warmer and kinder. She personally fed him Yellow River melon, which was sliced into small pieces. He could feel the sweet juice running from the corner of his mouth. He thought again of Xingxing. Since arriving, Xingxing had not yet tried a real Yellow River melon. When he left, he'd have to take a couple to her.

"What sort of painting was taken from Cave Seventy-three?"

Dazed, he heard someone ask and he struggled to remember its name. A painting appeared before his eyes, the one he had seen in Xingxing's picture book, but for the life of him, he couldn't remember its title.

Memory is often flawed.

When Wuye saw Xingxing, he really couldn't remember if he had confessed to the ridiculous crime. All he could remember was that during the last two days of his confinement, half the time he couldn't tell what was real or when he was hallucinating. "Cave Seventy-three" became an oft-repeated signal, encountering which his mental processes would shut down. Finally, the signal vanished. By the time the same words were asked in different way, he was inured to all questions.

In a word, by the morning of the fifth day, he discovered upon awakening that the red room had vanished as if it had never existed. He found himself in the yellow office where he had been interrogated. The door was wide open, there was no one there and no sound. He shouted several times, but no one responded. He stepped out of the office to find the hall empty. So he simply left the building. He examined the building carefully. It was an old gray-colored building that looked like it had been constructed with the aid of Soviet experts in the early 1950s. Then he walked toward the courtyard; spiderwebs hung outside the reception room. He paced back and forth for a while at the entrance and, after determining there was no danger, he sneaked away.

21

Xingxing was assailed by a deep fear.

It was that woman again! She had determined from Wuye's description that it was that woman who resembled the Bodhisattva Guanyin, the one who had advised her. Suddenly she felt that things did not look good.

Wuye may not have succumbed to her hypnotism, but he definitely said something or confessed to something. Otherwise it would have been impossible for him to flee from that scarlet cave.

Why was it scarlet in color?

Her hair stood on end as she thought of that red dream of hers. She felt a pain in her heart as if she saw Wuye cut his own wrist and the blood spurt out.

22

Wuye shoveled the last mouthful of millet porridge into his mouth. He looked tenderly at Xingxing.

She found that look intolerable. If she didn't hide behind the opposite emotion, she'd end up in tears. All men have tempers, but she could not imagine what Wuye would be like if he lost his.

Perhaps it was best for a middle-aged woman to live with a younger man. It was right in terms of sex and every other angle. She recalled the middle-aged men she had known. They were all quite charming, but totally lacking in youthful passion.

Wuye's purity was obvious from his health and cleanliness. She loved purity more than maturity. To her Xiaojun was a pure young man who had never grown up. As for herself, she was nothing more than a young girl by his side. Her immature subconscious affected her behavior.

"The name of that nasty skinny woman is Ahyuexi . . ." Wuye seemed to recall something, his eyes blurred. "What kind of people are they . . . They spoke noisily, but I didn't understand a word. Their clothes were very unusual . . ."

"Where did they keep you locked up? You certainly must remember that."

"I do remember."

"Sleep first, then take me to see the place." Xingxing covered him with a blanket and tucked in the corners. Then she bent over and kissed him on the forehead.

"There was one other thing that surprised me," he said, sitting up.

"What's that?"

"Ahyuexi is a descendant of Yu-Chi Yiseng. That's what the Bodhisattva Guanyin told me."

V.

The Transformation of the Western Paradise

I

According to Mahayana Buddhism, there are countless Buddhas in the ten directions and the three periods.[1] Each Buddha has a land he has taught and enlightened; these lands are called Buddha realms. These Buddha realms, unlike the mundane world of men, are pure and unpolluted, and hence called pure lands. Passing from this world through hundreds of thousands of millions of Buddha lands to the West, there is a world called Ultimate Bliss. The founder, called Amitabha, teaches the Dharma in this world. Those born in this land of Ultimate Bliss endure no sufferings but enjoy every bliss. The ground is yellow gold; the railings and trees are formed of gold, silver, and other precious objects. There are also gold and silver pools of the seven jewels, filled with the clear, sweet and cool waters of eight meritorious virtues. The bottoms of the pools are spread over with golden sand. In the pools are lotuses the size of carriage wheels in all marvelous colors. In the country there are always rare and wonderful birds that sing with marvelous voices, speaking the Buddha-dharma. Those who live in this country possess limitless life and all have unshakable faith.

There is a school of Buddhism called Pure Land Buddhism in which the practitioners dedicate themselves to being reborn in the Western Paradise. The form of practice is quite simple. All one needs to do, regardless of how much evil one has done, is merely invoke Amitabha's name and they will vault across the three periods to be born in the World of Ultimate Bliss.

---

1. Ten directions refer to east, south, west, north, above, beneath, etc. Three periods refer to past, present and future.

Pure Land Buddhism has been extremely popular throughout history for this reason.

2

The door to the Tantric Cave was locked. Zhang Shu rode his creaky old bike around behind the cave to look at the crystal-clear blue sky. He took out his special guest pass and held it up to the blue sky like some inexplicable sign.

There was no one there, so the pass was useless.

He felt like breaking the rusty lock with a good swift kick.

He came after he heard Xingxing's account. Actually what interested him more than the cave was that descendant of Yu-Chi Yiseng. He wanted to find her and get the real story about Cave 73.

He hung around until he no longer saw any point, at which time he decided to go to the small shop and check out the stone rubbings. Some of the stone rubbings in the area were exquisite but difficult to buy. He turned and saw those two old dogs that Wuye had described as Buddhas barking and biting at each other. He saw they were quite old and barked with great effort but still insisted on biting at each other's necks.

The small shop was open, so he entered. He saw her at once. He was sure it was the skinny woman Xingxing had described to him. But he harbored no ill will toward her and initially was inclined to like her. The young woman was of the Yi nationality. Her long hair reached to her waist. She wore an apricot-colored band around her head for whatever reason; otherwise she was dressed entirely in gray. Her skin was a bronze color and her skirt was gray, the lower hem of which was fringed and came to just above her knees, revealing a pair of thin but lovely legs. She had a narrow waist and long arms, and her chest was flat. Such a svelte young woman was rarely encountered in the hinterland. She had a certain attractiveness, especially when her expression became serious. Her thin face, with the long bridge of her nose, her sharp chin, and high forehead all denoted a sharp mind. She had long eyes and her eyelashes were long and black. Her lips, while moist, were colorless, and pressed together resembled a white peach leaf. She stood straight as a ramrod behind the counter. If she didn't speak or move it was easy to take her for a plastic mannequin.

Zhang Shu devised a plan as he walked around in front of the counter. The thin woman stood there, silent and expressionless.

"May I take a look at that book of paintings?" He leaned on the glass counter, head in hand, his bristly hair sticking through his fingers. He wanted to attract her attention, whether by making her angry or happy.

He flipped through the book and let her get another for him. This was a book on Dunhuang printed in Japan. It was quite beautiful but cost more than two hundred yuan. He looked at it for a while and then gave it back to her.

"Too expensive," he commented.

He kept on this way until he had looked through every book in the place. Then he asked to look at the rubbings. After looking at each one, he offered his harsh criticism.

But she remained unmoved.

"Do you have rubbings from the Tantric Cave?" he suddenly asked, looking her in the eye.

She didn't utter a word.

"Did you understand what I said?" He repeated himself, gesturing. After a long while, after he had lost all hope, she suddenly spoke.

"How much are you willing to pay? she asked.

3

So she could speak Chinese after all!

He was as startled as if he had just heard a clay Buddha speak. He quickly replied that he urgently needed a rubbing from the Tantric Cave and as long as it was the real thing, price didn't matter, acting as if he had loads of money. Only then did the thin woman size him up, and after that she clapped her hands twice without any expression. A coarse-looking man appeared immediately from out of the back room and the two of them began chattering in a language Zhang Shu could not understand. Then the woman gestured for him to follow her.

She led him down into a dirty, dilapidated basement. Several times while walking down the stone steps he nearly slipped and fell on the filth. With each descending step, his nervousness and curiosity increased. When they arrived at the bottom he almost fainted from the stench of what smelled like nitrate fertilizer made from years of urine. He quickly covered his nose and then shoved his hands in his pockets. The thin woman turned on the light as if nothing were the matter and opened a greasy cabinet.

In alarm, he looked around for fear lest he be carried away like Wuye. But there was no one else to be seen. The thin woman thrust a pile of stone rubbings under his nose.

He wanted to examine them upstairs, but the woman refused. By the dim light, he could see that the rubbings were awkwardly executed and depicted Amitabha Buddha in a number of different positions, which were ugly like bent earthworms. They were without a doubt also fakes.

"How much for one?" he asked.

She raised five fingers and then added a zero.

"It's really hard to imagine that a descendant of Yu-Chi Yiseng could be so greedy," said Zhang Shu, enunciating each syllable.

The thin woman raised her eyebrows. It was only then that he realized she was capable of facial expressions. Before he could think, he saw the flash of a blade and felt something hard and sharp against his belly.

"Tell me what you are doing here!" Her Chinese was better than Yu'er's and the old woman who guarded Cave 73.

Although this incident would affect Zhang Shu for a long time afterward, he was exceptionally calm at the time.

"Put the knife down. We can discuss this."

She didn't lower her knife and looked as if she were going to cut his belt.

He then told her the intensely interesting tale of Yu-Chi Yiseng and Lakshmi. Naturally, he repeated some of the legend Yu'er had told him, but later he found out that it was the last few words he spoke that moved the thin woman.

"Actually, before I heard this story I was much more interested in

Yiseng's painting. I've heard that he is famous and the representative of the Tang dynasty Yutian School of painting. He was esteemed by the Taizong Emperor of the Tang dynasty and that large frescoes by him can be seen at the Ci'en Temple and the Feng'en Temple in Xi'an, as well as at the Dandan Temple in Hotan, Xinjiang. I think it's unfair that a painter of his stature has not been recognized as he should be in the history of Chinese art. I want to do research on him and his relationship with Dunhuang . . ."

At that point, the thin woman's beautiful eyes were wide open and fixed on him. He felt that the hard object at his waist had eased off a bit.

4

When Xingxing was still in primary school, she saw part of a fresco titled *The Transformation of the Western Paradise* in her sister's history textbook. Later, she saw the same painting in a variety of books. If she closed her eyes, she could still picture the composition, the flying bodhisattva, the red and green lotuses, white cranes, and mandarin ducks, but now that she found herself standing before the genuine article, she was profoundly moved.

The Transformation of the Western Paradise was located in Cave 220, a cave of great importance that dated from the early Tang. It was a square cave with a compound ladder ceiling, the center of which was painted with beautiful peonies. Waves of rolling grass and hanging curtains were spread all around on which were painted a thousand Buddhas. An inscription above the door to the cave indicated that it dated from the second year of the Chuigong reign period (AD 686).

The huge fresco titled *The Transformation of the Western Paradise* was executed on the south wall of the cave. Amitabha is depicted with attendant bodhisattvas Guanyin and Mahasthamaprapta surrounded by a multitude of bodhisattvas and devas. The Buddha appears solemn and dignified. In the foreground of the painting are a pair of dancers. The graceful dancers are in the classic posture of "heavenly musicians playing the pipa." On ancient Persian-style carpets, peacocks dance gracefully and cranes call with their necks extended. In the upper part of the fresco yakshas fly scattering flowers, and musical instruments played by themselves; below, blue ripples spread in the pools where red lilies and green lotuses set off each other. Divine children sat properly with palms pressed together or played in the water. Waterside pavilions faced rows of buildings with terraces thronged with dancers and musicians as a multitude of Buddhas descended on clouds to enjoy the dancing and marvelous music.

The artisans of old were so imaginative.

Xingxing thought of her dream of the World of Ultimate Bliss. When she was a child, her maternal grandmother had told her about the World of Ultimate Bliss, after which she had a dream in which she penetrated the toilet in their house and made her way through a labyrinthine path full of twists and turns until she suddenly came out into the open. The first thing she saw was a beautiful wood of tall tress and bushes, all a bright and shining just washed green. Bright red berries were hidden among the leaves, shining like stars. The ripe fruit fell continuously to the ground where they immediately turned into red gems. Continuing on a natural flower garden in which the untended flowers grew in a riotous profusion of color. On nearly every blossom was an exquisitely wrought bird. The blood-red plumage of the birds was clearly the color of the underworld! Even more strange was that each bird held a berry like a red gem in its bill. The darting colorful birds looked like they would shatter at any moment in the air. And the brilliant red of the flowers looked liked coagulated blood, their crystal blue and dark green looked like they had been soaked through with seawater. What at first sight appeared to be flowers turned out to be birds and beasts. Amid all those colors stood a white archway on which was written: The World of Ultimate Bliss. Beyond the archway was a huge natural fountain. The shimmering drops, like a dream, sprayed water on the trees and flowers, the drops trembling with exquisite sound, and with that of the wind, flowers, trees, birds, and beasts combined to compose a heavenly music.

Thinking about it now, the biggest difference between the World of Ultimate Bliss in her dream and *The Transformation of the Western*

Paradise was that the latter included countless Buddhas and men in the five directions and ten worlds while the former included just herself and a serenely quiet and beautiful land. As far as she was concerned that which was profoundly moving could only be contained in silence. It would be better to say that the scene in her dream rather than belonging to the World of Ultimate Bliss actually belonged to nature, a mysterious and untouched region.

That day, she had Wuye take her to find that gray building where he was held for five days and five nights. Full of confidence, Wuye took her to the place, but they were startled to find themselves in front of a pile of gray rubble and a bulldozer at work. Wuye stopped a laborer and pressed him about it, as if hoping to confirm his memory for Xingxing. Indifferently the laborer replied that the building had been demolished two years before and that there was no gray Soviet-style building from the '50s in the area. Wuye blanched and looked utterly defeated. Xingxing tried to comfort him while having doubts about everything he had told her, attributing it to an illusion produced by the Bodhisattva Guanyin through hypnosis. She was enveloped in foreboding and since that day had been urging Wuye to leave.

She felt that the most absurd part of her dream was finding the way to the World of Ultimate Bliss via the toilet in her house.

5

Shortly after Xingxing arrived back at the guesthouse, Chen Qing came over to deliver a note from Zhang Shu inviting her to have dinner with him at the best restaurant in Dunhuang. He stated in the note that it was to thank her for giving him four copies of frescoes of Lakshmi.

Without the slightest hesitation, Xingxing decided to go. First, because Wuye had gone to the Yulin Caves to see that friend of his who had become a monk; second, and most important, she hadn't had a decent meal in ages and had been eating plain and simple food and felt like a square meal.

Zhang Shu was already there when she arrived. The lights were dim and the music soft. The half-drawn curtains produced a sumptuous red glow. He smiled when he saw Xingxing. Then he motioned for the waiter and asked Xingxing to order.

Xingxing's eyes ran over the seafood dishes, but her finger opted for common meat dishes. Dishes costing more than twenty yuan were rarely encountered in Dunhuang restaurants. Zhang Shu insisted upon ordering two local specialties—moss and black mushroom meat roll and *niang pizi*, a kind of noodle dish.

"How can you afford this? Did you strike it rich?" asked Xingxing, looking at him inquiringly. As she had said it, she suddenly realized her crisp voice didn't harmonize with the atmosphere here.

"Food is much cheaper here than in Beijing. You have to look at it this way," said Zhang Shu, leisurely opening a blue and white porcelain bottle and taking a sip of Sanpaotai, a local specialty in which longyan, red dates, and *gouji* are steeped in tea, making for a refreshing beverage. Zhang Shu was partial to the beverage, but after ordering it, he recalled that Xingxing didn't drink tea.

"You have tea and I'll have wine," said Xingxing, pouring herself a glass of Rose Fragrance Wine, a product of Xinjiang.

"I seem to recall that you don't drink any stimulating beverages."

"That's true, but there are special occasions."

"Such as?"

"When I'm feeling particularly proud of myself or when I am very disappointed." Xingxing smiled and lifted her glass. "But today, it's simply to complement the food."

"Good. Bottoms up for the food!" Zhang Shu lifted a glass in fun. At that moment a young waitress gracefully approached to serve their food.

"What have you been doing the last two days?" he asked, as he moved the dishes around, full of zest.

"Nothing really. I did some more sightseeing and copied some paintings."

"Have you seen any good paintings?"

"*The Transformation of the Western Paradise,* but I don't really like it all that much."

"Why?"

"It's too busy and too mannered. There is nothing mysterious about it."

"I actually like the painting. It's a great work on a large scale." He ate. "I heard that Director Tang of the Cultural Research Center is having it copied. His idea is to protect some of the originals and display the copies for the tourists."

"It's a good thing we came when we did."

"Actually, copies sometimes are quite valuable, especially when there is no original available." He smiled as he looked at her.

"Your words can go into a book of famous remarks."

"This is an age of substitutes because there are so few of the genuine article."

"Another brilliant remark." She smiled and her eyes shone.

"That is why when I see the real thing, I value it all the more." He spoke with some effort.

She looked away from his eyes.

"It's true, Xingxing. I often think of death these days." His voice was very low, and she had to strain to hear him. "The fear of death increases when a person hits middle age. Don't you think so? We have given away our youth. Now, no matter what, we should never give any more away to anyone ever again. That way, on the day we die, we can say that we have enjoyed life to the fullest."

His voice grew ever fainter, and she could see tears in his eyes.

He lifted his wineglass, drained it, and poured another. She put her hand on his trying to restrain him.

"Don't drink any more, okay?" Her eyes pleaded with him.

Zhang Shu gently moved her hand away and threw back another glass.

"I always wonder why life is so messed up. I don't love those who love me, and the ones I love don't love me." He was becoming more talkative and his gaze more insistent. "Think about it: I'm forty and don't have much interest in living. I can't take it lying down and want to keep on struggling . . ."

She looked at him without saying a word. She had completely lost her appetite.

"Thanks for the paintings," he said, drinking straight from the bottle.

"Don't mention it; it was nothing. For us painters it's nothing."

His eyes were becoming slow-moving.

"Three of the eight distresses of Buddhism include parting with what we love, meeting with what we hate, and unattained aims. Many things in life do not go as we wish." She looked straight at him. "There is a common expression that puts it really well: 'A good man can't get a good wife, but a worthless scoundrel can get a gem.' In my experience, a good man and a good woman will never walk together forever . . ."

"Why not?" His face darkened.

She shook her head.

He didn't believe her at the time. He thought it was just a common expression a woman was likely to use. But later, he came to believe it.

6

Many years later, I ran into Xiao Xingxing at a relatively unimportant occasion. By then she was close to forty. I had my doubts about Zhang Shu's feelings. There was nothing special about her; she was just an ordinary woman. You couldn't call her pretty, and there was nothing special about her temperament or her talk. She was cute, though. Applying the word *cute* to a woman of forty ought to be taken as a huge compliment. I must confess, though, that she did seem young and full of life. It was sort of like that song that says, "With her embrace, you will never age."

But most people are afraid of such women, regardless of their spirits or bodies. They have their own way of doing things, and for most men they exist perpetually behind a veil of mystery. Decades later the woman behind the veil might still be young and attractive, but the man has long since been withered by time.

I believe Zhang Shu's defeat can be attributed to the fact that he put her on too high a pedestal. Actually, women are essentially all alike. Xiao Xingxing, in particular, possessed all the female weaknesses: strong on the outside, but weak on the inside, and, while putting up a strong façade, she was in sore need of protection. Moreover, such women seemingly all end up "in a forced marriage." To court them, a man must be forceful and patient.

Unfortunately, Zhang Shu didn't understand this at the time.

7

It was at that moment that Ahyuexi entered Zhang Shu's life.

This silent girl was as quiet as a tree. One heard very little from her save the sound of the sweep of her beautiful head of hair.

Unexpectedly, Zhang Shu learned a lot from Ahyuexi about Dunhuang and Yiseng, obviously some of which was secret family legend. He believed it had a lot of research value. He did find it strange, though, that Ahyuexi knew much more than Yu'er.

She came to see him every day, to watch him write. She always quietly opened the door and quietly sat down beside him. If he didn't feel the breeze from her fan, he never would have known anyone was sitting by his side. Sometimes, when he could not hear her breathing, he grew afraid.

"Ahyuexi."

"Huh?"

"Take a break. I'm not in the least hot."

But the fanning and the soft breeze continued. He glanced at her face and saw how serious she looked. It was as if seeing him engaged in something so sacred that it was an honor for her to fan him.

"Ahyuexi."

"Huh?"

"You have a pretty name." Her earnestness touched him and he wanted to make her happy.

Sure enough, she smiled, showing her fine teeth. She lowered her thick lashes. She was as beautiful as she was charming.

"Who chose your name?"

"My father."

"Zhaxi Lunba?"

". . . How do you know that?" Her dark gray eyes suddenly grew round as saucers.

"If I'm right, then your mom is the woman who looks after Cave Seventy-three. You also have a younger sister by the name of Yu'er."

"Don't mention those two good-for-nothings to me." Ahyuexi was suddenly on her feet, straight as a blade and cold and detached.

"Ahyuexi, why do you hate them so much? Tell me. Didn't your mother keep you even after remarrying? . . . When did you leave them? Who was your stepfather?"

"My stepfather is a wolf with a human face!" Ahyuexi lowered her head. "His name is Dayejisi."

8

Ahyuexi's story was a long one, as long as a silent deep gray river.

Ahyuexi's father was Zhaxi Lunba, a Tibetan, and her mother was Guonu, a member of the Yugur minority. She was born in glorious Dunhuang and seemed to have been fated to lead an unusual life.

Everything happened by chance. For example, if her father Zhaxi Lunba hadn't become interested in Dunhuang and moved there to further his research, he never would have met Guonu nor would have Ahyuexi been born. And if Zhaxi Lunba hadn't died, Guonu would not have married Dayejisi nor would have Ahyuexi left home.

Ahyuexi was six years old when Guonu remarried. Two years later the Tibetan nobleman Ciren Lunba came to Dunhuang to take his granddaughter, Ahyuexi, away.

For the first three years, she led the life of a princess.

The Lunba were an influential clan in Tibet. When the British Army invaded Tibet in the early twentieth century, the Dalai Lama fled to Mongolia, and the Lunba clan had the power to decide in matters of life or death.

The Lunbas lived on Chaosheng Avenue, in a two-storey stone house from which they could see the pilgrims coming to Lhasa. Each wing of the house possessed a small shrine, where oil lamps had burned for ages on the carved wooden altars. Seven bowls of holy water had to be changed several times a day, because the spirits might come to drink at any time. The family supported four Buddhist masters, and when anything significant occurred, they would be expected to come and say prayers in rotation.

Ciren Lunba often took Ahyuexi to the Jokhang Temple. The old nobleman was one of the temple benefactors; otherwise he would not have received such special treatment. Ahyuexi wore a crown of gold and precious stones and earrings six *cun* in length (the longer a person's earrings, the higher their social status), and with the other members of the clan, male and female, young and old, would make her way on horseback to the Jokhang Temple.

Smoke-blackened columns supported the huge roof. Swirling incense smoke filled the interior of the temple; gold images of Buddhas on the four walls were enshrined and worshiped. In front of them was a strong metal folding screen of coarse mesh. The first Buddha was covered with the jeweled offerings of countless supplicants. Candles had burned for ages on pure gold candlesticks; they had burned for more than a thousand years and had never gone out. A visitor would be ecstatic listening to the drums, gold horns, Dharma gongs, and bagpipes that played on and on as well as the swelling tide of sutra recitation.

Young Ahyuexi would often accompany her grandfather to the top of the temple where they would gaze out over the infinite blue sky. She dreamed of riding a kite on a windy festival day over the snowy mountains to see her mother.

On her tenth birthday a number of guests came to their house. Her grandmother also pickled a lot of fine photinia flowers. The photinia flowers of Tibet grow tall and beautiful. People pick the flower buds, which have not fully developed, wash them, and seal them in glass jars filled with syrup. The flowers slowly swell in the jar, filled with syrup. After opening the jar, they make excellent sweetmeats. Of course there were also *zanba* and milk tea, things the Tibetans had to have, but which Ahyuexi wasn't very fond of.

Ahyuexi's fate was decided on that day.

Two elderly and prominent lamas dressed in red and gold robes held a map of the stars and began to emit a low guttural sound not unlike the large dharma horns. The sound slowly rose in pitch like a golden wire screeching in the wind. The moment the sound abruptly ended, she heard several syllables explode: la-de-rui-mi-qiao-nan-qi-ge. She saw two tall pointed hats of Buddhist masters glowing golden yellow.

9

Xiao Xingxing met Director Tang a month after she arrived in Dunhuang. Tang Renxia, the director of the Dunhuang Cultural Research Institute, was well connected with the Chinese art world and was of noble character and high prestige. As a young man, Tang Renxia studied art in France, and while there he met and married his now-ex-wife Ai Lu. Just after liberation and burning with enthusiasm to return to China to take part in reconstruction, he and his wife divorced. They had a daughter by the name of Wei.

Tang Renxia's eyes lit up when he saw Xingxing. According to him, something about Xingxing reminded him of Wei. Xingxing carried a personal letter of introduction from the director of the Central Academy of Art. She scrutinized this legendary figure.

Tang Renxia was very amiable, and though he was in his sixties or seventies, he didn't show his age in the least. His eyes sparkled, but he had very slight bags under his eyes. His forehead was broad and smooth. Xingxing found him exceptional.

"I've seen your paintings. I was in Beijing at the time of the Halfway Exhibition." Tang Renxia gestured for her to have a seat. "Your works exhibit intelligence, you are very skilled, and have a great future ahead of you . . . since you are here, I'll get to the point. We're currently assembling a team to make a copy of *The Transformation of the Western Paradise*. What do you say? Are you interested in joining?"

Xingxing smiled broadly. "Director Tang, to tell you the truth, I'd love to help with the copy work, but I'm not that interested in that particular painting."

"Which one are you interested in?"

Xingxing narrowed her eyes and like a naughty child eyed Tang Renxia as if whatever she said would be refuted. "I'm interested in the Yuan Dynasty frescoes in Cave Ten. Would it be possible to . . ."

Cave 10 is a Tantric Cave.

"No, that's out of the question!" Tang Renxia waved his hand, rejecting the idea decisively.

"Why?" asked Xingxing, her eyes turning cold.

Tang Renxia smiled. "Cave Ten is not open to the public. You were lucky enough to see it. You should be happy. But you are insatiable."

"You didn't answer my question."

Tang Renxia sipped his tea. "Tibetan Tantricism is a sensitive issue. The Tibetans have their religious beliefs, much of which we do not understand, so it is best to say as little as possible about it. We don't want to increase ethnic tensions . . . in the past there were many problems. You don't understand how serious because you are too young."

"I'm not trying to say anything; I simply wish to copy two paintings. Rest assured, I wouldn't use them as source materials in my own work to publish. If you believe me, I can make two extra copies for you . . ."

Tang Renxia waved his hand repeatedly. "No, no, Comrade Xingxing, there's no point in discussing the matter!"

They argued for quite a while. As dusk approached, someone entered—the woman who looked like Guanyin.

"It's you, Bodhisattva!" Xingxing shouted, pleasantly surprised.

But the woman nodded without varying her professional smile, almost as if she did not recognize Xingxing, then she turned leisurely toward Tang Renxia.

"What's 'out of the question'?"

"This is Xiao Xingxing from the Central Academy of Art. She would like to copy the frescoes in Cave Ten."

The woman smiled. "I was just coming to see you about this. Something has happened at Cave Ten. It is already closed, even for those with special passes. We also have some clues relating to the painting theft at Cave Seventy-three."

Tang Renxia said with gratitude, "That's great, Chief Pan. You have been working very hard. Come, let me introduce you. Comrade Xingxing, this is Department Head of the Cultural Administrative Area, Comrade Pan Sumin. She's the guardian deity of the Dunhuang paintings! Ha-ha-ha . . ."

"Hello, we've met," said Xingxing, extending her hand.

The woman cleared her throat a couple of times as if to decline before reaching out to touch Xingxing's hand with her fingertips, which felt very cold to Xingxing.

"Really?"

"Have you forgotten? I was lost in the vicinity of the Tantric Caves. You are . . ."

Pan Sumin placidly raised her eyebrows and with a look of compassion said, "I'm sorry. I don't remember."

Xingxing felt the woman was lying, but why would she do so?

"You said a thief had been apprehended at Cave Seventy-three?" Xingxing thought of Wuye and was filled with suspicion. Wuye had described that "Bodhisattva Guanyin." Then was it the same woman? Observing the faint crow's-feet at the corners of the woman's eyes and her perpetual smile, she felt she was looking at a mask, one carved with fixed lines, behind which was concealed the unknown.

"Not yet. I said we have some clues." Pan Sumin smiled placidly.

"Do . . . you know someone by the name of Wuye?" Xingxing asked, closely observing the woman's expression. But her face, which was as smooth as a mirror, didn't change; her eyebrows didn't even twitch.

"No," she replied placidly.

10

Xingxing hurried back to the Sanwei Mountain Guesthouse.

She couldn't say why, but she felt a plot was taking shape like a black cloud around Wuye, one that could descend at any moment and crush him. She had to save him, she had to.

She ran back to her room, but when she arrived there she suddenly heard a burst of charming laughter from within. She threw open the door and stood transfixed.

There was Yu'er, in splendid attire, reclining on her bed. She wore a headdress of pearls and precious stones. She was dressed in a thin green silk gown with a black vest embroidered with flowers and butterflies. A gold necklace inlaid with rubies hung heavily in the folds of her clothes across her left shoulder. It seemed terribly heavy composed of a good deal of gold and rubies.

Where did she get such jewelry? Xingxing wondered. Then her eyes fell on Wuye, who was blushing furiously.

Wuye was there! Every day he bought groceries and brought them back and prepared food and rice on the hot plate. Many a day, Xingxing could smell the aroma of his cooking from far off. Sometimes she felt she owed him something and wished to repay him by cooking a huge repast for him, but had never had the opportunity.

The aroma of cooking always triggered her imagination. She would think of that gray building in the western suburbs of Beijing and her cute little boy, Little Weiwei and Mousheng.

Mousheng was a good cook and liked to cook. But he seemed too wrapped up in it, for as soon as they sat down to one meal he was already talking about what to prepare for the next. Every time this happened, the food would suddenly stick in her throat and it would take her some time to get it down.

Every time she took wing, he'd pull her back to earth. She wasn't entirely against this for each time she took flight, she would be troubled by some vague fear, and then look back to earth and its warmth and security. Being on the ground for some time, she would begin to worry again.

She yearned to fly freely, to return freely to earth, and then fly again into the sky.

But she had nothing today. She didn't have the aroma of good cooking nor did she have Wuye's warm eyes.

"Sister Xingxing! Why is Brother Wuye's face so red? Ha-ha-ha . . ." Innocently, Yu'er laughed again with great charm. "I only sang a Yugur song I had learned for you. I didn't kiss you or bite you. Why are you blushing so?" After she spoke, she suddenly leaped behind Wuye, grabbed him by the head, and planted a big kiss on his hair.

Wuye and Xingxing were both stunned.

Wuye smoothed his hair, and blushing even more furiously, muttered something. But Xingxing could see that he wasn't upset by any of it.

Xingxing suddenly felt as if she were being pricked by a needle. That day, Wuye had inserted a shining needle in her belly. That was a warm, genial needle. But this one had pierced her heart.

"Right. Director Tang wants to see me about something. I'll be going. Yu'er, make yourself at home." She spoke calmly, turned, and in a daze seemed to hear Wuye shout after her.

II

She didn't know where she was going. She really didn't know where she should go.

Dusk had fallen over Sanwei Mountain. The last light of the setting sun shone faintly in the distance. She suddenly felt old. She became muddleheaded and dazed and faced a darkness deeper than that before her eyes. She walked aimlessly, becoming a doddering old woman. The pain in the bottom of her heart spread, and as it spread the pain increased.

She wanted to shatter herself against the distant mountains, like a cloud behind the mountains that breaks into pieces and is carried off on the wind into the boundless distance.

It seemed fated. Those whom she loved, admired, needed but dared not touch were always taken away by someone who didn't really love them. She recalled that woman of ten years ago. She was as thin as a sorghum stalk and her face reminded one of some animal in a zoo, but she had a glib tongue. She flirted at the right time, giggled just right, made secret overtures perfectly, and was generally gifted at baffling men. She had met her by chance when she and Xiaojun had gone on business to the northeast. She remembered that the woman was called Xiazi.

But after returning to Beijing, she discovered, much to her surprise, that Xiaojun had quite a different view. His pure, piercing eyes were befuddled.

Once at a friend's party, Xiazi kissed him on the forehead in front of everyone. Xiaojun for his part didn't seem in the least upset. He just smiled, blushed, and said, "Don't do that or Xingxing might get mad." Everyone laughed. Xingxing quietly slipped out amid the laughter, feeling heartbroken and bleeding and totally helpless.

A person's heart could not be broken twice.

Later she was reconciled with Xiaojun, but that scar remained. She couldn't tolerate having something she treasured so much become a joke exposed to all. It was the same as being naked in public. She didn't say all of this to Xiaojun, and many times she had to lick her wounds alone in silence. She loved him so much, but to a degree she was unwilling to tell him.

But he found out later. On that rainy night when they parted, they had to climb over the high wall around the office in Xiyuan. He squatted partially to let her step first on his knee and then his shoulders to help her up on the wall. Her muddy rain boots soiled his bleached-out army clothes. Then he nimbly climbed over the wall and reached up to her with his arms open wide.

She would always remember that happy moment.

She closed her eyes and jumped down into his strong, warm arms. He didn't release her at once but held her for a moment. She could feel his heart throbbing and his rapid breathing. Then he slowly grew more composed. That purity possessed only by young men made him seem even more admirable. He kissed her. Tears shone in his clear, pure eyes.

"Do you have to go?" she whispered, knowing what she said was nonsense. She wasn't going to bring up her feelings, but as soon as she spoke, she burst into tears.

He looked away in silence. She could see that he was clenching his jaw.

"Tell me what do you wish for more than anything else?" After a while he looked down at her in seriousness but with warmth.

She looked up at him, tears in her eyes.

"To . . . die . . . for . . . you," she said, pronouncing each word.

12

She had thought about those four words for a long time.

At the time, she was still a young girl of seventeen, but thoughts of death had entered her mind many times.

As far as she was concerned, death was more seductive than frightening. Many times she tried to imagine what it would be like after death. She imagined that death perhaps would bring the love she couldn't get in life. She would think and think, and then her tears would fall silently.

Really, if she could meet someone in this life she could die for, life would not be in vain.

This thought or "complex" was buried deep in her heart, supporting her through those difficult times. But today she no longer believed in this "complex," but still it would assert itself sometimes, disturbing her cold mind.

That rainy night of mud, that high wall, that heartbreaking first kiss, were now all so distant and could not be looked forward to, like something from another century. If she were tell this to her child or her child's children, they'd all stare at her wide-eyed and wonder what she was talking about, believing perhaps that it was a fairy tale.

13

Every night, Ahyuexi would arrive as silently as the moonlight.

During that time, Zhang Shu always felt as if he were dreaming. Their lovemaking seemed not to involve any physical desire, totally unlike with Yu'er. Ahyuexi was quiet and even when she climaxed, she never uttered a sound, as if she had reached a high level of "silent cultivation." This gave him a sublime sense of sex.

He thought of his wife. Every time they made love, she initiated it, but she preferred to be passive. Once she said to him, "If I have to initiate things, I get no pleasure out of it. Please, why don't you initiate things for once?" He thought it was ridiculous. But after he met Yu'er, he understood. He suddenly felt that a civilized person ought to marry a natural person, for two highly cultured people would never be able to experience the fullness of love because culture might serve as an obstacle.

He felt he was able to go even further with Ahyuexi. Not only did he experience happiness, but he also experienced something mysterious and acquired food for thought. He was repeatedly pulled into a deep gray dream world by her twining deep gray long hair. The dream world was filled with seduction, where a moon hung high in the sky, which was broken and misshapen, with the angles of a multifaceted diamond. It was the moon over Mingsha Mountain. The mountain lay silent under the moon. The silence enwrapped him and seemed to inform him of life's difficulties and the inevitability of death. He frequently went to savor death's beauty in the black of night.

That day Ahyuexi untied the bright apricot-colored band on her head, revealing a large scar on her otherwise broad, smooth forehead. The thin center of the scar seemed to move. It didn't look like skin but more like a clear strip of wrinkled paper pasted there.

"What's this?" asked Zhang Shu, touching her scar with his little finger.

"That's a celestial eye."

"A celestial eye?"

"Uh-huh." Her deep eyes were expressionless.

On the day of Ahyuexi's tenth birthday, after the two noble elderly lamas had cast her fortune, she was taken to a small, dark chamber. Three lamas in golden robes entered. In Lhasa, the color of a monastic's robes is related to their status. Most monks wear red robes, from chestnut red to brick red, depending on the rank. Only high-ranking monks who had been called upon to serve in the Potala Palace were allowed to wear a golden robe outside their red one.

In the dark, she was unable to see their faces but did see that they carried a pouch of herbal medicine. One lama placed the pouch on her forehead while another bound it tightly in place. Then she was left alone in the dark for a long, long time.

She was terrified, and she recalled what her father had said: "Child, you and I are different. You are a person with insight. The Potala Palace contains a record of your reincarnation . . . you will suffer, but in the end, you will successfully . . ."

The three lamas once again appeared out of the dark. They opened a box and took out a steel instrument that looked something like a drill, but one that seemed to have many fine teeth. The oldest lama bent over her and whispered solemnly, "Child, today we are going to assist you in opening your celestial eye. You may feel some pain, but you must be conscious if it is to be completed." So saying, he signaled to one of the other lamas to grab her and then aimed that instrument at a point on her forehead and began turning it. She grit her teeth. The drill penetrated her skull with a squeak and the monk operating the drill stopped. Then one of the other lamas handed him a hard strip of wood, which he inserted into the hole he had just made. At that moment she experienced a severe pain on the crown of her head and nearly fainted. But at that moment, she smelled some unknown fragrance and saw a five-colored light appear before her eyes.

"So that's called opening a celestial eye?" said Zhang Shu, smiling sarcastically.

"Yes."

"What can you see with that celestial eye of yours?"

"I can see a lot, but I cannot tell you." She spoke with great earnestness. "I don't want to be like some people these days who go around saying they can see things other people can't see, like street magicians."

"What about me can you see?"

She looked at him for a while and said, "You are good. Your intelligence is inspired, which in our language is called a 'silver band.' However, you appear not to have been well recently. You were sick and had a fever and headache."

"Anyone can see that I have been sick." Zhang Shu smiled with disdain. "That celestial eye is nothing but feudal superstition."

She was startled. "Superstition you say? So you don't believe in the human soul? We are taught that when a person sleeps, their soul becomes a silver band, casts off the flesh, and floats away. When a person dreams, this is what the soul experiences. When I look at you now, I can see a light around you. By the color of the light I can judge whether you are a gentleman or a jerk, intelligent or stupid, healthy or not, but you can't see my light. This is not strange; it is like a solar corona that can only be seen with a telescope, unlike a solar eclipse which can be seen by one and all. Can you say a solar corona doesn't exist simply because you cannot see it?"

Zhang Shu looked at her in amazement. This dark-skinned girl had received an unusual education. She spoke logically and with an air of nobility.

"I can use my skill to enhance the effectiveness of the pyramid. Try; you'll get better real soon." She quickly tore up a hard cardboard box and cut the cardboard into ten four-sided pyramids on each side of which she pasted a round piece of red, yellow, or blue paper. Then on the bottom, she wrote something in a language he didn't understand, which he guessed was Tibetan.

14

Science and mysticism are but two sides of the same coin.

Science, as it has developed to this today, is returning to the mystical.

It was only years later that Zhang Shu felt that what Ahyuexi told him was not myth.

Today, Eastern mysticism is in good graces with the entire world. Its value transcends categorization as either philosophy or religion, making it a focal point of cultural research. Zhang Shu subsequently wrote two articles after leaving Dunhuang: "The Yutian Style of Painting as Represented by Yu-Chi Yiseng" and "A Brief Discussion of Tibetan Tantric Qigong," which were both praised in academic circles. Subsequently, Zhang Shu joined the ranks of scholars. Naturally, Zhang Shu did not forget to whom he was indebted for the two articles. He included Ahyuexi's name as coauthor, but it was deleted by the editor. Later, he sent copies of the magazines to her to express his gratitude. But it was like casting a stone into the sea—he never received a reply. This made him very uneasy. Even his wife, Wang Xiyi was very concerned about what had become of her. Although Wang Xiyi had her shortcomings, she did not suffer from one that most women suffered from: jealousy. She loved to laugh at what people didn't have, but was never jealous of what they possessed, especially after she saw Ahyuexi's photograph, from which she determined Ahyuexi was extremely intelligent and noble. She insisted that Zhang Shu get in touch with the woman for her, as she wanted to find a place for Ahyuexi in the drama troupe and so on. Of course, this all happened later.

The sun rises in the East, and Eastern mysticism is inextricably linked with the sun. Nearly all ancient civilizations possess creation myths that are related to the sun. Humanity views the sun and light as the primal creative force. And Tibet, on the ridge of the world, is bathed in the full light of the sun like no other place on earth.

It is said that inspiration coincides with the solar cycle. The important discoveries of Newton, Leibnitz, Lomonosov, Krumlov, and Faraday that occurred at eleven-year intervals certainly did not occur as a matter of chance. In 1830, solar activity reached a peak, when Chopin and Mendelssohn both completed major works.

For thousands of years, yoga adepts have believed in a famous legend that holds that a huge storehouse exists between the base of the spine and the pelvis, which is called kundalini. It is the "serpent of life" that gives men strength. Normally it is asleep, but the yoga adept cultivates himself to awaken the serpent, which provides unusual spiritual powers, as is the case with those whose celestial eye is open. They can see the approach of death when the "silver band" that binds the soul to the body grows weak and breaks and the "light of life" begins to fade, starting at the top of the head. As Bateson said, soul is not for the flesh alone; worldly passage and information possess souls, too. Soul finds expression in manifold ways in which the individual soul is only a subsystem of the universal soul, while what is known as universal soul is but a dynamic state structured by the universe.

Then there is Einstein's famous paradox: "The most incomprehensible thing in the world is that the world can be understood."

15

Copying a large fresco is exceedingly difficult. Tang Renxia had thrown some light on the history of copying the frescoes in the caves. In his view, there was no strict separation between artists and artisans. He believed that a true artist should also be an accomplished artisan, at least possessing the skills of an artisan, but an artisan cannot necessary be an real artist.

His so-called skills of an artisan can be traced to before 1949. The Dunhuang Cultural Research Institute had already been established, though it was lacking in funds sufficient to purchase even average Mali brand poster colors and was entirely reliant on a few individuals to bring bamboo paper from the inland areas. They themselves had to add vitriol, mount, improve paintbrushes, and even mix their own pigments. When they went to the caves to make copies of the frescoes, they would have to use oil lamps or candles. Some of the paintings were quite high, and they had to climb up on ladders to look at them and then come back down to paint; sometimes they made dozens of trips up and down.

Each time he would reminisce with a number of old friends about those days, lofty sentiments would spontaneously arise. It was under these difficult conditions that they produced the partial copies of the world-famous frescoes at Dunhuang. That is why when Xingxing came to the copy room, the first thing they did after expressing their initial delight was to contrast their past misery with their present happiness for her benefit.

"Look, today the easels and drawing boards are all fit for use; electric lights have been installed in the caves; and rough sketches can be enlarged with a projector. The young people will never have to smell the coal oil lamps of our day."

Certainly the bamboo paper of the old days had been replaced by good quality alum paper specially made by Rongbaozhai. They got rid of poster colors and used mineral pigments—azurite, mineral green, cinnabar, and even gold foil and ink stick—all ordered from the Jiangsixu House in Suzhou. The ink sketch of *The Transformation of the Western Paradise* had been accomplished using projector enlargement. Once the sketch was completed, it was printed on paper, mounted on an easel, after which the colors could be applied.

Tang Renxia introduced her to two other colleagues. Then, smiling with satisfaction, he said, "Comrade Xingxing has finally compromised."

Xingxing forced a smile. She hadn't eaten, but she wasn't hungry. She looked at all the bodhisattvas, children, musicians, and dancers in *The Transformation of the Western Paradise* and thought of the scriptural texts from of Dunhuang in which it was written about those who are reborn in the World of Ultimate Bliss that, "Thinking of clothes a thousand styles appear; thinking of food countless aromas appear." Such a beautiful world was alluring, but getting there was no easy matter. The great bodhisattvas had good roots, had been born from lotuses, and would soon see the Buddha. But the aupapadaka, or transformation, children were different. It was clear that their good roots were not sufficient; they had to wait in a lotus for at least a short kalpa if not a long kalpa for the bud to open before they could enter the World of Ultimate Bliss. It appeared that the Buddha lands had a strict caste system. Even being saved had categories of gold and silver, didn't it? She thought of that childhood dream and that secret channel to the World of Ultimate Bliss and had to smile. Yes, who could see the connections between a crack in the wall and the World of Ultimate Bliss?

That evening, Xingxing climbed to the highest part of the easel and began painting with a special sketching brush. Standing below her, Old Lu kept reminding her, "It's best to pause while doing the floating belts of the flying apsaras and the draped robes of the bodhisattvas. They can't be done in a single stroke. Take a look at this Tang dynasty fresco—the fingernails of the human figures must be set deeply in flesh. It's best to apply the brush in a circular motion. The liniments must flow. Do you know how they painted the folds in clothing during the Tang dynasty?"

"Naturally with an orchid-leaf stroke," replied Xingxing, without turning her head.

"Right." Old Lu nodded. "Let me test you on another one: what sort of outlining was used in frescoes during the Sixteen Nations period?"

"Wire outlining was used on most of the early frescoes," said Xingxing, turning around this time. During the period of the Sixteen Nations, human figures were slim and the folds in their gowns numerous, so naturally wire outlining was used; human figures of the Tang dynasty tended to be fleshy, the lines dense and lively, so the orchid stroke was used; brushwork in the Yuan dynasty was much richer—human figures were traced using wire outlining whereas the folds in clothing were done using a gourd-pouring stroke; beards, eyebrows, and sideburns hair were done with a flowing silk stroke. . . . Am I right?"

"Right, right," said Old Lu, nodding rapidly, his eyes filled with delight. "I never imagined such a young woman would know so much about fresco paintings in Dunhuang."

Tang Renxia laughed loudly. "Comrade Xingxing once restored paintings. Old Lu, save your questions for our Weiwei. Do you think you can catch Xingxing, that she doesn't know her stuff?"

"Such talent is hard to come by. So you restored paintings," commented Old Guan, who had been silent the whole time. "Perfect. We are having some problems in copying some aspects of the paintings to make them look old. Perhaps you can help."

"Have you used methods such as cutting with a knife, rubbing with mud, brushing with the hand, or affixing paper to make them look old?" said Xingxing as she painted the long, flowing sleeves of an apsara.

"We've tried all those methods, but they did not achieve the desired effect," commented Tang Renxia. "There are plenty of ideas . . . but we have to spend a lot of time trying them out. A French group is coming, and the higher authorities want us to finish this painting before they arrive. That's not much time, is it? It's wonderful that you can help out."

16

Xingxing slowly sank into her world of color.

Old Lu and Old Guan were accustomed to working through the night without sleeping, but on this particular night they felt very tired. Their fatigue was a result of Xingxing's presence. Despite Director Tang's glowing recommendation and Xingxing's outstanding show, the two old men didn't have much confidence in her. They were among the best fresco copyists in the country, and they were deeply attached to the frescoes at Dunhuang and were conscientious and meticulous in their work.

Xingxing swung her legs from the scaffolding without making a brushstroke for some time. The frescoes at Dunhuang never ceased to amaze her. Those of the Sixteen Nations were unaffected and straightforward; those of the western Wei and Northern Zhou, lovely and refreshing; those of Sui and Tang, resplendent and magnificent; those of the Song and the beginning of the Five dynasties, brightly colored; those of the western Xia, cool and refined; and those of the Yuan, simple and elegant. The use of color in the early frescoes was free and unrestrained and very lively; after the Tang dynasty, the first sketch was very accurate and precise; the color was applied by filling in, or even neatly scraping between the lines and in some cases a narrow white line was left between the colors and the black outline. Such details were a headache for the copyists.

Xingxing began to apply the final hue, but getting the color just right was very difficult, especially on a painting of such scale. Standing beside her, Old Lu mentioned that in some copies, they had got the hue wrong and the entire painting ended up looking much older and dimmer than the original. It seemed that the artisans of old had used the brightest primary pigments undiluted.

Painting was very absorbing. But Xingxing just couldn't calm her mind today. That scene in her room would assert itself like a montage in her mind's eye. She knew that nothing had happened and that nothing would happen, but she just couldn't stand that whole scene. She couldn't fool herself again. The only possible reason being that she had fallen in love with Wuye, a young man eleven years younger than herself.

She made up her mind to leave, to leave before the copy of *The Transformation of the Western Paradise* was complete. She would do it for him and for herself, for all good times must come to an end.

If one is doomed in life to be parted from those one loves, then it would be best to leave, and leave early, that way some beautiful memories would be preserved.

Would she have been happy if she and Xiaojun had married back then? She had her doubts now.

The wind whipped up that night. It was a cold, piercing wind to her. She became a small solitary leaf in the wind, blown through a world of green, blue, red, and white. Falling slowly to the ground these colors coalesced to form a blood red. She herself was dyed the same color, a blood-red leaf, just like the maple leaf that her sister gave to her when she was thirteen. Later the maple leaf dried up and turned a scabby brown. . . .

Later, after it happened, Old Lu and Old Guan recalled that it was early in the morning and they wanted to get a little more shut-eye when they vaguely heard a voice say, "Just like a fallen leaf." Those were the very words. That's when they saw Xingxing lying on the ground, her back toward them, her black hair soaked with blood.

17

It had been a while since Chen Qing had told a story. That night, the night Xingxing fell from the scaffold, he told the story of the Lotus Girl.

Legend had it that in ancient times there was a big mountain at Dunhuang on which lived two Daoist priests. The one who lived on the south side of the mountain was called the Daoist Priest of the Southern Grotto, and the one who lived on the north side was called the Daoist Priest of the Northern Grotto. One summer the Daoist Priest of the Southern Grotto went to bathe in the spring at the foot of the mountain where he encountered a doe giving birth, but strangely, she did not foal a deer but rather a beautiful baby girl. Seeing a stranger, the deer fled. The Daoist Priest of the Southern Grotto quickly picked up the infant girl and took her home and raised her as if she were his own daughter. Time passed quickly and the deer girl grew into a lovely young woman. One day the fire went out and the Daoist Priest of the Southern Grotto told the girl to get some embers from the Daoist Priest of the Northern Grotto. The deer girl headed north, but strangely, with every step she took a lotus blossom sprouted, the fragrance of which wafted into the Northern Grotto. Smelling the fragrance, the Daoist Priest of the Northern Grotto came out and was transfixed. The deer girl bowed to him and said, "Please, sir, I have come for some coals." The Daoist priest of the Northern Grotto replied with a smile at once, "No problem, all you need to do is circle the Northern Grotto forty-nine times." So that's what the deer girl did. With each step a lotus sprouted and the grotto was filled with the blossoms, the fragrance all-enveloping. After that, everyone called the deer girl Lotus Girl . . . and that's where the expression "lotus blossom sprouting at every step" comes from.

VI.

My Mind Is Buddha

I

Tradition has it that once when the Buddha was speaking the Dharma on Mount Grdrakuta, he picked a flower and showed it to the multitudes assembled. None of his followers knew what he meant and looked at one another in confusion. Only Mahakasyapa understood and smiled. The Buddha saw that Mahakasyapa had understood and, extremely happy, announced, "I possess the true dharma-eye and a liberated mind. The reality that is devoid of phenomenal characteristics and the sublime wisdom of the Buddha exist beyond words, this I now hand over to Mahakasyapa."

The text above tells how the Buddha chose Mahakasyapa to be his successor. Of all the Buddha's disciples only he was able to understand the Buddha's wordless transmission of the highest Buddha Dharma. This highest of dharmas is contained in the profound aim of the Zen school: mind-to-mind transmission, my mind is the Buddha.

The Zen School is the most Chinese of all schools of Buddhism. It altered Indian Buddhism through the use of Chinese social ethics and thought, making Buddhism, which was a religion that renounced the world, into a worldly path that emphasized everyday ethical relations.

Bodhidharma's successor was Hui Ke, the Second Patriarch of Chinese Zen Buddhism. Tradition has it that Hui Ke went to Shaolin Temple and every day went to seek the Dharma from Bodhidharma, who remained facing the wall without uttering a word. Finally one day when there was a heavy snowfall, Bodhidharma spoke, "Those seeking the Dharma do not see the body as the body. The day red snow falls from the sky, I will transmit the Dharma to you." Hui Ke pondered this for a long time before he suddenly cut off his arm, dyeing the snow red, which he then presented to Bodhidharma, who then transmitted the Dharma to him.

Three years after Bodhidharma died, Song Yun of the Western Wei dynasty (535–557) was returning from a mission to the West when he met Bodhidharma in Pamir. He was walking alone and carrying a single straw sandal. Song Yun asked, "Master, where are you off to?" Bodhidharma replied, "To the Western Paradise." Song Yun mentioned this upon returning to China. Bodhidharma's disciples went to the graveyard and found Bodhidharma's coffin empty save for a single straw sandal.

Naturally this is apocryphal. But Zen philosophy does have its quintessence. During the Tang dynasty, the Zen monk of the Linji Sect of Zen Buddhism, Qingyuan Weixin, said, "Thirty years ago, before this old monk practiced Chan, when I saw a mountain, it was a mountain; when I saw water, it was water. But later, after I had learned a little, when I saw a mountain, it was no longer a mountain, and when I saw water, it was no longer water. Today, I have a place to rest: when I see a mountain is once again a mountain, and when I see water it is once again water" (chapter 17 of the *Wudeng huiyuan*). The first part, "saw a mountain, it was a mountain," represents perception before beginning to practice Zen, the positive of objective world. The second part, which represents perception after starting to practice Zen, is the negation of the first part, or starting from here one enters a state of egolessness from the individual ego, where both I and the other cease to exist, a state wherein all is one. The third part represents the realization after enlightenment, the moment when the infinite is grasped from the finite. It is the negation of negation, a form of affirmation. It is only at this point that one finds the true self. Chinese Zen philosophy, in this respect, is similar to Hegel's notion of "the negation of the negation."

With careful consideration, one can see that the development of human society moves in a strange circle from affirmation to negation to the negation of the negation. Bach, in his *Musical Offering*, used the "endlessly ascending canon" repeating the same theme, a canon that is played with repeated variation to arrive back at the original tonality, but one octave higher. It is filled with the play of musical notes and writing.

It is a canon in all styles. There is a fugue of unusual complexity; there is beauty and profound feeling; it is also infused with great joy. It is the fugue of fugues, an arrangement that is self-contained and replete with the metaphor of wisdom. Human society is much like a fugue—there is tremendous variation, but it always returns to its starting point, forming strange circles, the wisdom of which charms. But the starting point returned to is never the real starting point.

2

Wuye received a lesson in honesty when he was quite young. His aunt demanded complete honesty from him. She was so afraid of him lying that she assumed he was lying even when he was telling the truth. It was only after interrogating him that she could determine if he wasn't lying. But sometimes even the interrogations were not reliable.

He wondered if she hadn't been lied to and deceived many times in life.

But now he was lying. After meeting Xingxing, he had narrated many nonexistent tales in his letters to his parents so that he might be able to prolong his trip to Dunhuang.

Now, as he sat by bed nine in room three of the Dunhuang City Hospital, as he tightly held the hand of the woman he loved, he felt this world incredibly true.

Strictly speaking, Xingxing was awakened by the desire to vomit. Her unconsciousness had been enveloped by that blood red until it became a frightening allegorical nightmare in which she found herself in a strange land filled with many huge bronze statues. The fierce-looking statues were all together in one place, where, under a bright sun, they cast a huge, mysterious shadow. In the shadow, a youthful form wavered. That youth was pure and good, heroic and strong. He looked like Xiaojun and also like Wuye. He was the perfect incarnation of a man that had come down through the ages.

Later she found that youth actually sitting by her side, tears on his long lashes. Astonished, she looked at his long lashes as if it were the first time she had noticed how long they were. Why were they so long, like those of a European or an American? Such beautiful lashes. Why hadn't her mother formed her more beautifully? Natural beauty was important, especially for a woman.

Her reluctance to love stemmed from her own sense of inferiority. It started when she was very young. She felt that the adults didn't like her.

For the longest time, her stubborn and supercilious spirit would not submit. In all things she demonstrated her intelligence, talent, sincerity, and charm. Her efforts were not wasted: in attaining success, she also obtained the attention of many men. But in the eyes of her parents and many friends and relatives, her older sister remained the older sister of childhood and she remained the younger sister. Her paintings were widely praised, but they were not prized by her parents.

She loved her sister. From a very young age, her older sister was her idol. She often unconsciously imitated her. But of course it was basically impossible for her to imitate her sister, because she and her sister were totally unalike. Her sister was traditionally minded and was meticulous in everything, large or small. She was serious and hardworking, and hated everything bad. She didn't joke around or talk idly. Her sister criticized her for everything, no matter how insignificant and, although she wouldn't necessarily obey her sister, she felt her sister criticized her out of love. Until one day three years after her sister had married . . .

At that time, she had painted some decent pictures and was a modestly well-known young painter. She had not been able to find a husband. Then one day her brother-in-law introduced her to a young man. After meeting him, she returned to discover that there was something not quite right with her sister. That evening her sister snapped at her for something insignificant; "Don't think you're such a hot painter! Don't think you're so great because you've painted a few lousy paintings!" Her sister cried until she was hysterical: "I wouldn't trade places with you for anything!"

She was stunned and baffled, and her sister's hatred and spite deeply pained her. She knew she had to get married.

"Xingxing . . . Xingxing . . . are you feeling a little better?"

The warmth of Wuye's hand flowed into her cold hand. She forced open her eyes to look at him. How long would this warmth last? The first time Mousheng held her hand, she felt the same kind of warmth. At that time she felt abandoned by the entire world. Only Mousheng, who was short, wore glasses, and smiled warmly, truly loved her. Confidently, she reached out her hand, willing to take that warm hand and follow it anyplace.

There was no way she could reconcile that Mousheng with the one who later viciously stabbed his finger at her and roundly cursed her.

One day, for some insignificant matter, Mousheng kicked the brown glass tea table. In an instant the table lay shattered in a million pieces at her feet. Her heart and hopes were shattered at the same time.

When he wasn't angry, Mousheng was telling her how she should clean the dishes and mop the floor. In the evening he would tell her to heat milk for the child, wash his face and feet, brush his teeth, and fold his blanket. It was always the same, and he would always find something to criticize her about. It always reminded her of the mother who had disliked and avoided her. She was nervous every day and felt exhausted, because if she slipped up in any way, Mousheng would put on that stern look and grow silent. That glum face wrecked havoc on her nerves and even entered her dreams.

Of course, there were happy moments. Whenever she cooked something particularly tasty or showed a new work, Mousheng would beam, then she could breathe freely. Mousheng would suddenly use a little money left over at the end of the month to buy her and the child small gifts. On her thirtieth birthday, he bought an Italian gold necklace for her. Later he would mention that necklace many times as if it were better than the jewelry of any other woman on earth.

When he placed the necklace around her neck, she smiled. She did so because she had to look pleased and not hurt Mousheng's feelings. But she wasn't smiling inside. If he suddenly took the necklace away, she wouldn't cry over it. She was that sort of woman: when she laughed, she was resplendent; when she cried, she sounded glorious.

"Hate brings together . . . love divides . . . is that the way to put it?" she muttered.

3

"What did you say?" he asked, pressing his ear close to her mouth.

"I . . . I said . . . if . . . if . . ."

She didn't finish speaking because she was afraid to upset Wuye. She wanted to say that turning things around as "hate brings together, and love divides" also makes sense. When two people who love each other are together, they slowly learn to hate, and separation would make them fall in love again. People wanted what they couldn't have; simply because it was denied, they wanted it. The more they were denied, the more they wanted it, but once attained, it became worthless to them.

"What are you thinking?" Wuye gently move the hair off her forehead. Her forehead was slightly furrowed. He looked at her lovingly. If they were to be together, he thought, he would make her once again glow with health.

"I was thinking, thinking about my son." She forced a smile, but in her heart she wanted to cry. Her little Weiwei would one day grow up, marry, and have children of his own. At that time, he'd have no need for a wrinkled old woman that she would become. But for now, he needed her love, protection, and support; she needed the same from him. There was no danger in the love of a child, it was as safe as that of a mother's or father's. But her parents didn't give her the love she should have had. What was missing from her childhood would hound her to the end of her life, making her an eternally abandoned child.

Another thing that was no threat was her love of painting. She loved what she did, but she had a growing feeling that it was all lies. Did a true occupation exist on earth? When she fell from that fresco, she understood it in a flash and found its glittering artifice unbearably vulgar. If Shakyamuni were alive, he would be enraged at the sight of it. It encouraged people to forsake material desire in the here and now and replace it with a desire for the world to come. Eventually, it would be impossible to free oneself from any sort of mundane charm. Only the World of Ultimate Bliss in her dreams was real.

"Drink some milk. Xingxing, you haven't had anything to eat in two days," said Wuye, lifting a spoonful of milk to her lips. She turned away.

"How about some watermelon juice?" He lifted a small bowl of pink watermelon juice. She shook her head. "Have you . . . been . . . here . . . long?"

He lowered his head without replying.

"The young fellow hasn't left your side," said the nurse who came to change medicine interjected.

"Why?" Xingxing asked him after the nurse left. She seemed fully conscious. Her eyes shone coldly like two black gems in water.

"What do you mean why?"

"Why are you so . . . good . . . to me?"

Wuye bit his lip. A large blue vein throbbed at his temple.

"I love you," he said in a near whisper. His voice was a bit hoarse as if his throat had gone dry. "I fell in love with you the minute I laid eyes on you . . . didn't you feel it?"

He suddenly raised his eyes, looking wronged and resentful, like a child who has done something good that goes unrecognized by the adults.

Xingxing was overcome with a feeling of oppression. She grit her teeth, afraid she'd be swallowed by that feeling. The tide of feeling rose and as she was about to go under she violently thrust out her hand and latched onto the boy for all she was worth. There was no shock—his hand was cold and sweaty.

She opened her mouth to speak, but her words were swallowed up by her tears. Their hands trembled as the hot tears flowed.

4

Ahyuexi entered as Chen Qing began to tell a story. Zhang Shu had already transcribed a thick notebook full of Dunhuang tales, for which he had invited the old man drinking seven or eight times. Fortunately, Ahyuexi had brought the liquor the last two times, saving him some money.

In days of yore, there was a country called Yutian, the citizens of which were particularly fond of silk. But in those days the value of silk shipped from our Central Plains to the Western region was worth more than gold. There was a high official by the name of Yu-chi Mu, who offered advice to the King of Yutian, saying, "We can think of a way to acquire mulberries and silkworms from China and bring in those who can cultivate the trees, raise silkworms, along with some silk artisans to produce our own silk." The King of Yutian was delighted, and the two of them came up with a marvelous plan.

It is said that in those days, the Central Plains was thinking of establishing an alliance through marriage with the Western region. Thus the King of Yutian sent an emissary for that purpose. That emissary was none other than Yu-Chi Mu.

The emperor was more than happy to see the marriage. Yu-Chi Mu for his part paid a private visit to the princess to ask her to acquire the mulberry seed and silkworms for the Western region, a task to which she readily consented.

After a time, the princess set off, camel bells ringing, a vast and mighty horde escorting a relative of the emperor's. They arrived in Dunhuang and stayed for several days and then left for Yumenguan.

The officers and men guarding Yumenguan rigorously cross-examined anyone going through the pass. They carefully inspected the baggage of the escorts and serving women and even the baggage of her highness the princess.

After going through the pass, Yu-Chi Mu asked, "Your Highness, did you bring the mulberry seeds and silkworms?"

The princess removed the gold crown from her head and from her piled hair removed the silkworms and then opened a medicine bag from which she extracted the mulberry seeds. Mixed together in this way, they had not been detected.

Delighted, Yu-Chi Mu asked, "What about the silk workers? Who will come and pick the mulberry leaves and raise the silkworms?"

The princess smiled and pointed to a group of attendant women. "Is there a woman from the Central Plains who cannot pick mulberry leaves and raise silkworms? They are all very good at it."

Yu-Chi Mu roared with laughter and quickly informed the King of

Yutian to make ready to welcome the princess with magnificent pomp
and ceremony.

It was only after that that the raising silkworms, mulberries, and silk
making spread to Yutian, and from there to India, and on to Europe.

5

"That's very interesting. The Yutian princess married the general guarding
the Hexi Corridor, and the King of Yutian married a princess from the
Central Plains."

Late at night, Zhang Shu looked up from his desk and gazed tenderly
at Ahyuexi.

"Ahyuexi, I heard that in her youth, your mother was as beautiful as
the princess from Yutian. But now . . . How did she come to look the way
she does? Can you tell me your mother's story?"

"What is there to say? She looks that way on account of karma."

"What do you mean, karma?"

"She and that bastard she's with killed my father."

"Ahyuexi! Don't talk such nonsense unless you have proof!"

"It's not nonsense. Someone who knows the story told me."

"Who?"

Ahyuexi opened wide her slanted eyes and examined him for a while.
"Bodhisattva Pan," she replied with some hesitation.

"Her again! Pan . . . Su . . . min." He frowned. He couldn't say exactly
why, but that bodhisattva face more and more resembled a mask, a rubber
mask.

"The year I tuned ten and had my celestial eye opened, I began
practicing yoga at the temple. My grandfather asked the best vajra
master in Lhasa. He himself initiated me and I studied vajra breathing,
precious vase *qigong,* and vajra chanting . . . the master said I was the most
promising yoga adept. But four years later, my grandfather died and his
property was confiscated. By then, the master had transmitted everything
he knew to me. It was then that my mother sent someone to Lhasa to get
me. I had no choice, and I missed my mother, so I returned to Dunhuang.

When I got back, I saw how much my mom had aged, but Dayejisi was just as young as ever. I urged her to leave him, but she said my little sister was still young and needed a father. I could see that she was afraid of him, so we argued. One day when I came home from the market, I found Dayejisi home alone. In a very nasty way he told me that I had been eating for free off of him and demanded that I polish his shoes. When I bent over to pick up his shoes, he attacked me from behind, trying to tear open my clothes. I pulled the knife I carried with me and threatened him. He squealed like a stuck pig. All of Dunhuang heard him. Bloodied, he ran out of the house to report me. That evening people from the Public Security Bureau showed up and took me away in handcuffs.

Her face was cold and expressionless, as if she were talking about someone else.

"Did you run away later?"

"No, I was rescued by the Bodhisattva Guanyin."

"The Bodhisattva Guanyin? You mean Pan Sumin?" Zhang Shu asked, growing more alert.

"Yes, around here we all call her the living Guanyin because she is always helping those who are suffering!" She smiled piously.

"Would you tell me how she rescued you?"

"I was still young then and didn't understand things. I had been locked up several days without a drink of water. Practicing yoga helped to get me through it. One day I was taken out for interrogation. Bodhisattva Pan was sitting there. After the interrogation, she took me away."

"She's not afraid of Dayejisi?"

"No. He's more afraid of her."

"Why should he be afraid of Pan?"

"He's afraid of her the way a wolf is afraid of a hunter and an evil ghost is afraid of a bodhisattva."

"Is she really a bodhisattva?"

"She is a bodhisattva incarnate. She got me out nine years ago and has always been good to me."

"Good to you in what way?"

"What a strange question!" she said, arching her delicate eyebrows.

"Good is good. She looks after me like my own mother. She encourages me to go to school and do a little work each day. After I turned eighteen, she found this great job for me."

"Huh! More like raising a slave," snorted Zhang Shu.

"What did you say?"

"Nothing. What I mean is if she really treated you well, why aren't you still in school?"

She looked anxious.

"How . . . how can you blame her? She herself has a family. Where would she get the money? Besides, I practiced yoga from an early age, so going to school or not is all the same. Even though I never went to high school, she taught me to read the sutras such as the *Sutra on the Passage of Time* and the like. My teacher never taught me, but she did." Once again her face shone with a pious light. "Now I feel close to the Buddha, which is not the sort of happiness many people have."

"Ahyuexi, I like you the way you are." He took her in his arms and pulled her arms behind her. She looked like a beautiful long-necked vase. "But why are you so tough, without any pity? Is that what you learned from the Buddha?"

"Brother Shu, no matter how nice you are, you are still a Han Chinese. You know only the Buddha of the Chinese, but not ours. Your Shakyamuni became our Vairocana Buddha, just as your Guanyin became our Contemplating Ease. Even Lakshmi's features . . . oops! I've said too much."

"I know what you are getting at. What you mean is that in Tibetan Buddhism, many Buddhas and bodhisattvas are depicted as fierce and angry, including even the beautiful Lakshmi, right?"

"Yes, Brother Shu. You are very smart."

"But why is that?"

"I think . . . it's because our Buddha is more real. He possesses all sorts of Dharma-bodies . . ."

"Just like there are all kinds of people."

"Yes. The *Wisdom Sutra* tells us that in this world, nature is empty and the phenomenal unreal. That is profound wisdom."

"I understand. Nature is empty means that everything is formed through cause. There is no real self nature; the phenomenal is unreal means that empty nature doesn't mean that it is nothing; the appearance of the unreal exists. In other words, the reality we observe is empty but that which is commonly considered illusory is real. So, from this perspective, the Buddha is the Buddha. He possesses various Dharma-bodies, some angry and some pleasing, but all alike without significance. Right?"

"Yes." Then she shook her head. "No, not entirely. I said that our Buddha is more real, which means that the Buddha of Tibetan Buddhism esteems natural strength more and that's why there is a joyful Buddha . . . Do you believe in the simultaneous cultivation of two states?"

Everything was quiet. Zhang Shu felt that her speech had a highly hypnotic effect. Lakshmi suddenly appeared in his mind's eye. She was both beautiful and ferocious, but he didn't know which was best.

6

Ahyuexi's was a simple beauty.

A simple beauty of black or gray.

One day, as the sun was going down, Zhang Shu saw her sitting beside Yueya Spring. The setting sun coated her with a gold patina. Her deep gray hair stirred in the evening air, wafting a light fragrance. Her face was still and her eyes closed, like a serious female Buddha of unique character.

He recalled how one day she had told him that she worshiped Green Tara. Tibetan Tantric Buddhism had always seen the female as symbolic of wisdom, and, for thousands of years, the Tibetans have respected and worshiped the Green Tara most. The Green Tara is in some ways similar to the Chinese Guanyin, but with apparently vaster spiritual powers and who handles more things. Zhang Shu could see from a tanka that Ahyuexi had brought that Tara's skin was deep green. She was pretty and half naked and was draped with red and purple jewelry and sat on a lotus flower. Her teacher had told Ahyuexi that by worshiping Green Tara she could not only benefit herself, but also help others liberate themselves from suffering.

Sitting in meditation this evening, who is it she seeks to pull from the sea of suffering? He smiled wryly as he thought about this. No, so many forms of happiness were immersed in that sea of suffering. By rescuing someone from that sea, you were rescuing them from suffering and happiness, love and hate, life and death, love and desire and entering a world without all that. Perhaps that world was a good place, but it would never be a place he would seek out.

He knew that Ahyuexi was visualizing Green Tara. She said that when she was first initiated, she had visualized Green Tara, who was the chief object of her worship. Her right hand was lowered in the alms-giving mudra. In her left hand she held a blue lotus blossom. It was as if a hand held a precious vase above her from which poured a warm fragrance that flowed down along her deep gray hair, moistening her entire body. At that moment a green light burned around her and she felt she became Green Tara. And like Green Tara she remained behind in the cycle of life and death to help others and not enter nirvana.

But why was it that she couldn't forgive her mother and her sister?

"Pan Sumin told me that that bastard Dayejisi seduced and was in league with my mom. They did him in. The only thing is that no proof has ever been found . . ." That day Ahyuexi sat cross-legged beside a mandala she had painted and quietly told him all of this.

"She knows?"

"Of course, she knows! She's our bodhisattva and everyone here tells her the truth . . . My mom, that cheap bit of goods, told her so herself. She suspected that Dayejisi had sent someone to kill my father. But shortly after that, she married Dayejisi. For two years before my dad died, the two of them fought constantly. They had a reputation in these parts . . ."

"Your mom has only one eye. Who made her that way?"

"I don't know, but it's said that it was karmic retribution for when she poked out the eye of Lakshmi in that painting handed down by the family."

"Who said that? Was it your Bodhisattva Pan again?" snorted Zhang Shu sarcastically.

"That's none of your concern. I feel like I have two mothers—the one of my youth who was gentle and pretty and the one here when I returned from Tibet, mean and ugly. Did you notice how much money Yu'er seems to have? She dresses well, but she's nothing more than a carpet weaver. My mom makes even less money. So where did the money come from? A painting was stolen from Cave Seventy-three. Bodhisattva Pan says that my mom and Yu'er are most likely behind it. They're rolling in money now! You've seen Yu'er's necklace, haven't you? It's made of gold and jade."

"If that's the case, then why latch on to Wuye and not let him go?"

"Mom and Yu'er aren't the main culprits. That Xiang Wuye is an expert in stealing frescoes. He knows all about what sort of resin to use, and he also confessed to the crime. Bodhisattva Pan recorded her interrogation of him."

"Confessed? Stealing important cultural treasures carries extremely severe punishment. You've got to be kidding?" said Zhang Shu, suddenly restraining himself.

"Who said anything different? Bodhisattva Pan said to release him and get to the bottom of things, then arrest him. She said that he wasn't going to run off."

"That Pan Sumin is really sharp." He thought of that compassionate-looking woman and his hair stood on end. "But there's still a problem. What about that painting of your family's that you just mentioned? It's that painting titled *Lakshmi Bathing*, right?"

"How do you know about that . . . you're . . . in it . . . with them . . ."Ahyuexi suddenly pressed her lips tightly together, her eyes afire. "Have . . . have you slept with Yu'er?"

He was stunned. He never thought she would be so sensitive.

"Answer me. Did you sleep with her?" Her long, dark gray hair flared and stood like the antennae on a water sprite.

He didn't utter a word.

"Oh . . . you did, you did! You slept with her!" Her voice suddenly grew hoarse. As if a severe pain swept over her, she suddenly collapsed in a heap. He was frightened by the sight of her ashen face. He took hold of her, but she slipped from his grasp like a struggling fish. As they struggled, she did not strike out, but feebly resisted. She loved him deeply. This was the main difference between her and Yu'er.

"Yu'er is not a true yoga adept. She was never initiated . . ." She looked up at him through her bleary eyes, struggling to speak.

She cried for a long time. Touched, he stayed with her.

At that time, amid the golden light and the breeze, she sat quietly beside Yueya Spring, reflected in the water like a Green Tara with a blue lotus, praying for his future.

7

Every day, Xingxing repeated the same thing: "You'd better leave, Wuye."

Wuye always gave the same reply: "I'll leave tomorrow."

But the days slipped by and Wuye was still there.

That is until that day, the day the copy of *The Transformation of the Western Paradise* was completed. The brief romance of Wuye and Xingxing suddenly came to end when they parted. It was a complete break, and they never saw each other again. They departed for two different worlds.

That day, the Research Center held a banquet to celebrate. The banquet was, of course, held at the best restaurant in Dunhuang. Xingxing thought the *Sanbaotai* was very good. And then all the liquors, some of which she knew and others she did not, had wonderful bouquets. Director Tang specially seated Xingxing next to Pan Sumin, no doubt a great honor. Both protested the seating arrangement. They avoided each other's eyes and when they couldn't avoid each other, they would force a smile. Xingxing pretended to listen to Director Tang's remarks and twisted her neck until it ached. Actually, she was watching the main door, watching for Wuye's arrival, because she had secured a place for him.

". . . and I would like to thank our guest from Beijing, Comrade Xingxing, a young woman painter. She was particularly helpful in completing the copy of the huge fresco *The Transformation of the Western Paradise*. Moreover, her assistance was voluntary. Let's hear it for her!"

Applause erupted and all eyes moved in her direction. She felt flustered when she heard her name, but now it was even worse. She had to force a smile. She noticed Pan Sumin's placid gaze. To cover her discomfort, she hurriedly took a sip of *Sanbaotai,* but in doing so, upset Pan Sumin's long-stemmed wineglass.

"I'm sorry." Xingxing quickly used her napkin to wipe up the spill, but was prevented by Pan Sumin.

"A waitress will be here." She spoke coldly, "Waiter . . ."

". . . we would also like to ask Yu'er, the young Yugur woman, to sing . . ."

Director Tang was still speaking. People were coming and going. Among them, Xingxing saw the old manager, Chen Qing. Then she saw Wuye approaching.

He had a handsome walk. Perhaps because of his long legs, he looked comfortable and natural. He was his usual self: T-shirt and jeans but with a faded jacket this time. He was still paler than most people there and looked very serious, except when their eyes met, and then he smiled. Once again she found herself charmed by him. He really was a good-looking young man with a fine disposition. If he were a pop idol, hordes of young women would swoon before him. Unfortunately, Wuye would not get up on stage, no matter how you might threaten him.

Xingxing suddenly had a strange premonition. She turned her eyes away from him and saw that the seat beside her was empty. Her heart pounded. She had no desire to see her premonition materialize so quickly. This was followed by a feeling that disaster was about to strike.

Heavy-hearted, she looked at Wuye. He blushed and smiled at her as his legs brushed her knees. His legs trembled slightly and she trembled all over.

8

The first night after Xingxing was released from the hospital, she and Wuye became lovers.

It was unusually dry that night and when their flesh met, blue sparks flew, crackling in the dark. Xingxing felt thirsty and wanted to ask him to wait so that she could have a drink of water, but she never said anything. She stroked Wuye's soft hair. His hair was so soft and dry. She touched her own hair and found it as black and stiff as wire. Genes are such wondrous things. She and Wuye were so different, even in the smallest ways.

"It's hard to imagine, Xingxing, that your breasts could be so white and beautiful," he said, cupping her breasts in his hands and softly kissing her nipples. "They are like a girl's, but full. You have the most beautiful body I have ever seen."

"How many female bodies does a doctor see?" Xingxing's gentle eyes glowed mischievously.

He flushed red. He blushed so easily. Despite acting calm and experienced, Xingxing could tell that it was his first time. He was still a virgin. As far as she could tell there were two types of men when it came to women and love: one was the letch and the other was the aesthete. Wuye was of the latter type. His eyes, which kissed every part of her body, were filled with praise, worship, and adoration, enough to satisfy a woman's vanity.

"You are strange, Wuye. You're a strange guy." Xingxing smiled and bit her lip, her eyes filling with tears.

"What do you mean, strange? I meet the most beautiful, most intelligent, most attractive woman and fall in love with her. Nothing could be more natural. How can you call it strange?"

"One day you will have your regrets. I'm eleven years older than you, and not very good looking."

"Why are you always talking about such things? Why do you doubt me?" He grew more anxious and the blue veins on his neck stood out, throbbing.

"I believe you. I believe everything." She grabbed his hand and kissed it, the moist hand of a young man around twenty years of age. "But . . ."

"No buts!" He clasped her tightly to himself, with all his youthful ardor. He thought of the story of the Garden of Eden. God had said that Eve was the bone of Adam's bone and flesh of his flesh.

"Wuye, I'm married and have a child."

"I know." The tears shone in his eyes. "Everything is up to you. If you think it's too much trouble, I'll leave and go far away. But regardless, I love you. I'm free to love, and you are free to accept or reject my love."

"Love and freedom have never coexisted." Xingxing hung her head in silence. "Love and freedom are a paradox, an eternal paradox."

She recalled a quote from Sartre: "Love is the most futile thing in that it is the possession of a freedom. Though all lovers demand this oath, they also hate it. He wants to be loved freely, but this freedom must be a freedom without freedom."

She suddenly felt afraid of herself. Goodness. Is this how she loved Wuye? Was her love that calm and rational? Who was it that she really loved? Was it Wuye? Xiaojun? Or some figment of her imagination? She didn't want to think about it anymore. She knew that a person who had lost hope in love was beyond hope.

9

When Yu'er entered, the whole dining hall seemed to light up. She was accompanied by her mother who carried an odd-looking stringed instrument. Her clothes were unusually pretty. To her pure Yugur dress, some alterations had been made. She did not wear the usual vest over her embroidered silver-white gown. She wore a heavy necklace of coral and shells. Her brown tresses hung down like two streams of gold in which she wore a large red rose. The white and red served to highlight her brown skin. Her deep amber eyes blended with the gold.

There was no band, no microphone, nothing modern, but as soon as she opened her mouth, it was as if she were in the middle of the most modern music hall. It was as if there were loudspeakers positioned all around the restaurant that were a bit static and raspy at first. But as soon as she opened her mouth, her voice was unusual. Those from the big cities applauded vigorously. Between numbers, Yu'er picked up a glass, drained it at one go, said thank you, and continued singing. Without a delay, the entire restaurant erupted in applause. Yu'er began to enjoy herself and danced as she sang. She was barefoot and four strands of pale purple beads were strung between her toes, and her fingernails were all painted the delicate pink of a new moon. She began to gyrate, sometimes she would raise her ten interlaced fingers before her face; sometimes she would raise both arms and spread them. Her soft curves undulated more rapidly and in her mad gyrations, she uttered a marvelous trill. She was like a kite on a long, thin string scudding here and there. A scudding golden illusion. The audience seemed to rise and fall with this illusion. Handfuls of colorful flowers were tossed at the illusion, creating a rainbow of color in the golden light.

The old woman strummed the odd stringed instrument. Xingxing couldn't determine how many strings it had, but felt that its sound had a certain magical power. It allowed Yu'er's sometimes gloomy and sometimes unrestrained voice to expand and contract, rising and falling like a tide, by turns bitter and happy.

> *We were from the distant West,*
> *Our ancestors told us,*
> *Our home would be Xizhihazhi*
> *The sacred black ox led the way*
> *To the Bazi Mound.*
> *Atop the Bazi Mound,*
> *A patch of rosy tamarisks*
> *Can be seen in the desert.*
> *It was an auspicious place*
> *We've remained here since then*
> *And became the Yugur people of today.*

Xingxing could see a tear rolling slowly from the dry corner of old Guonu's eye.

10

With wine and song, Yu'er pushed the banqueters toward insanity.

Later, everyone began to dance madly. Xingxing signaled with her eyes to Wuye. The two of them were about to leave when Yu'er approached as if on a breeze. Yu'er smiled sweetly at Xingxing and then turned quickly to Wuye. She took up the wine bottle and poured a glass and raised it in a toast: "Brother Wuye, I know you don't drink, but according to the etiquette of the Yugur people, wine offered in a toast must be drunk. If you don't, I'll sing you a song that will never end."

Wuye blushed the color of a ripe persimmon. He had no idea why he had become so popular. His eyes dulled and he dared not look in Xingxing's direction. He was not conscious of the presence of anyone else in the hall save Xingxing. He vaguely sensed that Xingxing nodded at him. He then gulped down the draught. It was like a cold snake descending his gullet. Then as if the poison suddenly spread, his eyes teared up and vaguely noticed that the glass was untouched.

"Drink up, Brother Wuye."

He heard her charming voice. Her words reverberated in his mind. He felt afraid and powerless to prevent it. It was just like that mysterious incantation from the red room, which, repeatedly pronounced, became thoroughly enervating.

"Drink up, Brother Wuye!" "Drink up, Brother Wuye!" "Drink up, Brother Wuye!"

Repeated over and over, the words became a hypnotic spell. He felt confused. It was as if he were drinking from a bottomless glass. He felt everyone was staring at him with mocking smiles. A grown man like him couldn't drain the glass. He felt humiliated. He drank without stopping, clutching the glass till it nearly shattered in his hand.

Then a hand covered his glass.

"Don't drink it!"

He heard a familiar voice, but he didn't know whose it was. He tried to shove that hand away, but it clung to the glass. Through his heavy eyelids, he saw a woman standing before him. It looked like Xingxing, but it also looked like Yu'er. He didn't say a word but tried to force the hand away. Yet still it clung. Between the two weak hands, the glass shattered into white fragments, cold and wet. His dream was shattered by a loud noise and then he found himself covered with a sticky white fluid.

II

Xingxing's hand was bleeding. As she had struggled with Wuye over the glass, it had shattered and one piece had gashed her palm.

But she didn't feel any pain. In fact, she felt a violent pain in her heart as if her heart were bleeding unseen.

She never dreamed that Wuye would push her with such force and then drink madly despite everything. He looked at her liked a cornered beast. She couldn't stand playing such a role in such a place in front of everyone. They were performing like a couple of clowns stripped naked. She hated him for forcing her into such a position.

Then she thought of Xiaojun and that intolerable situation at the party. Perhaps she was too sensitive and there was nothing to fret about. She wished she could replace her heart of flesh and blood with one made of rubber or some other substance so that she would never be hurt.

No, she didn't hate Yu'er. In fact, it was just the opposite. She thought Wuye and Yu'er looked beautiful when they were together. In such a boisterous setting, she preferred to stay in the background, quietly observing. At such times, her soul seemed to leave her body and float freely in the air. She could see her own body and could see the difference between a beautiful woman and an average one.

Later she saw Yu'er drag Wuye out to dance. Yu'er's face was pressed against his and her eyes glistened, watery. Wuye's face was a furious red. Wuye seemed to be looking all over for something.

Xingxing felt more sober than ever before.

12

At the time of Director Tang's banquet, Zhang Shu was in his little room wrestling with the legends Ahyuexi had told him about Yu-Chi Yiseng and Buddhist painting. After hearing what Pan Sumin was doing behind the scenes from Ahyuexi's own mouth, he immediately went to find Wuye and tell him everything and help him come up with ways of dealing with the situation. But for some reason the young guy seemed confused, as if he were dreaming. He began to have his suspicions. Perhaps he had a strategy but didn't tell anyone around him. He had never encountered a person who behaved in such a way when their life involved such danger.

He accomplished a lot that day. By ten that evening, he had recorded and arranged everything she had narrated. Then he splashed his face with cold water and took a letter off the desk. It was from his wife. It was different from the two previous letters. The wording was more affectionate and showed more concern; it was also more timid in tone, as if she were afraid of making him mad. He was certain that something had gone wrong for her. Every time something like that happened, she was more conciliatory, but after things were straightened out, she would be her old self again.

Shu,

> *I miss you.*
>
> *From morning till night all Gugu asks is why isn't Daddy home yet? I don't know what to tell him.*
>
> *Do you miss us? I'm sure you don't. You know I don't have the best temper because I've always been spoiled. Even if I want to change, I can't do so overnight. How can you be so mean to just leave us here alone? I take care of everything at home now and my hands are showing it. I can't even play the piano anymore. You once called me a spoiled princess. So now you want to turn the princess into a Cinderella?*
>
> *Shu, no matter what happens, I still love you. Come home. Your name is Shu (forgiving). Can't you forgive me?*
>
> *We miss you.*

Yixi

Gugu

He knew that this was his wife's special way with words to which he always surrendered. He knew what was between the lines. She wanted him back to take care of everything. But he was softhearted.

It was at that moment that Xiao Xingxing knocked on his door.

13

"Zhang Shu, I'm leaving."

She held the door, smiling as she did the first time they met. She appeared straightforward and simple. And as always, she shouldered her inconspicuous bag.

"What? So suddenly?"

"Yes, I just made up my mind."

"You really are impulsive."

"I have a Buddha nature." She smiled. "It's as they say: born and dying naked and with no attachments in life."

"What time is your train?"

"Eleven o'clock."

"Oh, that's in just another hour. Have you told . . . everyone?"

"No, no one knows." Xingxing became serious. "Zhang Shu, I have a favor to ask. Please tell Wuye to hurry back to Beijing, the sooner the better."

"I know. I've been pushing him, too." He frowned, "You didn't even tell him you're leaving?"

"No. He was dancing and having such a good time. I didn't want to bother him," she said as if unconcerned, looking down. He then noticed that her eyes were a little swollen, as if she had cried recently.

"You can stay here another half hour, and then I'll take you to the station on my bike. It's not far from here."

"Zhang Shu, do you know that I've had a new dream recently? I dream I go to an ancient land, which is covered with bronze Buddhas under a glaring sun . . ."

"That must be India."

"India? I don't know. I told you before that all my dreams come true. I think I should go in search of that land in my dreams."

"Good luck." He forced a smile, but he suddenly felt sad.

14

The climax of the banquet actually occurred when Ahyuexi arrived, by which time Xingxing had left. Her back ramrod straight, Ahyuexi drove right in and went straight up to Yu'er and Guonu. Her speed and vigor, in addition to a sense of mysteriousness, left everyone stunned.

She whipped out her shiny knife and pointed it at Yu'er's chest, nearly making Director Tang, who was nearby, faint. The noisy chatter filling the room suddenly ceased. Before anyone could say anything, the young woman, as slender as a reed, asked, "Was it you who sold the painting?"

Yu'er's amber eyes flashed fire: "You're the one who sold it! I don't know who switched paintings!"

The shiny blade turned to Guonu. "Then it was you, you good-for-nothing."

Old Guonu frowned, and it was hard to tell if she was laughing or crying. Her lips trembled, but she didn't say anything at once. Yu'er shouted, "How can you treat your mother that way? You call her a good-for-nothing, then that makes you a good-for-nothing, doesn't it?"

Before she finished speaking, a slap landed on Yu'er's face. Yu'er shrieked and began to cry. Everyone in the dining hall stood up. Half drunk, Wuye recognized her as the young woman who had once trussed him up. With a drunk's courage, Wuye rushed forward and, with his finger inches away from Ahyuexi's nose, said, "What gives you the right to hit people?"

Ahyuexi sneered, "Oh, the painting thief. I didn't go looking for you and here you are!" The words were no sooner out of her mouth when she reached out and grabbed Wuye by the scruff of his neck. Wuye wasn't quick enough to dodge her. Then another hand flashed like a treasured sword, falling with a speed that left everyone speechless. Ahyuexi pulled her hand back leaving the other hand to strike nothing but air. Wuye

looked—it was Yu'er who had helped him. He was more or less sobered
up by then. But Ahyuexi wasn't willing to let it go at that. In a flash, her
arms swung above her head and a foot struck deftly at Yu'er's belly. She
quickly avoided the blow and thrust with her right palm. For a while the
two of them went at it, fists and feet flying.

At that moment, Dayejisi entered through the revolving door.

One-eyed Guonu suddenly dashed her string instrument to the
ground, her face twisted in anger.

The sound of the shattering instrument silenced the entire hall.
Everyone stood stock-still where they were standing.

15

Dayejisi bowed his head and clasped his hands in front of him in a
prayerful gesture as if no one were around. Director Tang and several
others who knew him stood up and greeted him. But Dayejisi stood in
the same position. Chen Qing by that time had managed to pull Ahyuexi
away. When Ahyuexi saw Dayejisi, she spat and angrily said, "Listen to
me, you two good-for-nothings! You've got one month to come up with
that painting; if not, you'll be sorry!" She vanished as suddenly as she had
appeared. She brushed against Dayejisi on her way out and threw him a
hostile glance. Dayejisi pretended not to notice and kept his head bowed
and his hands folded before him, like Ananda.

Yu'er rushed over.

"Dad, did you see everything? Just ignore her. She . . ." Yu'er shouted
through her tears.

"Yu'er, shut your mouth," roared Guonu.

"Mom!" Tears and snot ran down Yu'er's face. "You're still partial to
her, even though she repeatedly calls you a good-for-nothing!"

Chen Qing could see that they would soon be arguing, so he hastened
forward to intervene. Even Director Tang and Old Guan were on their
feet, shouting, "Sister, calm down, calm down . . ."

"She's still my beautiful daughter even if she curses me!" Her voice
trembling, Guonu continued, "I let her down! Go find Bodhisattva Pan

and let her talk to her. Let's go, Yu'er. Do you want to come with me or should my beautiful daughter? Then let's go. She has been wronged for so many years . . ."

"What do you mean, go get Bodhisattva Pan? Can she handle her?" Yu'er muttered and then somewhat unwillingly followed Guonu.

Chen Qing stooped down to pick up the pieces of the stringed instrument.

From start to finish, Dayejisi kept his eyes shut and his hands clasped before him, without uttering a word.

16

Later, someone who was a bit tipsy asked Dayejisi to tell fortunes. Dayejisi smiled and replied, "Your servant only wishes to tell the fortune of one person only. Sorry, sorry!"

He searched until his eyes lit on Wuye. "Come, come, come, young benefactor. Let me examine your face and tell your fortune."

Wuye was momentarily overwhelmed. The great Abbot Dayejisi chose him out of nearly one hundred present. Somewhat drowsily, he glanced around but didn't see Xingxing. He felt something was vaguely amiss. There was something at the back of his mind that irritated him and prevented him from using his head.

Dayejisi examined him closely, then took his hand and scrutinized it. Suddenly, Dayejisi went pale and asked, "How old is the young benefactor?"

"Nineteen."

"Ah, that's too bad!"

"What do you mean, sir?"

"Would the young benefactor like me to tell the truth?"

"Of course, please tell the truth."

"Then come to my place at eight o'clock tonight."

"Why can't you tell me now, sir?"

"It involves a secret of yours. This is not the time to speak."

"I have nothing to hide. Go ahead and speak."

Dayejisi seemed to hesitate a moment. "Well then, okay, since the young benefactor is not afraid, I speak according to the facts."

At that moment the entire dining room fell dead silent. Dozens of eyes were fixed on Dayejisi, even the servers carrying trays stood with their mouths open.

Dayejisi joined his hands and bowed his head and said something that startled everyone present.

"The young benefactor did something for which he has a guilty conscience. To put it more clearly, he stole something. If the young benefactor does not confess, he will meet with sudden death. I see the young benefactor spurring his horse along a precipice . . ."

"Nonsense!" said Wuye, clenching his fists and turning red.

"There's no need for the young benefactor to get angry. Listen carefully to what I have to say. The young benefactor has a 'hanging needle' line running from the spot between his eyebrows to the top of his head. Above, it cancels out the 'palace of life' and below it cancels out long life. It is a line of great disaster. Moreover, there is no horizontal line to obstruct its baleful influence. At a certain age, the line will prove fatal. There are moles in the center of the forehead as well as to the left and right. These indicate that you have offended Heaven in the extreme. You will be struck by three bolts of lightning. The first will strike official position, wealth, and accuracy of speech, leading to loss of position and defeat; the second will strike the three Yins and the three Yangs causing you to lose your parents; the third will strike the Palace of Fate, long life, and the Gate of Life, leading to death. You will have a chance only if you come clean and confess, and make amends for past wrongs. Otherwise you will certainly die."

Wuye lashed out with his fist at Dayejisi's bald pate, but Dayejisi didn't bat an eyelash. Just as Wuye's fist was about to land, he suddenly parried the blow. Wuye seemed to suddenly lose all his strength, his face went pale, and he slumped to the ground.

The hall exploded.

17

Wuye was carried back to the guesthouse. As the alcohol wore off, he vomited for a long time.

Later he felt a little better. He struggled over to the desk where he found a note. He didn't look to see who it was from, but he knew it was from Xingxing.

> All banquets must come to an end. I think maybe we should take this opportunity and part before the last course is done.

It was actually ten-thirty at night, and Xingxing had just gone over to Zhang Shu's room. If Wuye had made the least effort to think about it, there is a good chance that things would have turned out differently. But at the time, Wuye was so agitated. He sat at the desk without moving. It was ages before he raised his head, his eyes filled with tears. Then in a fury, he tore the note into little pieces and then kicked the door, splintering the rotten wood. Later he found that his toenail was oozing blood, but he felt no pain.

Being trussed up by Ahyuexi, Dayejisi's threats, and the guidance of that woman, who looked like Guanyin, were all aimed at one thing: to force him to confess that he had stolen the painting in Cave 73. Goodness! And for what reason?

But all of this was nothing compared to Xingxing leaving without a word. No, she didn't love him! What she loved was not him, but a ghost! A reincarnated ghost! His heart cried out, but as the warmth induced by the wine retreated, all that was left was a cold numbness.

All banquets must come to an end. Yes, that old woman, who watched over Cave 73, was once the beautiful Guonu. Once, she was deeply in love with a man named Zhaxi Lunba. Later, he died and their banquet came to an end. Later, there was a new banquet that included Dayejisi and two unusual girls. Later, this banquet, too, came to an end. Not only did it come to an end, but it also became a matter of intense hatred.

18

That night, Wuye didn't make the last train to Beijing. He packed his bags and sat the entire night through in his little room. Around two o'clock in the morning, Chen Qing showed up and reminded him to turn off his light. He turned off the light and continued to sit in the dark until the alarm sounded at about four in the morning. Someone knocked.

The knocking was neither urgent nor slow. It struck him that someone of importance was knocking. Fear gradually settled upon him. Although the knocking was unhurried, it possessed an all-encompassing power.

"Is Xiang Wuye staying here?"

It was a woman's voice. Although the knocking was in no way urgent, it raised goose bumps all the same. He leaped up. He felt disaster was upon him.

19

Consensus was never reached on how Pan Sumin managed to take Wuye away. Zhang Shu told me that when he realized Wuye had once again disappeared, he had called the relevant authorities at once. Then he had gone to see Old Guonu and Ahyuexi, hoping to learn something from them. Old Guonu was sick in bed . . . she had been ill ever since the evening of that unfortunate banquet. Zhang Shu surmised that she had been unable to withstand such a grievous attack of nerves.

Zhang Shu expressed all his suspicions in a long letter to the Dunhuang Public Security Bureau, but for some reason he never received a reply. Six months later, he heard that Xiang Wuye had been condemned to death for stealing first-class national cultural relics.

He sat smoking for a whole night in his living room. He guessed that Xingxing, in some part of the world, had learned of this.

20

Actually, to this day, Xingxing has never heard about it. Later, she really did go to India. It that noon of intense sunlight, among those bronze Buddhas, she hesitated a moment and asked me, "You're so close to Zhang Shu, did you ever hear him mention someone by the name of Xiang Wuye?"

I nodded as my heart pounded.

"How is he?" she asked, seemingly without a care.

"He's . . . doing well." I don't know why I lied. "He has probably already graduated."

"Oh . . ." She swallowed with some effort. She smiled like a little girl, "Give my regards to Zhang Shu. Next year, I'll return to China for the Dunhuang conference."

She wore that cap of hers as if she were being roasted by the sun. It was a very, very hot day.

21

The day Zhang Shu left Dunhuang, the only person to see him off was Chen Qing.

As usual, he rode that creaking bike of his, but the view was not as attractive as when he first arrived. The snow still glittered on the Qilian Mountains; the sky was still so high and far away.

Chen Qing had borrowed a bicycle. They chatted as they pedaled all the way to Yang Pass.

"Two brothers we meet, fated from a previous life." Chen Qing took the little bottle of liquor that Zhang Shu had given him from his pocket and took a swig. Zhang Shu was a little taken aback when he heard the words *two brothers*. Later, thinking about what Old Guonu had said, he relaxed a bit. He wondered if he didn't look very old.

The last Dunhuang story he heard was the Treasured Thoroughbred of Shouchang.

"It was in these parts, to the east of Yang Pass," said Chen Qing as he dropped the kickstand and shaded his eyes with his right hand. The furrows on his brow deepened in the sunlight. "There was a city. The remnants of the mud walls are still visible today. In the past this was called Shouchang City. To the south of the city, there was a lake that was called Shouchang Sea.

"In the past, someone captured a treasured steed on its shores and presented it as a gift to the emperor. It was a majestic beast! It was shiny black, and its hoofs snow white. The emperor received the horse on his birthday and was so delighted that he called the animal the Thoroughbred of Shouchang. He gave it a golden halter and a jade bridle.

"Who could have foreseen that the horse would not eat or drink after entering the emperor's stables. Every day as the sun set behind the mountains, the horse would neigh at the clouds of dusk, making people cry. The stable master was overcome and informed the emperor.

The emperor asked, "What ails the steed?"

"Your Highness, the steed suffers from homesickness."

"Nonsense! How can a beast suffer from homesickness?"

"Beasts, like men, long for home. For example, the geese fly south in the autumn and the swallows return north in the spring. The horse is accustomed to the West and also has a hot temperament, so naturally it is attached to its home. I beg of Your Highness to let it go."

The emperor lowered his head and thought for a while.

The stable master continued, "Everyone knows of the emperor's love of horses, and only this steed has been recognized by the emperor. If you set this horse free and allow it to return home, then everyone will know that the if the emperor who so esteems horses let this one go, Your Highness will receive even better horses in the future. If this horse cannot return, then all horses under Heaven will avoid Your Highness. Please consider carefully."

His Highness had no choice but to let the horse return home.

The horse neighed and then sped off to the west.

By the time the sun was about to set, it had returned to Yang Pass. Standing on the mountain summit, it saw that it still wore the halter bestowed by the emperor. With anger it shook its head, sending the halter flying one hundred and eighty *li* away. It landed on a peak, which was later called Dragon Halter Peak.

As he spoke, Chen Qing drained the little bottle. He laughed and clapped Zhang Shu on the back and said, "You look like a treasured steed that is homesick to me."

Zhang Shu laughed. He clasped Chen Qing's hand, then he mounted his rickety "treasured bike" and rode off.

POSTSCRIPT

Several years later, I was part of a Chinese Writers Association group that visited the Mogao Caves. We stayed at the Yueya Spring Guesthouse. At dusk I made my way alone to Sanwei Mountain nearby, but didn't see any guesthouse around there. I vaguely heard from the locals about a time a few years back when there were some problems involving national cultural relics. There was also an incident of officials in charge of cultural relics and a temple abbot, who were involved in selling relics.

Sunset on Sanwei Mountain was indeed beautiful. Rays of light appeared and disappeared through the infinite layers of a sea of clouds. I thought of the "Sanwei Buddha light" Zhang Shu had described to me.

That evening, the entire group climbed Mingsha Mountain. The sand was still warm, having soaked up a day's sunlight. From the summit we saw the solitary moon in the deep blue sky. I suddenly imagined a blond beauty sitting quietly on the summit, a painting scroll in hand, looking up at the moon. It was an irregular, diamond-shaped moon.

That moon was part and parcel of Zhang Shu's mysterious dream.

The shape of the moon is forever changing. Everything under Heaven is constantly changing. People are being born, people are dying, but Heaven is always the same.

Heaven is eternal. Yesterday's moon will never reappear in the sky. From this perspective, then, Zhang Shu's dream is perhaps real.

9 781416 583905